Praise for the novels of Chris Cavender

Rest in Pizza

"Charming . . . two lovable, dynamic protagonists
and a warm small-town atmosphere."
—*Publishers Weekly*

"The increasing mastery of action and flow suggest
that Cavender is hitting his stride."
—*Kirkus Reviews*

"These cozy pizza mysteries have been truly
outstanding and this particular one will leave the
reader once again wanting a whole lot more of the
great writing and cool plots that Chris Cavender
continues to serve."
—*Suspense Magazine*

A Pizza to Die For

"Just like a pizza with all your favorite toppings,
this series will satisfy even the most finicky cozy
readers. Fans of Laura Childs and Joanne Fluke
will most likely enjoy this series as well."
—*RT Book Reviews*

Pepperoni Pizza Can Be Murder

"The small-town setting, the small-business focus
and the relationship between sisters Maddy and
Eleanor are all reminiscent of Joanne Fluke's
Hannah Swensen mysteries."
—*Booklist*

"Cavender is an ace at writing cozies. His characters are all believable, especially the relationship between Eleanor and her sister, and his plots are rock solid. Sure to appeal to fans of food cozies."
—*Library Journal*

A Slice of Murder

"Pizza lovers will relish Cavender's delightful first in a new cozy series . . . A lively pace and a thrilling climax."
—*Publishers Weekly*

"Cavender introduces a promising cast of characters."
—*Booklist*

"The camaraderie of the Timber Ridge, NC, sisters is reminiscent of Nancy Martin's Blackbird siblings."
—*Library Journal*

"A delightful mystery—as filling as a big slice of warm pizza."
—*Armchair Interviews*

Books by Chris Cavender

A SLICE OF MURDER

PEPPERONI PIZZA CAN BE MURDER

A PIZZA TO DIE FOR

REST IN PIZZA

KILLER CRUST

THE MISSING DOUGH

Published by Kensington Publishing Corporation

CHRIS CAVENDER

KILLER CRUST

KENSINGTON BOOKS
www.kensingtonbooks.com

KENSINGTON BOOKS are published by

Kensington Publishing Corp.
119 West 40th Street
New York, NY 10018

All Kensington titles, imprints, and distributed lines are available at special quantity discounts for bulk purchases for sales promotion, premiums, fund-raising, educational, or institutional use. Special book excerpts or customized printings can also be created to fit specific needs. For details, write or phone the office of the Kensington Special Sales Manager: Attn. Special Sales Department. Kensington Publishing Corp., 119 West 40th Street, New York, NY 10018. Phone: 1-800-221-2647.

Kensington and the K logo Reg. U.S. Pat. & TM Off.

ISBN-13: 978-0-7582-7153-2
ISBN-10: 0-7582-7153-0
First Kensington Hardcover Edition: January 2013
First Kensington Mass Market Edition: November 2013

eISBN-13: 978-0-7582-9153-0
eISBN-10: 0-7582-9153-1
Kensington Electronic Edition: November 2013

10 9 8 7 6 5 4 3 2 1

Printed in the United States of America

There's no better feeling in the world than a warm pizza box on your lap.

Kevin James

Chapter 1

I never imagined that one of my pizzas might ever actually kill someone, even if it had been tainted by someone else's hand. But that's what happened when my sister, Maddy, and I tried to win twenty-five-thousand dollars in a competition that quickly turned into a deadly struggle to learn who our allies were, and exactly who the enemy was trying to ruin our lives forever.

"Eleanor Swift, it's so good to see you again," the man known as Laughing Luigi said as he walked into my pizzeria, A Slice of Delight, one winter day in Timber Ridge, North Carolina. Funny, I wasn't happy at all to see the middle-aged, heavyset man with bushy black eyebrows and thinning hair visiting me. We had a history, and it wasn't a good one. At least it was a slow time for us, just before our afternoon break, so thankfully the restaurant was deserted. Maddy was in back working in the kitchen, and I was out front. It wasn't our usual arrangement, but I thought that it was good for us to shake things up every now and then.

I studied the man with the dark complexion and wondered what he was up to. The buoyancy he was portraying was certainly against his nature. Despite his name, I'd never heard him chuckle once, let alone laugh out loud. The feeling of joy in seeing him again was most emphatically not mutual, given the fact that the last time our paths had crossed, I'd been doing my best to break his nose with a green pepper. Of course, I hadn't been trying to inflict any real damage on the man; I'd just been trying to tell him what I thought of his offer for my pizzeria. He'd been trying to buy me out for months, wanting everything from my conveyor oven to the tables out front, and I was tired of him not taking no for an answer. One day he pushed me too far, and that explained the impromptu attack of the killer green pepper.

"Luigi, did you come here all the way from Charlotte just to order one of my pizzas? I make my own dough by hand every day, you know."

His face tightened slightly at my dig, if only for a flickering moment, but I knew that I'd scored a direct hit. Luigi, well-known throughout the South these days for his frozen pizza dough, tried his best to ignore the fact that I refused to use his product, Laughing Luigi's Pizza Dough, in my pizzeria. Funny, but he wasn't laughing at all when I'd reminded him that I still made my dough the old-fashioned way, from scratch.

He did his best to let it go. "As delicious as that sounds, Eleanor, I'm here for another reason entirely."

I shook my head. "Some people just don't get it, do they? No means no, Luigi. I wouldn't sell A Slice of Delight to you years ago, and I'm not going to do it now. What's it going to take to get my point across? Do I have to upgrade my weapon choice and use a metal napkin holder this time?" I picked one up from a nearby table, and pretended to test the heft of it in my hand. I probably wouldn't throw it, but it felt good being armed nonetheless.

"No violence is necessary, Eleanor," he said as he held his hands up, his palms extended outward. "I'm here for another reason altogether, and one that shouldn't necessitate violence."

I couldn't imagine what that might be. "If you're not here to order a pizza, and you're not trying to buy my restaurant, I can't imagine what the two of us have to talk about."

A smile blossomed on his lips, and for the first time ever, I believed that I heard a faint chuckle coming from him as he asked, "How would you like the chance to win twenty-five-thousand dollars? Would that interest you, or should I go on my way?"

"Go on. I'm listening," I said. I had to give him credit; he sure knew how to get a girl's attention. As I waited for him to explain himself, Maddy Spencer, my sister and number one employee, came out of the kitchen. She stayed back there as little as she could get away with, and was always eager for any excuse to cut her shift as our chef in back. I couldn't really blame her, though. My rightful place was in the kitchen, and my sister thrived on her contact with our customers, but every now and then, it was good for folks to see the owner out front.

My sister started to say, "Eleanor, we're getting low on—" but her voice faded when she saw Luigi standing there. "What do you want, Luigi?"

"Maddy, I see that you are as delightfully refreshing and direct as ever," Luigi said.

"Yeah, I'm a real breath of fresh air. I asked you a question. What are you doing in our pizzeria?"

"I was just about to explain everything to your sister," he said. "You might as well hear what I have to say as well. After all, it affects you just as much as it does her."

It was clear that Maddy wasn't all that interested in hearing what he had to say. "Yeah, well whatever it is, let me save you some trouble. We're not interested."

I put my hand on my sister's shoulder. "Hang on a second, Maddy. Let's at least hear him out."

Maddy looked at me as though I'd lost my mind, so I quickly added, "Luigi just told me that we could have a chance at winning twenty-five grand."

Maddy looked at me for a moment to see if I was kidding, and then she turned to Luigi for a second or two. Without saying a word to him, she looked back in my direction and asked, "And you actually believe him?"

"The jury's still out on that," I answered. "But we should at least give him a chance to explain, don't you think? He was just about to give me the details when you walked into the dining room."

"Go on then," she said as she turned back to Luigi. "Explain it to us both." She glanced at her watch, and then added, "You have exactly three minutes."

I glanced at my watch and saw that in three minutes we'd be set to close, but I wasn't going to throw him out, not if what he was saying was true.

If Luigi was put off by Maddy's open rudeness, he didn't show it. "In all honesty, I don't need that much of your time. To honor the fifth anniversary of my pizza dough company, I'm holding a competition among the top four independently owned pizzerias in North Carolina. Since we're holding the competition here in town, I thought it would be quite fitting to invite you ladies to join my little contest."

"What's the catch?" Maddy asked as I started imagining what I could do to the pizzeria with that kind of money. The dreams were alluring, but I wasn't sure I wanted to put my pizza up against such stiff competition. It wasn't that I didn't believe in the food I offered my customers, but I had no delusions of grandeur. I wasn't classically trained in any aspect of pizza making. As a matter of fact, my late husband, Joe, and I had pretty much learned how to make pizzas in the restored Craftsman-style cottage we'd rehabbed together. Did I stand a chance against other pizza makers, and was I willing to find out just where I stood when my pizza was compared to theirs?

Luigi did his best to smile as he said, "First of all, I can assure you both that there's no hidden agenda here. The competition will take place over two action-packed days. Each of the competitors will present pizzas that use my regular crust, my thin crust, and my new deep dish pizza crust dough. For the final stage of the judging, you will each present a

pizza of your own choosing, both in crust and toppings. For all intents and purposes, it will be a level
playing field. You'll each be working in identical
kitchenettes on stage, so that only your knowledge
and skill will determine who is the very best and
wins the grand prize."

"Why are you having it here in our town?" I
asked, suddenly wondering why Luigi had settled on
Timber Ridge when he could have just as easily
picked one of our state's large cities instead. I knew
that the publicity and media coverage would be
much better in Charlotte or Raleigh. Even Asheville
or Greensboro would offer more access to television
cameras and newspaper reporters.

"Why not? I can assure you that it has nothing to
do with you being here," he said. "That's just a
happy coincidence. So, what do you say? Are you
interested? Believe me, I understand completely if
you choose to decline."

"Why would we do that?" I asked. "Is there
something that you're not telling us, Luigi?"

He shrugged. "I thought it would be obvious. I
shouldn't have to remind you that it would place a
great deal of pressure on you both if you're compet-
ing in your own town."

I hadn't even thought about that, but now that I
had a chance to consider it, I realized that I had a
real decision to make here. It would be prudent to
balance out the odds of winning against the risk of
public humiliation if I lost. Timber Ridge was a
small town, and if I made a poor showing of it, I
knew that I'd be hearing about it for the rest of my
life. Still, when it came right down to it, it was a
small stick and a pretty wonderful carrot. Was it

really that tough a decision to make? "We'll do it," I said quickly.

My sister, almost always the bolder of the two of us, said to me gently, "Maybe we should find out more about who the competition is going to be before we just jump into this."

"Does it really matter? We know that they must be good, or Luigi wouldn't have invited them." I looked at him and asked, "Am I right?"

"I've personally sampled pizzas from each restaurant, and I can vouch for their quality down to the last pizza chef."

"And the rules are the same for all the contestants, right?" I asked Luigi.

"They are. I can assure you of that," he answered.

I turned to Maddy. "Then I really don't see how we can expect anything more, can you? What do you say, Sis? Are you with me on this? We could give the pizzeria the sprucing up we've been wanting to do for years."

"With that amount of money, you could gut the entire place and start over," Luigi said.

"We happen to love our pizzeria just the way it is," Maddy told him.

Luigi looked around and said, "Of course. I completely see it. There's a certain charm here that is irresistible. Leave the dining area as it is, and replace that conveyor oven of yours with a wood-burning or gas-fired oven. The possibilities are endless, and you'd be amazed by how far you'll be able to make twenty-five grand go."

I looked at Maddy. "If you're not behind this one hundred percent, we'll walk away from the offer right now. Are you with me or not?"

"You don't even have to ask. Of course I am," she said. "If this is something you want, then let's do it."

Maybe I should have listened a little closer to the hesitation in my sister's voice at that moment, but the chance of winning the competition, not to mention the money, was enough to blind me to all but the most obvious signs. "We'll do it."

"Excellent," Luigi said as he pulled a sheaf of papers from his briefcase. "Just sign your name at the places marked on this contract, and you'll be my final contestants."

I accepted the papers as Luigi magically produced a pen. Before I could take it from him though, my sister snatched it from his hand and looked hard at me. "Eleanor, Bob needs to look this over before you agree to anything in writing," Maddy said. Bob Lemon was the town's best attorney, and he also happened to be Maddy's fiancé.

She glanced at Luigi and asked, "You don't mind if she has a lawyer look this over, do you? I'm sure that you've got nothing to hide."

Luigi shrugged. "I don't mind a bit. I'm staying at Tree-Line tonight, so you can find me there. It's a lovely new resort, isn't it? That's where we'll be holding the competition, so I'm here to make all of the arrangements. If you decide to sign the contract, have it back to me by nine A.M. tomorrow, or I'll just have to assume that you've changed your mind and decided not to participate after all."

I couldn't believe that after what had happened between us in the past, Luigi was actually offering us a wonderful opportunity to compete for the title and the cash. I knew that I should at least make a gesture to show my thanks. "I've got a fresh pie coming out of the oven just for us. Would you like to join us for a slice?"

"Sure, why not?" Luigi said as he patted his pockets. What he was looking for I had no idea, but when he came up empty, he added, "On second thought, I'll have to pass. Thanks for the offer, but I'm afraid I've left my medication back at the complex, and I can't eat without it. I'll leave you both to enjoy it, and to start making plans for what you'll do with the money if you win. Until tomorrow, ladies," he said with a smile as he left the pizzeria.

Maddy looked at me the second he was gone and frowned. "Dear sweet sister, have you totally lost your mind? Were you really going to sign that thing without having Bob look it over first? That's not like you, to just throw caution into the wind like that."

I just shrugged, since we both knew the answer to her question. I'd been blinded by the lure of the prize, and I was very glad that Maddy had been there to step in.

I leafed through the extensive document, and then asked her, "Do you think Bob will mind going over this for me on such short notice? Will he even have time to vet it for me?"

Maddy grinned. "He will if I ask him to do it myself. There has to be some advantage to being engaged to the best legal mind in the county."

"I would hope that you have more reasons for your engagement than just the odd free bit of legal work." My sister was getting married again, something that wasn't all that foreign to her, given her previous trips down the aisle in the past, but I knew that she was a firm believer in the institution. Why else would she have participated in it so many times, given the ultimate results? I hadn't cared for several of the men she'd married before, but I was a huge fan of Bob's. Though they hadn't even discussed a date for the wedding yet, the two of them had already fallen into a state of premarital comfort with each other that suited them.

"Are you sure I shouldn't ask him myself?"

"No, I'll handle it," she said as she pulled out her phone and stepped into the back. I pulled our lunch from the conveyor oven, plated it, and then sliced it. As I waited for Maddy to rejoin me, I looked around the pizzeria's kitchen. It was hard not to plan my improvements, but I knew that I was getting ahead of myself.

I had to win the contest first, and if I knew Luigi, the competition was going to be pretty fierce.

"Well, this doesn't look too bad," Bob Lemon said half an hour later as he finished examining the contract Luigi had supplied for the competition. Maddy and I had eaten our pizza while we'd waited for him, and I'd offered to make him something to eat for his trouble, but he'd declined. I hadn't expected such quick results, but my sister had asked him nicely, and he'd promptly responded. Bob tapped the document with his index finger, and then said, "There is one thing, though."

I frowned. I'd been hoping that there wouldn't be any glitches to the contract, but knowing Luigi even as little as I really did, I wasn't all that surprised. "How bad is it?"

"That's entirely up to you. If you win the competition, Luigi has the right to use your likeness, the name of your pizzeria, and just about anything else he wants for PR purposes for up to three years after the contest is completed."

"What can he do if I lose?" I asked.

Bob grinned. "He can't even mention your name under his breath."

"Sold," I said as I reached for the contract.

"Not so fast," Bob said. "There are a few other lesser things you need to keep in mind. You'll also be responsible for all taxes on the winnings. I'm guessing, just off the top of my head, that that will be somewhere between a third to half of your winnings, when all is said and done."

I grinned at him. "So, you're telling me that the only downside of winning is having my pizzeria advertised for free all over the South, and to top it off, I get somewhere between twelve and seventeen grand out of the deal if I win."

"That about sums it up."

I laughed out loud. "I'll take that deal any day that ends in *y*. Let me sign this thing so I can get it into Luigi's hands before he changes his mind."

Maddy stepped between us before I could take it, though. "Bob, are you certain this won't bite my sister down the road?"

He considered her question, and then answered, "Let me put it this way. If any problems I haven't mentioned arise down the road from her executing this agreement on my advice and counsel, I will represent her free of charge."

Maddy kissed him, and then she said, "You weren't going to charge her anyway, though, were you?"

"Most likely not," he said with a laugh. "Now, if

you ladies will excuse me, I have a case to prepare for tomorrow."

"Thanks for everything," I said as I reached up and kissed his cheek.

Bob smiled after the kiss. "Wow, I can't help but wonder how many men besides your father could say that both of you had kissed him within minutes of each other."

Maddy and I said in perfect unison, "Just one. Jimmy Hickman."

Bob replied, "From the dual expressions of distaste I'm witnessing, I'm guessing things didn't fare quite so well for young Mr. Hickman."

"Believe me," I said, "There are details about that you don't want to know."

"You're right, I don't." As he started to leave the pizzeria, he turned to Maddy and asked, "Are we still on for tonight?"

"We are. Thanks again, Bob."

"My pleasure," he said as he left the pizzeria.

"You finally got yourself a good one there, Sis," I said.

"You don't have to tell me." She rubbed her hands together, and then said, "We have thirty minutes left on our late lunch break. What do you want to do with the time we've got left?"

"You can do whatever you want to, but I'm going straight to Tree-Line to deliver this contract to Laughing Luigi before he can change his mind."

Chapter 2

Maddy and I walked into Tree-Line, the brand-new hotel complex on the edge of town, and headed toward the front desk. One step inside the lobby explained the name of the luxurious new complex. Huge posts fashioned from giant trees stood out in the expansive space, highlighting the timber frame structure that was the loveliest shade of tan I'd ever seen. The walls were covered with pine stained butter-scotch that highlighted the beams, and the floors featured a warm slate of grays and greens that radiated high-end comfort. Light wafted gently down from several skylights, and I felt as though I were in Montana instead of my corner of North Carolina. The complex hadn't even officially opened yet, and we'd all been waiting eagerly to tour the facility during their grand opening. I wondered how Luigi had managed to snag a room while they were still working out the last-minute glitches that any operation that big must be experiencing, and then I realized that the presence of his pizza competition would bring the hotel and restaurant a great deal of free publicity. No doubt it would carry a lot of weight with the eccentric owner. As I looked around more, I could see that a fire was going in the massive two-sided see-through fireplace across from the reception area, and large, comfortable couches and chairs were arranged all around it. Large windows showed views of the surrounding mountains, and even though the leaves had left the trees in colorful bursts of explosion a few months before, it was still a majestic sight.

All in all, it was quite a place given its proximity to Timber Ridge, but I knew that the owner, a man named Nathan Pane, had more money than the annual budgets of seven counties, so if anyone could afford to build a complex this spectacular, it was him. His niece, Gina Sizemore, was a striking brunette in her mid-twenties, and though we'd had a rocky start when we'd first met, we were now friends. If I looked closely enough, I could still see the evidence of some of her scars from the fire that had nearly killed us both. Though Gina claimed that I'd been the one to rescue her from the fire, I knew in my heart that she'd saved me by confronting a killer, and I also realized that there was no way I'd ever be able to make it up to her.

"Hey, Gina," I said as Maddy and I approached the reception area. "How are things going? The place looks unbelievably beautiful. You've done a magnificent job with the property."

The hotel manager came out from behind the desk and hugged me fiercely. "I was wondering if you were ever going to come out here and take me up on my lunch invitation." She glanced at my sister and said, "Hey, Maddy."

"Hello. Eleanor is right, by the way. This place is truly magnificent."

She nodded her thanks as she looked around with great pride. "It truly is lovely. I told Uncle Nathan that he didn't have to go to these extremes, but he wanted to give Timber Ridge something back for all of the years he's lived here, and I couldn't stop him." She smiled as she added, "Not that I tried too hard to rein him in. We both win, after all. I get my dream job running this place, and by building Tree-Line, he gets to keep me close."

"How's he doing, by the way?" I asked. "I haven't seen him since he finished the house restoration." Nathan owned a great deal of the land around us and had more wealth than most folks realized, but one of his favorite things was a Craftsman-style cottage that echoed my own. My late husband, Joe, and I had done the rehabbing ourselves on ours as we'd tried to get the pizzeria going, but Nathan had hired a crew of experts. I wouldn't have traded places with him even if he'd thrown in a million extra into the deal, though. The home where I lived alone now was one of the best reminders I had of my late husband, and though I'd moved on and was dating a fine man named David Quinton, there was one corner of my heart that would always belong to Joe. One of the things that I admired most about David was his open acknowledgment and acceptance of that fact.

Gina smiled at the mention of her uncle. "The last I heard, he was thinking about buying an entire lake somewhere near Cashiers so he'd have a place to go fishing."

"What's he going to do with his own lake?" I asked. "That's a lot of trouble to go to just to not have to share a spot for your line. Surely there's got to be another way to go about it. Was he serious, or was he just pulling your leg?"

"Who knows? I'm never exactly sure, but with that man, you never know." She rubbed her hands together and smiled. "Now, let's go see about lunch."

"Can we take a rain check?" I asked. "Maddy and I just split a pizza, and I'm here to deliver something to one of your early guests."

"Don't worry about that. We can have lunch anytime," Gina agreed. "Could I help you find the guest you're looking for? We're doing a dry run before we open, so we invited some family and a few of my uncle's business partners to the event."

"Actually, I need to find Laughing Luigi." I turned to Maddy and asked, "Did we even know his last name?"

"You're kidding, right? I thought Laughing was his first name," Maddy said with a smile.

Gina's good nature faltered for a split second, though she quickly masked it. "He's in the auditorium at the moment," she said. That must have been when she realized the real reason that we were there. "You're entering the competition, aren't you?"

"We are," I admitted. "The bait he dangled in front of us was just too much to turn down. The possibility of twenty-five-thousand dollars going to a small-town pizzeria is something that I just couldn't say no to."

"Believe me, I understand," she said. "Before I knew about Uncle Nathan, I pretty much stayed broke with my expensive tastes. You know what's funny, though? Once I had real money, I lost a great deal of interest in spending much of it. What I'm doing here," she said as she gestured all around us, "is what matters to me now these days."

"Do you mind if I ask you something?"

She nodded. "Anything."

"You don't care much for Luigi, do you?" I asked.

She shook her head. "Honestly? No. But then again, it's not up to me to approve of him. He's bringing us a great deal of business and attention. I've just got a bad feeling about him, though," she added in a whisper. "I'm not sure why, but something's not right about all of this."

Maddy stepped in. "So it's not just me. You caught it, too, right?"

I had to laugh. "If you ask me, you're both imagining things. I'm not a big fan of the man, but Bob Lemon himself looked over this contract," I said as I waved it in the air. "With his approval, I signed it. After all, what could go wrong?"

"I just hope you don't find all of the answers to that question somewhere down the road," Maddy said.

"Seconded," Gina said.

Maddy asked, "I hate to ask, but is there a restroom nearby? I drank one too many sodas at lunch."

"There's one just around the corner, but you can use the one in my office. I really pampered myself designing it, and I've been dying to show it off." She pointed toward the fireplace and added, "Eleanor, Luigi's just down that hallway, through the first set of doors on the right."

"I'll catch up with you later, Sis," Maddy said.

As they left together toward Gina's office off to

one side behind the front desk, I started down the hallway to find Luigi and make A Slice of Delight's entry in the competition official.

All of that left my thoughts, though, the second I opened the door and walked inside.

From the sound of the loud voices coming from the stage, apparently Maddy and Gina weren't the only ones who had a problem with Luigi.

"You are a liar and a thief," a woman said as she waved a finger ominously at Luigi, "and you're not going to get away with this."

"I don't know what you're talking about," Luigi said. I doubted that was true. There was a smug grin on his face that testified otherwise.

"We were supposed to be invited to this mockery of a contest," the woman snapped. "I even signed your insane contract. You can't just capriciously pull our entry at the last second."

"As a matter of fact, I can, and I have. You signed the document in question, but did you actually read it?"

She was clearly agitated by his question. "How could I? It was full of confusing lawyer language and boilerplate clauses. I'd be amazed if anyone actually bothered to read the thing before they signed it. It was massive."

"I'm sorry, but I can't help you. If you were foolish enough to sign a legally binding contract without understanding all of it, you have no one but yourself to blame. Section seven, paragraph eleven states that at the sole discretion of the contest host, the invitation to the competition can be withdrawn up to one hour before it is set to begin. Since we are now three weeks away from the actual contest, I'm well within my legal rights to terminate your participation, and you have no recourse in the matter. Your invitation has officially been withdrawn, and your reservations have been cancelled. I suggest you deal with it, Mrs. Ford."

"This is not over, not by a long shot. Don't think you're going to get away with this, Luigi," she said, clearly distraught over being dropped from the competition without explanation. I had to wonder if it had anything to do with my earlier, and sudden, invitation.

"There's nothing left to discuss. It's over," Luigi said, and then I heard a slight laugh. It was a dark, ominous sound, without joy or hope, and I felt a chill run through me when I heard it. I doubted that I'd ever be able to forget the way that sound hit me, like a punch straight to the heart.

Mrs. Ford stormed off the stage and nearly knocked me over on her way out the door. "Get out of my way," she snapped just before exiting the auditorium.

"Is she a friend of yours?" I asked Luigi as the door swung silently shut behind her.

He was clearly not pleased when he realized that I'd witnessed the confrontation. "How long have you been eavesdropping, Eleanor?"

"I wasn't," I said curtly. "I'm sure that I missed most of it, but she wasn't very happy when she left, was she?"

"I can't be responsible for her state of mind," he said.

I doubted that was true, but I'd had enough battles with Luigi to know that I wasn't eager to get involved in one that in no way concerned me. "I came to give you this," I said as I walked up on stage and handed him the signed contract.

"Good," he said absently. "I'd hoped you would agree."

"I didn't understand everything, but my attorney made sure there weren't any bear traps in it. Aren't you going to tell me who that was who just threatened you?" I asked.

"She is of no consequence—a pizza maker whose ambitions clearly outreached her ability." He dismissed her without another thought and turned his back to the seats and faced the stage. "This is going to be incredible. Each set of two contestants will have their own mini kitchen. I'm bringing in small electric ovens for the baking, and every station will have a duplicate set of tools and supplies for the contest," he said as he painted the picture with words and gestures. "It will be the fairest contest that my company and I could design."

I turned and looked out into a sea of seats. "Is there really going to be an audience?"

"Of course there is," he said. "What did you expect? This is a big deal."

"I don't know. I just figured the competitors would make their pizzas, they'd be judged, and then the winner would get a check."

He shook his head. "Where's the flair, the drama, the showmanship in that? This is going to be a grand event!"

The man was clearly caught up in his own delusions, but who was I to set him straight? After all, he was the one putting up the prize money.

"It's going to be magnificent," he said.

"I can't wait."

"Well, you'll have to," Luigi said. "From here on, everything will be wrapped in secrecy until the evening before the competition begins. You'll all be staying at the Tree-Line as my guests, so you'll have to make yourself available for interviews before we begin, at the end of each stage's judging, and of course after the grand finale."

"We have to stay here?" I asked. "You know that Maddy and I have our own places in town," I protested. I wasn't all that thrilled with leaving my cottage, even with these luxurious accommodations that would be available to me free of charge.

"I'm sorry, but it's a part of the rules."

"Bob didn't say anything about that when he read the contract," I countered.

"That's because that particular document dealt with the competition itself, not the details that will be surrounding it. Besides, what are you complaining about? You will love staying here, and as an added bonus, I'll be picking up the check for your accommodations, and you'll get a daily stipend for food, no matter the outcome of the contest." He paused, and then smiled slightly. "Eleanor, don't tell me you don't relish the idea of gouging me, even if it's just a little?"

"We'll agree to those conditions. I'm sure this place will be fine," I said.

As I responded, his cell phone rang, and after glancing at the number, Luigi said, "It's my office, I need to take this. My VP of Marketing and Sales, a man named Jack Acre, will contact you soon with all of the details. I'll see you and your sister in three weeks."

I knew enough to realize when I was being dismissed.

It appeared that I'd just have to wait to find out what other hoops Luigi was going to make us all jump through in order to have a shot at his grand prize.

"There you are," I said to Maddy as I approached the front desk. "I thought you were meeting me in the auditorium."

"I was, but we got a little distracted," she said. "You should see her bathroom. You could practically live in it."

"I don't see how," Gina said. "Eleanor, I'm sorry. It was all my fault."

"No worries. The contract's been delivered, so we're all set. It appears that Maddy and I will be staying with you here at the complex during the competition, Gina."

"I know," she said with a smile. "I wasn't allowed to say anything until Luigi told you, but I'm thrilled to have you staying here with me. I have the best two suites in the house reserved for the two of you on our luxury floor. All of the contestants, Luigi, and two of his staff members have rooms reserved there, but I saved the nicest two for you."

"You didn't have to go to all of that trouble on our account," I said.

"You saved my life, Eleanor," she replied. "How much gratitude is too much for something like that?"

"Funny, but I still feel like you're the one who saved me," I said.

Maddy laughed. "Okay, I get it. You're both heroes. Now, tell me more about these suites. Can we see one of them?"

I smiled. "Maddy, we can't impose on Gina like that."

Gina shrugged. "I'd be delighted to show you if I could, but both of those suites are occupied at the moment."

"Please don't tell me Luigi is staying in one of them," I said. "I couldn't bear the thought of being in the same place that he ever stayed."

"Don't worry; he's not in either suite. As a matter of fact, we saved those especially for my uncle's most important guests, some real bigwigs," Gina explained.

I started to wonder about just how much these suites cost, but I decided to keep my reservations to myself. After all, when would I ever get the opportunity to stay in that kind of suite again on my own, especially without having to foot the bill?

Gina continued. "So, if you're not too full from lunch, I could have our staff show you a lovely array of fresh pies, cakes, and other desserts we're offering here. Believe me, they are worth every calorie."

I glanced at my watch and said, "We'd love to, but we've got pizzas to make."

Maddy bit her lip, and then said, "We could be a *little* late, Eleanor."

"Come on, Sis, we're going," I said with a grin.

She shrugged as she looked at Gina. "What can I say? I tried."

"No worries. You've both got rain checks."

"Ms. Sizemore," a man said as he approached us, "I'm sorry to interrupt, but the breakers in the conference room keep tripping, and our electrician is saying that it's something we're doing."

"I'll be there in a second, but call Henry Felding and tell him that I'm not paying him until it's fixed." She paused, and then added, "Never mind. I'll call him myself." She turned back to us as she said, "If you ladies will excuse me," and pulled out her cell phone to make the call.

Out in the parking lot, Maddy turned to me and said, "I can't believe how that fire changed Gina."

"Really? I can barely see the scars, and I know where to look for them."

"That's not what I meant, and you know it," Maddy said.

I shrugged. "Some folks can change on their own, but it's been my experience that for most people, it takes a truly traumatic event to jar them out of their lives enough to make them want to reevaluate how they've been living."

"I'm willing to admit that the very real possibility of being burned alive could do that to a gal," Maddy said. "And yet it didn't seem to change you at all."

"Don't be so sure about that," I said, remembering how it had led me to the point where I could finally start to let go of Joe and think about another man in my life.

"Well, if you've changed, I can't see it," she said.

"Maybe you just need new glasses," I said with a smile as we got into my Subaru and drove back to A Slice of Delight.

A part of me wished that the competition would begin tomorrow instead of three weeks from now. The suspense of who else would be participating, the challenges, and actually everything about the contest was almost more than I could take. But I knew that soon enough, Maddy and I would be drawn back into the joys and problems of running a pizzeria, and my worries about the upcoming competition would all fade, at least for the short term. With Greg and Josh, our two college men who worked when classes permitted, I knew we'd be able to handle just about anything that came our way at the Slice, but I also realized that there was no way I was going to be able to stop thinking about that prize money.

Even with the hefty cut taken off the top to pay taxes, it was still a lot of money to play with.

I just hoped that if I did win, I'd keep my promise to spend it on the pizzeria and not myself.

Chapter 3

"I keep forgetting just how amazing this place is," I said to Maddy three weeks later. The appointed eve for the competition to begin was finally upon us, and we'd come with our overnight bags to check into our rooms.

"Gina did a truly magnificent job," Maddy said as we both took in the hotel lobby's elegant yet rustic feel. Low whispers of jazz served as background music, and she'd added more soft lighting and a few large towering plants since we'd been at the grand opening nine days ago. After we checked into our rooms, which were as lovely as promised, Maddy and I headed back downstairs for the cocktail party that would introduce us to all of our competitors.

Gina and Luigi had decided to host our meet-and-greet party at the smaller and more intimate hotel complex's atrium annex tonight, since the auditorium had already been set up for the audience, and the kitchens were all organized on the contest stage, so we headed over there.

Apparently we were early, though, since no one else was there.

"Should we come back later?" I asked.

My sister shook her head. "I'm happy right where I am."

A waiter approached with flutes of champagne, and though I wasn't normally much of a drinker, I took one as Maddy grabbed one for herself. "You're drinking, too?" she asked with a smile.

"Why shouldn't I? I'm not driving anywhere this evening, and besides, it might help calm my nerves."

"And if that doesn't work, at least you got to drink some very good champagne." Maddy took a sip, and then she asked, "I wonder what the guys are up to while we're here at this elegant soiree tonight."

"Do you mean our boyfriends or our employees?" I asked. We'd given Greg and Josh three days off and had shuttered the doors to A Slice of Delight. My two young employees had protested that they could run the pizzeria without us, but I'd had my doubts. We'd certainly lose some money over the next few days of the competition, and maybe even a customer or two, but I didn't see any way around it. Besides, we had a one in four shot at winning the grand prize, and the lost days of revenue wouldn't mean much then. If we lost, I'd just write it off as an experiment that hadn't worked out.

"Take your pick. Strike that. I'm betting that Greg and Josh are off sulking somewhere because we wouldn't let them try to run the Slice without us."

"Don't kid yourself, Maddy," I said. "Knowing

them, they're probably skiing in the mountains right now. Their school is on break for the next ten days, and I refuse to believe that they aren't off somewhere taking full advantage of it."

"Yeah, you're probably right," she said as she took another sip. "How about the other two, though? It's a shame they're missing this."

"Believe it or not, David said something about them having dinner together before they join us here later," I said. "I can't believe Luigi would exclude them, even for this portion of the evening. It's not really fair."

"And that surprises you in what way, exactly?" She glanced around the room, which was finally starting to fill up, and then she asked me, "Where is our grinning host, anyway? You'd think that after shelling out all of this money, he'd at least be on hand to bask in the glory of it all."

I looked around the room and saw three other sets of people that had to be our fellow contestants, though no group had strayed enough to speak to another. It was amazing how eight people just disappeared in the space designed to hold about three times that. "Maybe he's off somewhere trying to figure out a way to cheat us all out of the grand prize," I said with a smile.

I was just joking, but Maddy took it seriously.

"If it happens, let me just go on the record right now to say that it wouldn't surprise me one bit," my sister said. She was interrupted from adding anything more by a nice-looking couple as they finally got up the nerve to approach us.

"Excuse me, but aren't you Eleanor Swift?" the woman asked, extending her hand. She was tall,

nearly six feet, and willowy, with long, straight
blond hair and hazel eyes.

"I am," I said. "I'm sorry, but if we ever met, I
don't remember you."

She laughed gently, a sound that reminded me of
wind chimes in a summer breeze. "There's no reason in the world that you should. I just wanted to say
how much I enjoy your pizza."

I smiled at her and admitted, "Well, I can't hear
that enough, so I appreciate your compliment. Are
you one of the competitors?"

"We are," the man with her said as he stepped
forward. "We're the Clarkes. I'm Jeff, and this is
Sandy. It's no secret why you're in the competition. I
agree with my wife. Your pizza is delicious." Jeff
was several years older than his wife, if my guess
was right. He was rather nice looking, with gray
coming in at his temples, and piercing blue eyes.

"You must be here for a good reason as well," I
said.

Jeff grinned at his wife. "Isn't that odd? Why is it
that neither one of us introduced our pizzeria?"

Sandy shrugged good-naturedly. "I've long given
up on trying to figure out some of the things we do."
She turned back to me and added, "We own the
Grinning Cat Pizzeria in downtown Asheville."

"Really? I've been there," I said, suddenly excited.
"I love your pizza, and your restaurant, and I'm not
just saying that." I turned to my sister and said, "I told
you we should have introduced ourselves to the own-
ers when we were there." Maddy and I had taken a
day trip to Asheville a few months before to shop for
Christmas presents, and while we'd been in town,
we'd stopped in and had the most delicious pizza for

lunch, something that was our normal habit while visiting other cities and towns.

"It's true. We were jealous," Maddy said after she introduced herself. "I don't know which I loved more, your sauce or your brightly decorated pizzeria. It's really eclectic, isn't it?"

Sandy laughed at the observation. "Most places we'd stick out like a sore thumb, but since we're in Asheville, we fit right in. One of our customers was wearing a T-shirt the other day that sums our town up perfectly. It said, 'If you're too weird for Asheville, you must just be too weird.' The city isn't all eclectic, but our favorite parts of it certainly are."

"The mosaic mural you have on the back wall is perfect," I said. "I take it you are both Lewis Carroll fans, given the name and the prominence of cat memorabilia. Why not just call it the Cheshire Cat outright?"

"Honestly, we both love the Alice books," Sandy said, "but our inspiration was actually our own cat. He had the oddest habit of holding his mouth so that it looked like he was grinning all of the time."

"He sounds delightful," I said.

"He was indeed," Sandy answered, a little subdued.

"I'm so sorry," I said.

"How could you know? He's been gone awhile, but we still miss him," Jeff said. After patting his wife's shoulder lovingly, almost as though he was reassuring her that he was right there beside her, he waved a hand around the room. "What is this all about, anyway? Is George waiting for everyone to get here so that he can make a big entrance?"

"I'm sorry. Who is George, exactly? Is he another contestant?" I asked.

"Luigi, I should have said," Jeff said quickly, trying to brush the question off.

"Hang on," Maddy said. "You're not getting off the hook that easily. Why did you call him George?"

Sandy looked uncomfortable about the direction the conversation was taking, but Jeff clearly wasn't a fan of our host, so he didn't mind sharing a little dirt about him. "I'm not surprised you didn't know. He makes a big deal out of keeping it a secret, but his real name is George Vincent. He thought Luigi sounded more authentic for a pizza maker before he moved to North Carolina, so he started calling himself that, and it stuck. I didn't think you could successfully give yourself a new nickname, but he somehow managed to do it. What I still don't get is how he has the nerve to call himself Laughing Luigi. What a joke." He gestured with his champagne glass toward us and asked, "Have you two ever seen him laugh, or even smile, unless he had something on the person he was talking to, or most likely, about? I know I haven't."

"He can be a bit abrupt at times, can't he?" I asked.

Maddy shook her head. "Sis, that's the nicest way I can imagine anyone describing the man. He's a boil on the nose of the world, as far as I'm concerned."

Jeff laughed at the description, and then he told Maddy, "You I like."

"You'll have to excuse my sister," I said. "She has a habit of saying whatever's on her mind, regardless of the circumstances."

"That's just one of my charms. You can't deny that I speak the truth, though," Maddy answered.

"Most likely more than you know," Jeff said softly. I wasn't entirely sure that particular comment had been meant for us at all.

"Isn't this resort lovely?" Sandy asked quickly, clearly trying to change the subject. I had to guess that her spouse had started drinking before this little soiree, since he hadn't been there long enough to ingest enough to get drunk already.

Jeff, suddenly realizing that he was distressing his wife, immediately obliged. "I don't mean to be rude to your hometown, ladies, but this place is just a little too grand for the likes of Timber Ridge, isn't it?"

"Jeff," Sandy said reprovingly. "You should apologize to Eleanor and Maddy. That's not a polite thing to say."

"But it's true enough," Maddy agreed. "We have a reclusive millionaire in town who built it for his niece."

"We don't know that's the full motivation behind it," I said. "I'm sure Nathan had other reasons to do it as well."

"Eleanor, you have to admit that it didn't hurt that Gina wanted to run a place like this, though," Maddy answered.

"Whatever the reason he had," Sandy said, "it's truly magnificent."

The other two duos must have noticed that we were chatting, because they drifted over to where we stood, and soon enough, introductions were made all around.

Maddy and I were offered extended hands by a

set of twin men in their early thirties. The men had matching dark hair and eyes, and were both about fifteen pounds overweight. How had they managed to do that in sync as well? I knew that twins shared a great deal that the rest of the world couldn't fully understand, but was it reasonable to think that they'd have the same eating habits? Beneath the surface of their jocularity, there was a feral look about them, and I wondered if it was based on their dispositions or their genetics.

"Hi, there. I'm Todd," one of them said.

"And I guess that makes me odd," the other twin said with a grin. It was clear it was a standard line of theirs by their practiced ease of delivering it.

"We're the Blackwell brothers," Todd explained, "And his real name is Reggie."

"Well, it's not my real name. For that, you'd have to call me Reginald Hallsworth Standard Blackwell."

"It sounds like there's a story that goes along with that name," Sandy said politely.

"There is," was all that Reggie would say in response, effectively killing the conversation.

Todd spoke up in the growing silence, though, and added, "We own the Pizza Pie Factory in Raleigh."

"And we're from Pizza Top in Charlotte," the other man said. "I'm Kenny Henderson."

"And I'm Anna Wright," the woman added. He was barrel-chested, and sported a mustache that matched his hair a little too perfectly, while his partner was a mere slip of a girl, barely into her twenties from the look of her, with mousy brown hair and eyes.

"Are you a couple, too?" Maddy asked.

They both looked instantly appalled by the suggestion. Kenny spoke up first. "No, it's nothing like that. Not at all. She's my assistant, and only my assistant."

Anna just nodded her agreement, and now the room was definitely filled with awkward silence.

No one seemed willing to add anything else of substance to the conversation after that, and we stood around a few minutes, each struggling to make small talk, when Luigi finally joined us. As I studied him approaching us, I realized that he did in fact look more like a George than he ever had a Luigi, and it was all I could do not to laugh out loud about the name and persona he'd taken on.

"Excellent. I see that you've all met," Luigi said. I made up mind to keep thinking of him as Luigi and not George, even though I knew better. It was the only way I could keep from laughing in his face. Still, it was good knowing that there was a chink in the man's armor.

He continued. "Please excuse my tardiness, but I've been seeing to some last-minute details about tomorrow in the auditorium. Gina Sizemore asked me to extend her apologies. I'm afraid we have to make a few adjustments to the setups before we're ready to begin. We've been tweaking everything all day to make sure that every station is identical, and we've modified the rules just a touch before we get started as well." Several of us were about to ask what the changes were going to be, but he held up his hands and added, "The adjustments we've made are outlined in the new packets you'll receive tonight in your rooms."

Two men walked in hurriedly, and Luigi gestured them over to our little group. It was clear that he'd been waiting on them, and I didn't doubt that he hadn't been thrilled about being upstaged like that.

"Come on. Get over here," he commanded, and they both dutifully joined us.

As they did, Luigi introduced them. "I'd like you to meet Jack Acre, my VP of Marketing and Sales, and Frank Vincent, our head of production." Jack Acre was handsome, not movie-star good-looking, but quite a bit above average. Even if I hadn't just found out that Luigi's last name was Vincent, it was obvious that he and the other man were brothers. I had to wonder if there was any resentment between them. After all, Jack had been introduced as a vice president, but Luigi had gone out of his way to tell us that Frank wasn't at that level.

At least Jack's smile was friendly, though there wasn't much warmth to it, while Frank just nodded in our general direction, keeping his gaze on the carpet.

"Jack, I need you to fetch my medication. It's in my room," Luigi said.

"Why don't you let Frank get it?" Jack said easily. "I'd like to have a word with the contestants myself."

"Because I asked you," Luigi said firmly as he gave Acre his key. "Frank, I'm sure there's something you need to be doing right now as well," he added, dismissing both men as effectively as if he'd ordered armed guards to throw them out. Jack seemed to take it all in stride, but for a brief flash, I saw a look of anger on Frank's face. It appeared he wasn't all that fond of being ordered around by his brother.

"What about those changes?" Kenny Henderson asked. "Why can't we get them now?"

I knew that I was going to have to start thinking of a way to associate these people with the cities they were from, or I'd be constantly confused. From now on, he'd be Kenny Charlotte in my mind, and his assistant was going to be Anna Charlotte. The Blackwells would be Todd and Reggie Raleigh, and Jeff and Sandy Clarke would be the Ashevilles. It probably would have sounded like a weird system to anyone other than my sister, but it had worked for me in the past, and I was going to stick to it.

"You'll all get them at the same time, and it will be in plenty of time," Luigi said as he glanced at his watch. "However, I'm afraid there's no time to go into that now. We have guests waiting, and besides your loved ones, there are members of the press here, as promised, so I ask you all to be civil to anyone who asks you any questions tonight. Have fun, and I'll see you all tomorrow afternoon for the first stage of the competition."

With that, he left us, despite questions being posed from us as he walked away. Luigi gestured to a pair of guards standing at a red velvet rope, and motioned for them to let the waiting crowd join us.

Before they could get there though, I heard one of the twins from Raleigh say as he handed his brother a folded ten-dollar bill, "You were right."

The other brother was smug as he said, "You rarely go wrong betting that a leopard is not going to change his spots."

"What does that mean?" I asked. "Have you two had prior dealings with Luigi, too?"

"Haven't we all?" the twin who'd just pocketed the bill asked. "I thought that was the real reason for this little show Luigi's putting on."

"We don't know what you're talking about," Kenny said, and Anna did nothing to dispute it. "We barely know the man."

"Sure. Right," the twin said. "How about you two?" he asked the Asheville couple. "You look like your paths have crossed his in the past, and I'm guessing that it wasn't all that pleasant for you."

I'd been watching Jeff and Sandy part of the time while Luigi had been talking, and I knew that what the twin was saying had to have been true. There was history there, whether they admitted it or not. What was Luigi up to? Was there really even a twenty-five-thousand-dollar prize? There had to be. Bob had made sure that it was in the contract.

So what exactly was going on?

Was it simply a competition for the best indie pizza in North Carolina, or did Luigi have something darker in mind gathering us all together like this?

After the deluge of reporters left, we were still waiting for Bob and David to show up.

"Where could they be?" I asked my sister.

"Maybe they're in the lobby waiting for us to find them," she said.

"Then let's go check on them. I don't know about you, but I'm getting tired of answering the same stupid questions. Where did Luigi find these so-called reporters, anyway?"

"I'm guessing grocery store fliers and middle school newspapers," Maddy said with a broad grin.

"Then let's go find our men," I said.

Maddy and I were leaving when we spotted Anna from Charlotte and Luigi off to one side in the corridor between the atrium and the main lobby.

"You can't stop it," she said fiercely.

Luigi answered sharply, "We both know better than that. I've told you before, and I'll say it again. I won't allow it."

"You don't have a say in the matter. Not really," she said, and then stormed off in our direction. I noticed that Luigi smiled a little as Anna left him to return to the cocktail party, and then he started back toward the auditorium where the contest would be held.

I stopped Anna before she could get past us and I asked, "Are you okay?"

"I'm fine," she said. "I suppose that I'm just a little overly emotional these days."

Maddy suggested, "Why don't you come back in and have a glass of champagne with us? It will make you feel better, I promise."

"Sorry, but no thanks," she said.

"If you don't like champagne, they've got some nice white wine instead," I suggested.

"No thanks. I really can't. Bye."

She left us quickly, and after she was gone, I asked Maddy, "Do you have any idea what that all about?"

"Who knows? Luigi surely has a way with people, doesn't he?"

"He's a real charmer, all right," I answered. "It's a

good thing he has Jack Acre for Marketing and Sales."

"If you say so," Maddy said.

"What's the matter? Don't you like him?"

"The jury's still out on him. After all, we haven't really had a chance to get to know him, have we?"

We walked out into the lobby, the central hub of the complex, but Bob and David were nowhere to be found. We were still trying to figure out where they were when Jack Acre approached us. "Have you seen Luigi, by any chance?"

"He was headed for the auditorium the last time we saw him," I said.

"Good," Acre said. "It took me forever to find his meds. The man's room was a real train wreck."

A second later, Kenny from Charlotte nearly knocked Jack down as he accosted us. "Where's my assistant?" he demanded of us.

"We haven't the faintest clue. It's not our night to watch her," Maddy said, matching Kenny's tone.

"I heard she was with you," Kenny said with a little less agitation.

"She was, but she's not here now."

"And you don't know where she went?"

"No, we don't," I said. I had a feeling Anna wasn't in any mood to deal with her boss after arguing with Luigi, and even if I knew where she'd gone, I wasn't about to rat her out.

"You've got to admit one thing, Sis," Maddy said to me after Kenny left and we were about to call our men to see where they were.

"What's that?"

"At least our lives aren't boring."

"I'll give you that. But why exactly is that a good thing?"

"I love working at the Slice, and you know it, but it's not exactly a hotbed of activity. The air around here is singing with energy."

"I can feel it too, but I'm not so sure that it's positive energy."

"I never said that it was, only that it was there. We'd better watch our steps around this gang. Like the woman said, we could be in for a bumpy ride."

I knew in my heart that Maddy could be right, but I wasn't at all sure why she was so happy about that.

I could have used a little bigger slice of boring before the contest began, and the drama really had a chance to start. Spending time a little later with Bob and David helped, but it was still tough getting to sleep that night.

Tomorrow was potentially the start of two of the biggest days of my life.

Chapter 4

When we walked up the steps of the stage the next afternoon, Maddy and I were falling all over each other with anticipation, anxious to begin. The contestants were allowed inside the auditorium, and we all got our first look at the stage. As promised, there were four identical pizza making stations set up, with individual ovens, refrigerators, prep tables and all the tools we'd need for the two days of the contest.

Maddy and I were still familiarizing ourselves with the layout when we heard Luigi say to the whole group, "If you'll all come together over here by the main judging table, we can get started."

We all did as he asked, and once we were gathered together, Luigi said, "Have you all read the rules and procedures changes?"

"Yes," one of the Raleigh twins said. "What does the section on judging mean, exactly, and why is there only one chair at the table where you're sitting right now?"

It was a question Maddy and I had discussed ourselves, asking it after we'd read the three changes to the contest that Luigi had sprung on us at the last second. One point in particular struck us as odd: it had said that the contest would be judged at the organizer's discretion, whatever that meant.

"There's only one chair for a very good reason," Luigi said smugly. "I am Laughing Luigi's Pizza Dough. As the CEO and main stockholder, everything in the company comes down to my decision, so I've decided that I, and I alone, will judge who wins."

"Do you mean that it's not even going to be a blind taste test?" Jeff Asheville asked him. "How are you going to prove that you're impartial?"

"You'll just have to trust me," Luigi said with a grin.

"And if I don't?" he asked.

"It's not too late for you to drop out of the competition," Luigi explained. "Is that what you really want to do?"

Jeff looked at his wife, who shook her head once. "No," Jeff answered. "We'll stay in it."

"I thought you might," Luigi said. "Are there any other questions?"

One of the twins started to say something, but his brother grabbed his arm and squeezed it so hard that the skin turned white under his grip.

"Nothing? Good. Get to work, and may the best pizza win." He motioned to the back door and said, "Let them in."

A number of folks filed into the auditorium, including quite a few faces that were familiar to Maddy and me. Had they come out to support us, or watch us as we failed? I smiled softly when I saw Bob and David fight for a seat near the front. At least we'd have two folks pulling for us. As I watched the people come in, I saw a familiar, but unexpected face in the crowd. It was the woman who'd had the confrontation with Luigi three weeks ago on this very stage. What was she doing here? Luigi must have noticed me staring into the crowd, because it didn't take him long to see her as well. "Excuse me," he told us all as he walked down the steps toward Mrs. Ford. She'd made good on her threat of not just rolling over after being dumped from the competition, and I couldn't blame her. Who wanted to miss out on a chance of winning twenty-five grand?

Fortunately, she was close enough to the stage so we could hear what was going on. It didn't hurt that neither she nor Luigi tried in the least to keep their voices down. She'd come ready for a fight, and I knew that Luigi wouldn't back down either. We were in for quite a show, unless I missed my guess.

"This is a public contest," Mrs. Ford said as Luigi approached. "I have as much right to be here as everyone else."

"You don't think we can throw you out?" Luigi asked. He was clearly unhappy with her presence there.

"I already talked to a lawyer. The only way you can exclude me is if you make everyone else leave, too. Is that what you want? I can see the headlines across North Carolina tomorrow. PIZZA DOUGH KING FAILS TO RISE. I've done a mock-up of a press release with that as a headline, if you'd like to see it."

She looked at Luigi smugly, mostly because she had him where she wanted him, and she knew it. I was certain that one of the reasons our sponsor was holding the competition was to promote his company, and contrary to popular belief, bad press was in no way better than no press at all.

Luigi turned his back on Mrs. Ford and rejoined us on the stage.

Without another glance, he turned to the audience and said, "Welcome to the first competition to find the greatest independent pizza maker in all the state."

Everyone applauded as Luigi introduced each team. When Maddy and I were introduced as the hometown team, there was an explosion of noise, and I was reminded yet again that we were under the microscope here in Timber Ridge. After the announcement, Luigi turned to us all and said, "Good luck."

Maddy and I started as each team leapt into action, but it started off badly, and then went downhill from there.

It appeared that we were going to fail, and do it epically, in front of most of our regular customers.

Before I even realized how late it was getting in the competition, Luigi announced, "Contestants, you have seventeen minutes left to present your entries in this stage of the contest using Luigi's regular, and most popular, crust." Maddy and I stared down at the disappointment of a pizza in front of us that we'd just pulled out of the portable oven. It had been like working in the middle of a circus trying to make the pizza, and we'd let the crowd, and all of the attention, get to us. The stage itself was jammed with pizza makers, Luigi, and a few photographers who always seemed to get in the way; plus, there wasn't an open seat in the auditorium as we looked out onto the sea of faces. There was nothing like looking back at an audience that was all gathered to watch us fail. The pizza in front of us was an unmitigated disaster. I was used to working with my own soft and pliable dough, but Luigi's was so stiff that it was all I could do to knuckle it into the pan. By the time I was finished with it, it looked as though a third grader had attempted to bake a pie, and unsuccessfully, at that. Maddy's veggie topping distribution and lopsided cheese application hadn't been much better.

We were both off our game, and we knew it.

As we studied the disaster in front of us, the Asheville team beside us pulled something out of their oven that looked ready for a magazine shoot.

"Do you see that?" Maddy whispered.

"I'm trying not to look. Is there any way we can salvage this thing?"

She looked down at our pizza and shook her head. "I don't think so. It's a complete and epic fail."

I glanced at the huge digital clock hanging over our heads like a sword. There was now sixteen minutes left, barely time enough to make and bake another pizza. "We might as well try something else," I said. I'd left a ball of dough out on the counter when I'd made the first crust, so I grabbed it and started shaping it into a round disk.

"At least this one's working up better into the shape I need," I said. "Get your new toppings ready."

Once the crust was complete, I took my sauce, the only thing I was allowed to supply myself, and spread it carefully on top of the dough. I slid the pan to Maddy, who added her toppings and cheese in a pleasing random pattern, and then I slid the pie into the oven.

Now all we could do was wait for the results, and hope that they were better than our first attempt.

"What should we do with this one?" I asked as I stared at the pizza gone wrong still sitting on our cooling rack.

"There's only one place this thing belongs," my sister said as she slid it off the pan and into the trash.

One of the Raleigh twins grinned in our direction as he saw what Maddy had done. "I hope that was just your warm-up pizza."

"Don't worry about us. We always make a really bad one first to get it out of our systems," I said, doing my best to smile as I said it.

"Then you're bound to win the whole competition now," the twin said. "That looked pretty hideous, and I doubt that it even tasted that good."

"Don't listen to him," Sandy from Asheville said beside me. "I don't know about you, but all of this attention is really unnerving."

"Thanks," I said. It felt good that even in the heat of battle, one of the other contestants cared enough to try to make Maddy and me feel better. I admitted, "I've never baked in a competition before. Have you?"

She laughed as she started cleaning her station, her perfect pizza parked in the warmer ready for judging. "Oh, yes. Jeff and I have done lots of these before. Don't worry. You get used to it after a while."

"I find that hard to believe," I said.

Sandy sneezed just as Luigi approached us. "You aren't coming down with a cold, are you?" he asked.

"No, it's just allergies," she said as she blew her nose. "There seems to be something year-round that I'm allergic to these days."

Luigi boasted, "I've never been cursed with them myself, but I know that allergies can be miserable. Are you taking anything for them?"

"I am," she said. "I just forgot to take one of my pills today."

"Well, carry on," Luigi said as he drifted over to the Charlotte kitchen to see what they were up to.

"Eleanor, come look at this," Maddy said.

"Excuse me," I told Sandy as I joined my sister at the oven. "What's going on?"

"It's not baking," she said.

"What?" I looked at the oven, and then opened it. Sure enough, while it had produced heat at one time, it was losing warmth, and fast. I checked the oven's settings, but it was still set properly to 425° F.

And then I spotted the cord. The plug was barely an inch from the power strip, and at a casual glance, it appeared to be fine, but somehow, it had become dislodged. As I plugged it back in, I glanced over at my competitors, but no one was watching me. Anyone could have done it, but I had a sneaking feeling that it had been one of the Raleigh twins or the team from Charlotte. It couldn't have been Jeff or Sandy, since I'd been talking to them the entire time, unless of course they were working with one of the other teams to eliminate us early. I had to stop being so paranoid. Chances were that not everyone on that stage was out to get us. It was most likely just an accident that the oven cord had been pulled out.

At least that's what I found myself hoping.

"Who unplugged our oven?" Maddy asked me, a fire in her eyes that I'd seen plenty of times before.

"It could have just been an accident," I said.

She clearly didn't believe that, not for one second. "Let me ask you something. How hard was it to plug the oven back in?"

"It took a little force to get it back in the socket," I admitted.

"Then it was no accident. We need to watch our backs, Eleanor. People can do nasty things when there's this kind of money involved."

"No harm done, though," I said. "I plugged it in again, so we're back in business."

She didn't reply, but just gestured to the clock instead.

"Don't worry, Maddy. It's going to turn out fine."

I just wished that I could believe it.

My sister and I both spent the remaining time watching the pizza, the power cord, and the oven itself, all at the same time.

When Luigi announced, "One minute left," I knew that I'd have to take our pizza out, even though I would have liked to have given it at least three more minutes in the oven. After all, having a bad entry to submit was better than not having one at all. I took the pizza peel, slid it under the pie, and pulled it out. After I transferred it to a serving plate, Maddy quickly cut it and plated the best-looking slice just as Luigi announced, "Time is now officially up. Competitors, present your slices here."

The others had all finished early, and they pulled their finished products from the warming bags, but I wondered if that might actually hurt them. The pizzas could be kept warm, but would they retain their crispness that long? At least ours was guaranteed to be fresh.

Luigi made a show of studying each piece before he sampled it, inspecting the bottom of the crust, the sides, and the toppings. After making notations on a clipboard as he inspected them individually, he tasted each piece. After he was finished, he compiled the scores and then picked up his microphone again. "In order of finishing, from last place to first, we have the following teams, named for the cities they represent. Coming in fourth, is Asheville." There was polite applause from the crowd, and when I looked at the husband-and-wife team, they appeared to accept the verdict, though I could see Jeff's clenched fists that denied his calm, outward demeanor. How in the world had we managed to beat them? I'd seen their pizza, and it had been a work of art. Could it honestly have tasted that awful, or was something else going on here? No matter. At least we hadn't come in last place.

"In third place, we have Raleigh."

One of the twins snorted, and I found myself amazed. Something was definitely wrong here. Was it possible he'd mixed the entries up, giving us a score that we didn't deserve? We had at least come in second, and perhaps won this stage of the competition today. When Luigi announced, "Timber Ridge is our runner-up," Maddy and I hugged each other as the crowd erupted in applause. It was nice to hear, since we were the home team, but Luigi's judgment was what counted. The team from Charlotte celebrated as the winners, and after a moment's pause, Luigi said, "That concludes this afternoon's compe-

tition. With the regular crust complete, this evening
we move on to the thin crust phase of our competition. Tomorrow morning the contestants will attempt a deep dish pizza, and tomorrow afternoon we
will have our final session, which will feature free-
style pizzas from each of the teams. Then tomorrow
evening, we will announce the winners! We'll see
you all back here in three hours for the next stage of
our competition."

"What are we going to do in the meantime?"
Maddy asked.

"I say we get something to eat. There's a greenroom set up with food for us, isn't there?"

"It's just cold sandwiches and cans of sodas,"
Kenny from Charlotte said as he pointed to a door
just off the stage. "Is there anyplace in this one-
horse hick town where we can get a decent meal?"

"There's a pizza place that's perfect on the downtown promenade, but it's closed for the competition," Maddy said with a smile.

"I understand the restaurant here at the hotel is
quite good," I said.

"Thanks, but we need to get away from all of this
to plan out our next pizza, and it's going to be tough
to do with all of you hovering around. We'll find
something."

Maddy watched them go and then turned to me
and said, "Someone doesn't play nice with others."

"Do you mean besides us?" I asked with a grin.

"Always. I hate to agree with Mr. Personality, but
he's right. Sandwiches don't sound that great to me
after slaving over those pizzas. What do you think?"

"We could always go to Brian's," I suggested.
"The diner's got to be better than what we can get

for free, and we can't really afford to eat in the restaurant here."

Just then, Gina approached us. "Hey there, I forgot to give these out today," she said as she handed us each a nicely embossed card.

"What are they for?" I asked as I studied mine.

"You can use them in our restaurant while you are our guests here. Meals here are on the house," she said with a grin, "and you can each bring a guest with you."

"That's really sweet of you, Gina, but we can't do that to your bottom line," I said.

"Speak for yourself," Maddy said. "I've heard nothing but raves about the place, and I've been dying to try it."

"Does everyone get these?" I asked.

"They get cards, but they aren't allowed to bring any guests," she admitted.

"I don't want you overstepping your bounds just for our sake."

"Don't worry; I'm not doing anything that my uncle hasn't requested. He's pulling for you two, you know."

"I hope he doesn't get his hopes up. We just got lucky this afternoon. That second-place finish was an absolute fluke."

"Way to talk us up, Eleanor," Maddy said with a grin that extended well past the wittiness of her remark.

"What are you smiling about?" I asked.

"I just found our two meal guests," she said.

I looked at where Maddy was pointing and saw David and Bob cutting their way through the crowd onto the stage.

Gina caught it, too. "I'll leave you two until later. Congratulations."

"Thanks," I said as the men approached.

After we collected quick kisses from our respective beaux, Bob said, "We're here to take you two out to an early dinner. Name the place, and it's our treat."

Maddy smiled softly at her fiancé. "Even if it's the restaurant here at the hotel? I hear that it's kind of pricey."

"Absolutely," Bob said. "Whatever you'd like." As an attorney, he could well afford it, but still, it was nice of him to offer.

"I've got an idea. How about if we take you two out instead?" Maddy asked.

"There's no need for that," David said. "We've got it."

"Well, if you insist," I said, "but Maddy and I happen to each have Golden Tickets, so it's all on the house if you let us pick up the tab."

"Even for us?" Bob asked.

Maddy grinned. "Sure. Gina said we could both bring a guest."

"Then count me in," he said. It was funny, but from the moment my sister had accepted his proposal, Bob had lost all interest in hurrying the process of the actual ceremony, much to Maddy's delight. I had a feeling they were in for a very long engagement, but if they were happy with their relationship at its current stage, it was no business of mine.

"Let's go," David said. "That's assuming that I'm your plus-one, Eleanor."

"It's normally dangerous to assume anything like

that, but this time, you happen to be correct," I said with a smile. I was happy to have David in my life, though I'd never forget my late husband, Joe. My new boyfriend was a lot like him, though most likely in ways that probably no one else but I could see. The most important thing was that he made me smile, which was a huge plus in his favor.

The restaurant was jammed when we got there, and I was afraid that we wouldn't be able to get our complimentary meals after all, when the maître d' said, "This way, if you please. We have a special area reserved just for you."

He led us to a table overlooking an outdoor fountain surrounded by benches, and as I sat down, I said, "I could get used to this kind of treatment."

"There's no reason you shouldn't, at least not while we're here for the competition," Maddy said.

"We could always bring you both here ourselves some other time," David said.

"Careful what you're offering. We might just take you up on it," I said with a grin.

"Hey, if I get a chance to spend some time with you, it's worth whatever it costs." Just then David looked down at the menu, and then added hastily, "At least if I don't mind not paying my other bills on time. This place is kind of pricey for Timber Ridge, isn't it?"

"When you consider that most of their clientele probably comes from out of town, it makes more sense," I said.

After we ordered, Bob said, "Congratulations on finishing second in the competition this afternoon, ladies."

I nodded my acceptance of his compliment, but Maddy barely noticed.

Bob asked, "I'm sorry. Did I say something wrong?"

"Don't mind her. We both feel like there's something just not right about this contest," I said.

"I'm glad you said it first," Maddy answered. "You saw the same thing as I did up there at the end, right?"

"I did," I answered.

"Well, don't keep us in suspense," David said. "What exactly happened?"

"Our dough wasn't even golden around the edges, let alone brown, and the veggies on top of the pie had to still be crisp and a little raw," I said. "It wasn't entirely our fault, though. Someone unplugged our oven on our second attempt, and we didn't have enough time to bake our pizza properly. The first pizza disaster was entirely on us, but the second was inedible. Honestly, we would have been better off submitting the first pie cold, mistakes and all, and yet we ended up taking second place in the judging."

"Could you two just be hypercritical of your own work?" David asked.

I considered it, but quickly dismissed the idea. "Sure, most of the time I'd agree that was a possibility, but we saw what we saw. There's no way we deserved second place, and anyone with a sense of taste would have put it in last place. Jeff and Sandy made a pizza pretty enough for a magazine shoot, and I'm willing to bet that it was as tasty as it looked."

"How is that possible, though? They came in last," David said.

"I'm guessing that Luigi's got his own agenda about this contest. We got second place because he was punishing the other two for something else they must have done. We know for a fact that none of the competitors here like Luigi at all."

"Then why did the Charlotte team beat you?" Bob asked.

A diner from another table nearby leaned in and said, "You're kidding, right? The fix is in. I thought everyone knew that Luigi has a stake in their restaurant."

"How do you know that?" I asked as I studied the woman in her thirties with frosted tips and a waistline thin enough to defy all logic.

"I'm the food reporter for the *Charlotte Touch*," she said as she handed Maddy her business card. Her name was Tina Lance, and if her card was any indication, someone had a very high opinion of her work to fork out for those cards.

"I've never heard of it," Maddy said flatly as she handed the card to me.

She shrugged. "We're new, but we're feisty. That's why I'm here. I'm going to expose Luigi for the fraud that he is."

"What do you mean?" I asked.

"First of all, his name's not Luigi at all. It's George Vincent, and he's using this contest to advance his own agenda. I'm sorry, but you never stood a chance."

"We already knew his real name," I said.

That seemed to take a bit of the wind out of her sails.

"If it's true that he's partnered with one of the

pizzerias, why haven't you reported him to the authorities?" Bob asked.

"All in good time," she answered as her check came. "I probably shouldn't have said anything to you, but I didn't want you to get your hopes up. Like I said, there's no way you can win. The whole thing is fixed."

After she was gone, I asked Maddy, "Do you believe her?"

"After seeing how he judged the competition before, I find it hard to believe that it's not the most reasonable explanation of what happened. I keep asking myself why she would lie to us, too," my sister said. "What does she have to gain by stirring things up like that?"

David broke in and asked, "You're kidding, right? She's a reporter. It's been my experience that they thrive on conflict. If she didn't see anything in this afternoon's contest, I wouldn't put it past her to try to make something happen so she could report it in the rag she works for."

Our food was delivered just then, and our conversation wove in and out of the critic's accusations as we ate. By the time we were finished with our excellent meals, I said, "I'm sorry to say that I didn't do that food justice. I tried my best to ignore what the food reporter told us, but I can't help wondering if what Tina Lance said was true."

Maddy grinned at me. "Let's assume for one second that it was all fact. In a way, she did us a favor. If we were destined not to win, it kind of takes the pressure off of us for the rest of the competition, doesn't it?"

Bob frowned. "You may look at it however you

choose to, but I'm not taking this so lightly. I've got a friend in Charlotte who owes me a favor. I'm going to have him dig into Ms. Lance's background, as well as check to see if her suspicions are true about Luigi and the Charlotte pizza makers."

"Don't burn any favors you might need later on down the road on our account," Maddy said. "In the end, it's just not all that important."

"If it matters to you, it impacts me," Bob said as he started to leave a tip. The waiter spied what he was doing, and then quickly returned it to him. "Thank you for the intent, but it has all been taken care of," he said, "gratuities included. Have a pleasant evening."

"Thank you," Bob said, and we all echoed it.

"Well, ladies, you have an hour and a half to kill before the next competition. Care to share it with us?" David asked.

"As tempting as the offers sounds, I'm afraid that I'll have to decline," Bob said as he glanced at his watch. "I'm due in court soon." He kissed Maddy good-bye, and after he was gone, David grinned at us both. "That suits me just fine. Now I get the both of you to myself."

"Be careful what you wish for," Maddy said with a grin. "Besides, I think I'm going to stretch out and rest before we get started again. Luigi arranged for us all to have rooms, and I mean to use mine."

"If you don't mind, David, that sounds great to me, too," I said.

My boyfriend just laughed as he shook his head and said, "I can't believe that I was just shot down twice in two seconds. If I didn't have an overinflated ego, something like that might sting a little."

I kissed him, and then gently shoved him away. "Don't worry. I'll make it up to you another time."

He grinned broadly now. "That sounds great to me. You know me. I just love rain checks!"

We took the elevator upstairs to our rooms after David left us, but we didn't make it inside right away.

There was something much more interesting than a nap going on in the hallway, something that neither one of us was willing to miss.

Chapter 5

"You'll do what I tell you to do, or believe me, I'll make you suffer for your disobedience," we heard Luigi say somewhere down the hallway. All of the contestants were staying close together on the same floor, along with Luigi and his employees, Jack Acre and Frank Vincent, so he could be talking to anyone.

I grabbed Maddy's arm and pulled her into the small room where the ice machine and a vending machine stood. I didn't want him to see us just yet. After all, we might learn a great deal more about the man if he didn't know that we were listening in.

"Who's he talking to?" Maddy asked me softly.

I shrugged. "Whoever it is hasn't replied, at least not loud enough for me to hear them. It could practically be anybody."

There was a moment's silence, and then Luigi

said, "I'm not playing around here. If you cross me, I promise you that you'll live to regret it."

I peeked around the corner as far as I felt comfortable going, but I still couldn't see anyone. The only way the conversation made any sense at all was if Luigi was standing in the hallway outside of someone else's room, and they were still inside. But who could it be? I leaned even farther out, and suddenly felt Maddy pulling me back. "We don't want him to know that we can hear him," she said.

I reluctantly agreed, though I was still straining for a clue about who Luigi was threatening.

I was about to poke my head out once again when I heard footsteps approaching quickly. I motioned to Maddy, and then forced myself back into the corner, where hopefully Luigi wouldn't spot me. Maddy followed suit, and I thought we'd be safe, unless the man had a sudden yearning for ice or soda and decided to take a detour into the small space. The elevator chimed once just past us, the doors slid open, and then a moment later, they closed.

I poked my head out again, and then stepped all the way into the hallway once I knew that he was gone.

"The coast is clear," I told Maddy.

She came out and joined me, and then we both looked up and down the hallway together. "Any idea where he was standing when he was talking to our mysterious stranger?" Maddy asked me.

I shook my head. "I don't have a clue. It could have been any one of these rooms. We didn't have much visibility past our own room."

Maddy frowned. "I didn't care for his tone of voice, and I can't imagine the recipient liked it any better. Luigi clearly threatened someone here. We just don't know who it was."

"We're just going to have to start knocking on doors and see who answers," I said.

"I'm not saying that you're wrong, but I'm just curious about something before you knock on the first door. What excuse are we going to use?"

I thought about it for a moment, and then said, "We've got the perfect icebreaker, really. We can talk about the competition."

She shrugged. "It's not great, but it's still probably better than anything I can come up with."

"Wow, stop it. Your extreme praise is going to make me blush."

"Just start knocking on doors, Sis, okay?"

I nodded, and approached the first door we hadn't been able to see. After three attempts, no one answered, and I was ready to give up on them.

"Wow, our plan needs some work," my sister said dryly.

"Maddy, not everyone is going to be in their room this time of day. Consider this a positive new bit of information. Whoever is in this room couldn't be our candidate."

She frowned. "Sorry, but I don't know that I can agree with that, Eleanor. What if they heard our knocking but decided not to answer? We can't just prowl the hallways hoping and waiting for someone to come out of their room. I can't imagine someone not calling security if they see us lurking around the corridors like a pair of criminals."

"You've got a point, but I'm still not willing to give up. Let's at least try a few more rooms, okay?"

"I've got your back. Knock on," she said with a shrug.

We actually had more luck with the next door. After knocking twice, the door was opened by Jack Acre. From his tousled hair and his exposed shirt-tail, it was clear that he'd been taking a nap. "Can I help you two?" he asked, rubbing the sleep from his eyes and trying to wake up.

"Sorry, we didn't mean to disturb you," I said.

He had the presence of mind to look embarrassed about being caught napping. "I don't ordinarily nod off in the middle of the day, but the boss insisted that I get my rest. As his second in command, if he's at the office, that means I have to be there too, even if the 'office' in question is the auditorium downstairs. You must have had some reason to knock on my door. What can I do for you?"

I hadn't really thought about someone not an active part of the competition answering their door. I was fumbling for something to say when Maddy spoke up. "Are we meeting before the competition again for every round, or do we just show up when it's time from now on?"

He flinched a second, but then he explained, "You have to be there at five on the nose. That's when everyone else is getting there, and anyone who isn't on that stage is disqualified immediately from the competition. You read the notes, right?"

"Parts of it were a little fuzzy," I said, though that wasn't really true.

"I told Luigi to let me handle drafting it, but he insisted that Frank do it. Now if you'll both excuse me, I might be able to catch another half hour of sleep before I have to go downstairs for the next stage."

After he closed his door, Maddy frowned at me and said, "We're not doing too well so far, are we?"

"We can't let that stop us, though. I'm not giving up just yet," I said. As we approached the next door, I started to knock, and then I heard voices coming from inside the room. From the sound of it, they were having an argument. Despite the heavy wooden doors, I could still tell that it was the married couple from Asheville, Jeff and Sandy. When I looked at the door, I understood why I could hear them. They hadn't pulled it all the way closed, so we could still hear their voices. I had to wonder if the door wasn't completely shut because Luigi had just left them. It could be for another, innocent, reason, but then again, they could be the folks we were looking for.

"I'm telling you, I didn't flirt back with him," Sandy said as I took another step closer to the door.

"It sure looked that way to me," Jeff said. "I won't tolerate another incident like what happened in Asheville. I should have punched his lights out then and there, and we never should have agreed to come here and compete."

"Jeff, you know we didn't have much choice. If we don't win, we're probably going to lose our restaurant."

"There are some things more important than that. I can't stomach the thought of that man putting his hands on you."

"I can promise you that it won't ever happen again, but I can't help how the man acts when he's around me," Sandy said.

"You don't have to encourage him, though," Jeff answered.

"Is that what you think? Do you honestly believe that I was trying to get us a better place in the order of finishes? If I did, I must not be very good at it, because we came in last, remember?"

"That wasn't because of the pizza we submitted, and we both know it. He was punishing us by putting us in last place, and there's nothing we can do about it," Jeff said.

"Honey, I love you, but you've got to find a way to get past what happened."

"You're probably right, but I'd still like to punch him in the nose the next time I see him," Jeff said. "I don't know what I was thinking when I agreed to come here, but we're not leaving now with our tails between our legs."

I was about to move on when Maddy surprised me and knocked on the couple's door frame instead. "What are you doing?" I asked her in a whisper.

"We still need to talk to them," she answered softly.

Sandy pulled the door open, and was clearly surprised that it hadn't been shut all of the way in the first place. From the redness in her eyes, it appeared that she'd been crying at some point.

"Hello, ladies," she said.

I was about to say something inane when Maddy said, "We were wondering if you'd seen Luigi lately. He was supposed to meet us up in my room, but he never showed up." It was a lie that could easily be discovered, but Maddy was probably right saying it. After all, given what we'd just heard, I couldn't imagine either pizza maker from Asheville confirming it with our host.

"We haven't seen him," Sandy said quickly.

"Funny, I could swear he was just down here." Maddy replied, pushing just a little harder.

"You're mistaken," Sandy said quickly as she tried to close the door. Was she trying to get rid of us?

"Sorry to disturb you," Maddy said as Jeff approached. "We also wanted to drop by to say that we think you two were cheated in that stage of the contest. Our pizza was a wreck, and yours was ready for a magazine cover shoot. What do you think happened?"

"We really shouldn't be fraternizing during the contest," he said.

"She means it. Your pizza really was a work of art," I said, not just backing up my sister, but saying it because it was true.

Jeff didn't appear the least bit mollified. "It's nice of you to say that, but there's only one opinion that counts, and Luigi torpedoed us." He shook his head as he rubbed his hand through his hair before adding, "I don't know how we can come back from this horrible start."

"It might not be as hard to do as you think," Maddy said.

"Why do you say that?" Jeff was clearly intrigued by my sister's statement.

"Think about it. If there's just one arbiter in the contest, what's to keep him from picking a winner no matter what the scores end up being? You read the fine print of the contract you signed, right?"

"I glanced over it," Jeff admitted. "Why? Did I miss something?"

"Since Luigi is the sole judge of the competition, if he decides to, he can throw out the results of the preliminary findings and pick a winner on his own at the very end."

"That's actually somewhere in the contract?" Sandy asked.

"It's buried in the warranties section under completely different wording, but I spoke to an attorney about it, and it's there, all right."

A ray of hope broke through Sandy's gloom as she took Maddy's hand and squeezed it. "Thank you so much. That's the best news that we've had all day." She turned to her husband and added, "See? I told you that we still have a chance."

"As a matter of fact, we all do," I said. "Good luck this evening."

"Best of luck to you, too," Sandy said as Jeff closed the door.

As soon as we were on opposite sides of the door, I turned to Maddy and asked, "Is that the truth?"

"That I wished them luck? Sure, why not? It's the sporting thing to do, don't you think?"

"I'm talking about the contract," I said.

Maddy nodded. "Bob read it again this morning, and he pointed the clause out to me. I thought it was only fair to tell them about it, too."

"You've got a good heart, Maddy," I said.

"Thanks. It matches my great legs, don't you think? Now, which door should we knock on next?"

"Let's just keep going down the line and see who we find on the other side," I said.

I started to knock on the next door, but it opened

before I had a chance to even touch it. The Raleigh twins, Todd and Reggie, were on their way out. As one of them double-checked the door behind him, the other looked at us and asked, "Were you looking for us?"

"We just wanted to ask you something about the competition," I said.

"Sorry, we don't have time right now," the other said.

And then they were gone before we had a chance to ask a thing.

We had just one more person answer the door before we quit, but they weren't associated with the competition at all.

We'd gained some new information in our little investigation, but we hadn't discovered who Luigi had been threatening, and our break time was quickly running out.

I glanced at my watch and said, "Maddy, we've only got forty-five minutes before it's time to go. What do you want to do in the meantime? I honestly don't think there's time for us take naps, do you?"

She shrugged. "Maybe not, but I'm going to rest for twenty minutes, and then grab a quick shower. It's not ideal, but I need something to pick me up before we compete tonight. This afternoon was a complete disaster, and we can't take the chance that Luigi's going to suddenly lose his sense of taste again."

"You're right about that," I said. "If you don't hear from me by the time you wake up, come knock on my door and be sure that I'm awake, okay?"

"You can count on me," she said.

* * *

The crowd was even larger this time when we walked into the auditorium three minutes before the contest was to begin again. We'd cut it closer than we'd meant to, and I made a promise to myself that Maddy and I would be on that stage a full ten minutes before each phase was to begin. I couldn't think of much worse than being disqualified for being late. Losing outright, even coming in fourth, would be better than that.

As we hurried up onto the stage, I glanced around at the other competitors. Everyone else was there, except the Charlotte team. If Kenny and Anna didn't make it in time, they'd be disqualified, and our competition would suddenly drop to two other pizza making teams.

Ten seconds before the digital clock ticked down, they appeared on stage, both breathless and disheveled from hurrying to make it in time.

The only problem was that Luigi himself was absent.

Where could the man be?

Finally, after what seemed like forever but was in fact just four minutes past our starting time, Jack Acre took the stage and took the microphone from the judge's table. "It seems that Luigi has been held up, but there's no reason to keep you folks waiting. Tonight's contest will center around our new thin crust dough, something we're all very proud of at Luigi's. Contestants, you have one hour to produce your best pizza and present it to the judge. Good luck."

Maddy looked at me and asked, "Where do you suppose he could be?"

"I don't know, and at the moment, I don't really care. We need to do better than we did this afternoon. I can't imagine Luigi being quite so generous with us this time."

"We'll be fine. We just had the jitters before," Maddy said as she looked past me and waved to someone in the crowd. I turned to see David and Bob sitting in the front row, and I waved to them myself. They both gave us their thumbs-up signal, and Maddy and I got to work.

The first thing I did was take the dough we'd been given and put it on the counter to rest and warm up a touch. That had been my mistake earlier, and I wasn't about to repeat it.

Maddy stared at me a few seconds as I stood there doing nothing, and then asked, "Have we decided to take the casual approach this time?"

I said softly, "This dough is different from ours on so many levels. It needs a chance to warm naturally if we're going to make a pizza worth eating. We have some time to spare before we prepare it."

"Just in case though, why don't we take more dough out of the fridge like we did this afternoon?"

We'd been supplied three premade balls of dough, so I did as she suggested and took another ball out of the mini fridge.

"Why not take out all three to be on the safe side?" Maddy asked.

"What if I'm wrong?" I asked in return, adding a grin. "We should leave it right where it is, just in case."

"That's what I love about you, Sis. Your confidence is so underwhelming sometimes."

"I don't know. I have more hope than I did when

this whole competition started. For whatever reason, we have a legitimate shot at the grand prize."

Maddy looked surprised by the comment. "Do you honestly believe that, even after what Tina Lance said?"

"The more I consider the possibility of a rigged contest, the more I find it hard to believe that Luigi would take a chance on monkeying with this competition," I said. "He's got too much at stake here, and too much to lose. I have a feeling that Tina was just trying to get a juicy quote from one of us for her article."

"Well, that puts the pressure back on us if it's true then, doesn't it?"

I smiled at her. "Come on, Maddy. We can do this."

"I'm game if you are."

"Why don't you prep the cheese while I test the dough?" I suggested.

"Good. At least that will give me something to do other than stand here looking pretty."

"Not that you're not great at that," I said with a grin.

As Maddy began grating and blending the cheese for our thin crust pizza, I checked the dough with my index finger, pressing it lightly to see if there was any bounce back at all. So far, there was no response. As I looked around at our competitors, I saw that every last one of them had already formed their pizza doughs into their pans, and were prepping their sauces and toppings. Was I making a mistake waiting? No, I had to believe that I was right, no matter how difficult it was watching everyone else work while we stood idly by. Todd and Reggie from

Raleigh were working with quiet efficiency, almost as though they were communicating on their own twin frequency without saying much of anything aloud. There was something underlying the serenity though, and I could feel the tension radiate off them like heat from a lamp. Jeff and Sandy from Asheville were quiet as well, but again, there was nothing peaceful about their behavior. If I had to guess, I'd say that their argument about Luigi was still brewing just below the surface. I'd never seen Luigi flirting with anyone the entire time I'd known the man, but that didn't mean that it hadn't happened. Just how far had the man pushed the Asheville pizza makers? It sounded as though Luigi had stepped way over the line with Sandy, and I could understand the way Jeff must have felt. Our last competitors were Kenny and Anna from Charlotte. I hadn't paid them much attention since they'd arrived so late, but it was clear that I'd missed something along the way. Kenny looked extremely upset about something, and Anna was really awkward around him, apologizing every time she got in his way, which seemed to be constantly. All in all, the stress and strain seemed to be showing on all of us in one way or another. If Tina Lance had been telling the truth, they would have the least amount of pressure on them of any team, but you couldn't tell that by watching them. I was scanning the audience for Tina Lance when Maddy nudged my elbow.

Chapter 6

"Check it already, will you?" she asked. "We're closing valuable time here." There was some real strain in her voice, and I knew that this prize was as important to her as it was to me. It wasn't just about the money, either. If we won, it would be something we could point to as a stamp of approval for our skills, even if it was just coming from Luigi.

I tested the dough, and it finally had some give to it.

"It's ready," I said.

"Finally," Maddy answered, the relief clear in her voice.

I took the dough, kneaded it gently in the pan, and then made sure that the crust was thin, and more important, uniform. When I had it right, I stopped adjusting it and added a touch of our sauce to the top of it. It was important not to use too much, something that could be overwhelming in a thin crust pizza, at least in my mind. I slid it over to Maddy, who added the cheese in a very careful and measured application. For tonight's pizza, we were going bold, making it a simple five-cheese blend with no other toppings. On the way to the competition, we'd debated long and hard about what to make, and she finally gave in to my opinion, something that was rare enough on most occasions to celebrate. I felt that in our earlier attempt in making our kitchen sink pizza, we'd used more toppings than we normally did at the Slice, but that seemed to suit our regular crust. With the thin crust though, I felt it was important to showcase the pie itself, and not the additions we might bring to it. Joe and I had experimented with dozens of cheesy combinations when we'd first opened A Slice of Delight, and we'd finally settled on a mix that Maddy and I still made ourselves at least once a week.

My sister looked at the nearly naked pizza, and then back at me. "Are you sure about this? Are we committing to this style?"

I looked around at the other entries, but I couldn't tell exactly what toppings they'd used on their pizzas. When I looked at ours before I got ready to slide it into the oven, it looked kind of naked to me, and for a second, I almost gave in to the temptation to load it up.

But just for a second.

"It goes in as is. Did you check the cord this time?" I didn't want any replays of what had happened earlier.

"We're all set, and I'm going to watch it the entire time," she said.

I opened the portable oven door and slid our

pizza into the oven. The regular crust had gone on top of the pizza stone inside, but this one was going in on a special pan made just for thin crust pizza.

There was no going back now. We were committed to our bare bones pizza.

I just hoped that I hadn't made a mistake.

As it was baking, Jack Acre joined us all on stage and summoned one member of each team together. I went for our team, as did every other lead pizza maker. Once we were together, Jack said softly, "This won't take a second, but Luigi is still missing, and he's not answering his telephone. Frankly, I don't know where he could be."

"Does that mean all of our work has been wasted?" one of the twins asked pointedly. "It's not fair, you know."

"Hang on a second," Jack said. "The competition is going forward. Provisions were made for emergencies, and this is covered. I'm going to judge tonight's entry myself, and I'm sure Luigi will handle tomorrow's two competitions once he shows up again. How soon will your pizzas be ready?"

We were the last ones, set to pull out our pizza in eleven minutes.

Jack nodded. "Very good. There's no need to wait any longer, then. Whatever you have baking now is going to be your entry for tonight's competition." He looked pointedly at Maddy and me as he added, "There won't be any second chances tonight. Do you all understand?"

I got the message, and I saw that some of the other contestants were nodding their approval of this change in rules. Had there been complaints about our second entry for the regular crust phase of the competition, especially after we'd taken second place? Knowing some of the teams we were going up against, it wouldn't have surprised me one bit.

That was fine with me tonight, though. I didn't need any more second chances. I nodded my agreement along with everyone else, and then Jack smiled. "Good. I'm glad we got that settled. I'm going to make an announcement, and then we'll turn off the big timer."

Jack Acre turned to the crowd as we rejoined our teams, smiled, and then said, "Ladies and gentlemen, we'd like to thank you for taking time out of your evening to join us, and we won't waste any more of your evening than we have to waiting for the full hour to pass. As soon as the final pizza comes out of the oven, the judging will begin."

Someone from the back of the room shouted out, "Where's Luigi?"

Jack held up his hands. "He's been unavoidably detained, but as his second in command, I'm taking over for him in his place. There's no need to worry. The contest will go on."

There were a few murmurs from the crowd, but there wasn't really anything anyone could do about it. Where *was* Luigi, though? He loved the limelight; that much was clear. So then why had he given up his opportunity to have a captive audience? It must have been important; that was all that I could say.

Maddy was still staring at our oven when I rejoined her.

"How's it looking, Sis?" I asked.

"We're good so far," she said as she kept her glances darting from the oven to the power cord and then back again, "but I'm not lowering my guard for one second. Has anybody pulled their pizzas yet?"

I looked around, and saw that the team from Charlotte was cutting their pizza already. It had an abundance of ham and pineapple on top, and the aroma wafting over to our station was heavenly. "The Charlotte team went Hawaiian," I said.

"I can smell it from here. Wow, that's going to be tough to beat. How about the Raleigh team?"

I glanced over at them and said, "Nothing yet. Asheville's pulled theirs out, though. They went with a kitchen sink pizza this round."

Maddy frowned. "How is a thin crust possibly going to hold it all?"

I had the same concern. There was a danger of losing toppings if a thin crust was overtopped. Then I looked closer at their pizza. "They've done a fine petite cut on all of the veggies. It looks pretty amazing," I admitted.

I noticed one of the twins removing their pizza, and my heart sank a little. "The Raleigh team went with straight cheese, too. Their pizza looks amazing." It did too, with bubbling brown and golden cheese covering the top of a perfect-looking crust. I knew right then that we didn't have a chance tonight against this competition.

"I'm not feeling so sure about my choice anymore," I said.

"Well, on the plus side, ours is almost finished, too. Let's not give up yet. Get the Parmesan and the grater ready."

It was our final touch, a light brush of olive oil on the exposed crust, and then a fine grating of fresh Parmesan cheese. Hopefully it would be enough to set us apart from the rest of the competition. I pulled our pizza out of the oven, Maddy and I put the finishing touches on it together, and then I cut it and plated a piece.

Jack nodded when he saw that we were finished, and he motioned us all to present a slice of each of our pizzas. I was so nervous my hands were shaking, but I managed to hold onto the plate as we each carried a slice to Jack where he sat alone at the judge's table. He looked pleased to be in charge, and I had to wonder if he'd found a way to distract Luigi himself just so he could preside over the festivities instead of his boss.

We put our plates down in front of him. He took a single bite of each slice, and then made several notes on his judging sheet.

When he was finished, he stood and addressed the crowd. "Tonight's fourth place entry is the team from Charlotte." He said it with a hint of satisfaction, as though the outcome had been predetermined in his mind. So much for Tina Lance's theory that the contest had been rigged. Or was the fix just in with Luigi? Without their silent business partner judging, it looked as though they might have to win this contest on their own abilities. That explained why the Charlotte team looked shocked by the announcement, as well they should. They'd gone from first place to last, putting them now squarely in the middle of the pack. "The third place entry tonight is from Timber Ridge."

I felt my heart sink a little. I must have made a mistake going with such a simple pizza. My fears were confirmed as Jack awarded second place to the team from Raleigh. That made the Asheville pizzeria the winner for the night. The tension melted a little between the husband and wife team as they accepted the crowd's applause, but it was clearly still there.

Jack finished up by saying, "Thank you all for coming. By my calculations, the race is dead even right now. In other words, the competition is wide open, and our contestants are in a dead heat as we go into the next round. Join us tomorrow morning for the deep dish entries, and again tomorrow afternoon for the final stage. Finally, be sure to join us tomorrow evening when we crown our champion pizza maker and award our cash prize."

Folks were starting to stand when our chief of police trotted up the stairs and took the stage rather unexpectedly. He grabbed the microphone from Jack and addressed the crowd. "If everyone would please sit back down, I have an announcement to make."

There were quite a few comments from the crowd, but I knew that Kevin Hurley wasn't about to say anything until he was good and ready. He glanced back at Maddy and me and I could see an apology in his glance for just a split second.

What was that about?

I found out soon enough as Kevin addressed the crowd. "I'm afraid I have some bad news for you folks tonight. There's been a murder here at the hotel today, and at the moment, nobody's going anywhere."

Chapter 7

"A murder?" I asked as the crowd began to rumble. "Did somebody kill Luigi?" I hadn't meant to say it out loud, but all of the contestants on the stage looked straight at me, and to make matters worse, Kevin did himself.

He shook his head in my direction with a look of consternation on his face, and then turned back to the crowd. "I'm sorry to say that tonight's host, George Vincent—otherwise known as Luigi De-Marcos—was killed in the contestants' greenroom sometime in the three hours between the afternoon session and the beginning of this evening's competition. My officers will be taking your names and checking your identifications as you leave the auditorium, so be patient with them. We'll try to get you all processed as soon as we can, but this is going to take a while." There were more grumblings from the audience, but Kevin asked as though he had perfect silence as he added, "I need to ask that if anyone had contact with Luigi at any point today, or went anywhere near the greenroom just over there, please step forward so we can have a conversation about it. Otherwise, everyone else should find their way to one of the exits."

For the most part, the crowd headed to the doors in the rear where Kevin's staff was waiting for them. He approached us on stage first, and I saw David and Bob heading for the stage as well, only to be stopped by one of Kevin's deputies. I wanted to tell her to let them up, but I wasn't in a position to make any requests at the moment.

Kevin gestured to the other contestants, and then gathered us together and said, "I need to speak with each of you individually. The sooner we get this over with, the sooner you can go back to your rooms."

"How did he die?" Kenny from Charlotte asked.

"Are you sure it was murder?" one of the Raleigh twins asked at nearly the same time.

Kevin held up his hands. "I'm sorry, but you all must have misunderstood me. I'm not answering questions right now; I'm asking them. I'm going to have to ask you to stop talking, to me and to each other, until I can interview you all." He pointed to me and said, "Eleanor, you're first."

"I'm going with her," Maddy said, taking my hand in hers as though it were an unbreakable bond.

"If they are going to together, then we are, too," Jeff said. "You aren't going to separate us, either."

"I said one at a time, and I meant it," Kevin said. "Eleanor, let's go."

I turned to my sister and said, "It's going to be fine, Maddy. I'll be okay."

"You don't have to say anything to him, you know," she said as she looked at Bob, who was still at the steps being blocked from joining us. "You're entitled to an attorney."

"I don't need one. I didn't do anything wrong," I said. It might have been a foolish response to make, but I didn't care. If Kevin wanted to talk to me, I wasn't going to hide behind Bob to keep him from asking me questions.

"Please?" I asked, and Maddy dropped my hand.

"Thanks," I said as I followed Kevin to the other greenroom on the opposite side of the stage. I was pretty happy that I wouldn't have to go over to the scene of the crime. The spaces were identical, though they were being used for different purposes. This room, instead of having a table, chairs, and snacks, was some kind of storage area. There were Christmas decorations stashed there, along with Valentine's Day hearts, and banners and buntings for the Fourth of July. Someone had crammed everything to one side and they'd jammed a small folding card table and two chairs into the remaining space.

I took the seat across from Kevin and said, "Ask away."

"Why did you assume that it was Luigi who had been killed when I made the announcement?" he asked, all semblance of affability gone from his voice.

"Why wouldn't I? He was missing his own contest for goodness' sake, and if you knew the man on any level at all, nothing short of murder could have kept him off that stage and wallowing in the spotlight."

"Exactly how well did you know him, Eleanor?"

Kevin asked, taking out the notebook and pen that were constantly with him.

I considered how to answer that, and finally said, "Not all that well, but our paths crossed for a long time. He tried to buy the Slice from me right after Joe died, but I turned him down cold. I might as well tell you now that we didn't leave things on good terms, so I was surprised when he invited me to participate in the contest."

Kevin jotted that down, and I knew that he'd be digging into my past soon. "Why did he hold the contest here? Do you know?"

"I asked him that question myself, as a matter of fact."

That piqued his interest. "What did he tell you?"

"He just said that there were reasons that didn't concern me, and then he wouldn't tell me anything else. Why, do you think that it's important?"

"It could be," he said. "Luigi's business is based in Charlotte, and there are a ton of venues he could have chosen there instead of coming to Timber Ridge. I didn't understand him coming here from the start, to be honest with you."

"I guess the only people who have a chance at answering your question are his employees or Gina herself."

"I'll follow up with all of them," he said as he made another note. After a moment's pause, he asked, "Eleanor, when's the last time you saw him alive?"

The question had a chilling ring to it. While I'd heard his voice upstairs on our hotel room floor, I hadn't actually laid eyes on him. "You want to know when I last saw him? It had to be just after the afternoon contest was finished," I admitted. I'd told him the truth, at least the literal fact even if I was doing my best to obfuscate the truth. If I was lucky, he'd blow right past it.

"I'm curious. Why did you place the emphasis on seeing him just now?" Kevin asked, not missing a beat. "Did he call you after the first stage was judged?"

"No," I admitted, "but Maddy and I were going to our rooms and we overheard him threatening some-one in the hallway."

"Were you planning on keeping that little tidbit to yourself?" he asked.

"I was just answering the question you asked me," I protested.

I could tell that he wanted to say something else, but after a moment, he let it go and asked me, "What time exactly did that occur? What did he say and who was he talking to?"

I told him everything that Maddy and I had heard, and then said, "You can ask Maddy for confirmation if you want to."

"I will, right after we're finished." Kevin took down my statement verbatim, and then asked, "And you honestly don't have any idea who he was talking to?"

I shrugged. "We couldn't see or hear anyone else from where we were hiding in the little ice and vending machine room, but after we heard that Luigi was gone, Maddy and I knocked on doors to see if we could find out who it might have been."

"You two just can't help yourselves from snoop-ing, can you?" he asked, a touch of ire in his voice as he spoke.

"The threats were real, Chief, and Maddy and I wanted to know what was going on."

"Who did you talk to as you were interviewing suspects?" Kevin asked.

"We spoke with Jack Acre first. I think we woke him up from his nap, as a matter of fact."

"Okay, who else was there?"

I didn't want to throw Jeff and Sandy under the bus, but I really didn't have any choice. "We spoke to the team from Asheville. Actually, they were fighting when we got there."

Kevin perked up again. "Do you happen to know what it was about?"

"Luigi was clearly their topic of conversation when we overheard them fighting. Jeff was upset about the way the man was acting toward Sandy."

"Flirting, do you mean?"

"It sounded as though it went way beyond anything innocent, and Jeff was clearly still furious with him," I finally admitted. I felt like a rat doing it, but Kevin needed to know everything if he was going to investigate this murder.

"Interesting," he said as he jotted it all down. After the police chief finished, he looked at me and asked, "Can you account for your time between two and five this afternoon?"

I knew that was the window of opportunity for the killer, and realized that Chief Hurley was asking me for my alibi. "I was with Maddy every second, but you're going to want more than that, aren't you?"

"If you wouldn't mind."

I thought about it, and then gave Kevin a nearly minute-by-minute accounting. He whistled as he finished writing it all down. "That's the most detailed alibi I've ever gotten."

"We were busy, and nearly the entire time, we were with other people."

"Then the magic time right now is between three-thirty and five," he said.

He checked his notebook, and after a moment, Kevin started to ask me his next question. I wasn't foolish enough to believe that he'd accept what I'd told him at face value, but I knew that as soon as he checked out my story, he'd believe me. He had no other choice, actually, and I was glad for every encounter Maddy and I had that afternoon.

Kevin looked up from his notebook. "Let's get back to your room search. Did you speak with anyone else while you were knocking on doors?"

"We saw the Raleigh twins, but they brushed past us on the way out of their room, and they made it pretty clear that they had no interest in talking to us. After that, we knocked on a few more doors, but nobody else answered. Hang on, that's not strictly true. We got one guy who wasn't there for the contest, so we stopped trying to figure out who Luigi might have been talking to after that."

"You two were busy," he said. "Think long and hard before you answer my next question, Eleanor. Is there anything else you want to add that might help me in my investigation?"

I hated being such a blabbermouth, but Kevin had a right to know. "When we were in the restaurant eating our meal, a woman named Tina Lance approached us. She's a reporter from a paper in Charlotte none of us had ever heard of, and she said that the contest was fixed from the start."

"Did she go into any more detail?"

I nodded. "Actually, she told Maddy, Bob, David, and me that Luigi was partnering with the Charlotte team, and that they were going to win the contest no matter who made the best pizzas for the competition."

"Did you catch the name of her newspaper?" he asked.

"It was the *Charlotte Touch*. She gave me one of her business cards," I said as I pulled it out of my blue jeans pocket.

Kevin took it, recorded all of the information from it into his notebook, and then handed the card back to me. "Wow, I can't believe all you were able to find out even before we found Luigi's body."

"You have to remember something. We weren't investigating a murder at that point. Maddy and I were just trying to find out if we had a chance of winning the grand prize. I suppose that's all off now," I said, realizing that all of the renovations I'd been planning in my mind had just gone up in smoke.

Kevin frowned, and then said, "I'm not so sure that's true. This fellow Jack Acre; you said he was in charge when Luigi didn't show up, right?"

"Sure, he ran tonight's contest round all by himself, but I can't imagine he has the authority to continue it with the company founder dead."

The police chief shrugged. "Don't give up hope yet. I'm going to see if I can get him to carry on with the competition without Luigi."

"Why would you do that?" I asked. "You're not just going to ask him as a favor to me, are you?"

He shook his head. "Think about it, Eleanor. If I

can keep my suspects here at Tree-Line without being forced to do anything in my official capacity, I have a better chance of solving this murder before everyone scatters to the four winds. Are there any other suspects you might know about that you haven't shared with me yet?"

I considered it, and then said, "Well, I heard Luigi scolding Jack Acre and Frank Vincent when I first showed up. They're two of his top employees, and Frank in particular looked at his brother with open contempt when he didn't think Luigi was watching. There's also a woman hanging around the contest who was spitting mad at Luigi for dropping her from the competition. I don't know her name, or anything about her, but you might want to find her and ask about her alibi."

"I've got to admit, you've done quite a bit of background work for me on this case." He hesitated, and then added, "Let me ask you something, Eleanor. You and Maddy are staying here at the hotel for the competition, right?"

"We were," I admitted, "but I can't imagine any reason that we wouldn't go back home now. This thing has lost its appeal for me with the murder and everything. I'm not even sure that I care if we win the money anymore." Even I couldn't tell for sure if I was lying or not at that moment. There was too much of a jumble in my brain, and it was still just sinking in that Luigi was dead. Just because I hadn't liked the man didn't mean that I wanted to see him murdered.

"What if I asked you to stay on here as a favor to me?" Kevin asked.

"Why would you do that?"

The chief of police took a deep breath, and then let it out slowly. "As much as it pains me to admit it, you and Maddy seem to have a knack for finding out things behind the scenes that I can't uncover in my official capacity. I'm not asking you to snoop, but if you're here anyway, you could always keep your eyes and ears open for things I might need to know."

"Chief, are you asking me to spy on the other competitors for you?" I asked.

"I am. Do you have a problem with that?"

I thought about it, and then shook my head and smiled. "No, I'm fine with it, and I'm sure that Maddy will be, too. I just wanted to make sure we were clear about it."

Kevin bit his lower lip, and then said, "This is in no way official, and you can't tell anyone but Maddy what you're doing."

"We're going to tell Bob and David; you know that, right?" I asked.

He waved a hand in the air. "I suspected as much, but no one else. There's one more thing, too. You can't take any unnecessary chances, do you understand me? I just want you to look and listen. Do not, I repeat, do not take any action without me. If you can't agree to that, then you can't help me."

"I'll do my best, but I can't promise anything," I said.

"You won't even give me that much?" Kevin asked.

"I could, but I don't want to lie to you. By the way, would you mind telling me now how Luigi died?"

"I'm not ready to release that information just yet," he said.

I couldn't believe he actually thought that was going to be a one-way street. "Come on, it's going to come out sooner or later. You might as well tell me now."

"At first glance, it appears that someone choked him with a piece of pizza," Kevin said. "That's not public information yet, so I'm trusting you to keep it quiet."

"Whose pizza was it?" I asked almost off the cuff.

"We're still working on that," Kevin said.

"As soon as you figure it out, I want to know. You owe me at least that much if I'm going to spy for you."

Kevin considered that for a few moments, and then nodded. "Fine. I know that's the best deal I'm going to get from you, and I don't have time to dicker anymore. Just be careful, and call me the second you sense trouble. Now go on, and send in your sister when you get back on stage."

I stood, and then said, "Thanks for believing in me, Kevin. It's nice to know that I'm not on your list of suspects for this murder."

Kevin shook his head slightly. "Did I give you that impression, Eleanor? If I did, I apologize. I'm afraid you and Maddy are still on my radar, just like every other contestant here. I have to confirm your alibi to know one way or the other, just like everyone else."

The relief dropped out of me in a rush. "Hang on a second. Let me get this straight. You're asking me for my help, but you still think I could have killed the man? If I had, what would keep me from lying to you about everything that might make me look bad?"

"I'd like to think that I know you well enough to be able to tell when you're lying to me," he said.

"I wouldn't put too much faith in that belief, if I were you," I said.

"What is that supposed to mean?" Kevin asked. "Have you made it a habit of lying to me in the past?"

I pretended not to hear him and just kept walking out the door. I had half a mind not to help him at all since he still considered me a suspect, but after all, I knew that I was going to dig into Luigi's murder regardless of what we'd just discussed, so why not take a chance on working with Kevin?

I walked back on stage and told Maddy, "He's ready for you now."

The other contestants quickly clustered around me, but I had my orders. "I'm not allowed to talk about anything we just discussed, so please don't ask me."

"At least tell us if the contest is over," one of the twins demanded.

"As far as I know, that hasn't been determined yet."

"How could they not cancel it?" Sandy asked. "A man died here today."

"All I know is that it's not up to me; that's all I can say."

At that moment, someone touched my arm, and I was relieved when I saw that it was Gina. "Eleanor, I need you for one second."

The others protested, but I gladly let Gina lead

me away from them. Once we were off the stage, Bob and David started to approach, but I shook my head slightly, and they got the hint immediately. I didn't know if Gina had just been trying to save me from the other competitors or if she really did need me, but I knew that it could be useful talking to her alone.

"I'm sorry about this mess," I said. "This can't be good for your complex."

She bit her lower lip, and then said, "I won't lie to you. It's really bad. Unfortunately though, it's a part of an hotelier's life."

"Murder?" I asked incredulously.

"No, not generally speaking," she admitted, "but people do occasionally die in the hotels where they're staying. Almost never this dramatic, though. Eleanor, I'm worried sick about what's going to happen to us here. My uncle hates publicity, and I'm afraid that he might just decide it's not worth the public relations storm we're about to face and just shut us down."

"Could he honestly just walk away from this kind of investment?" I asked. I knew that Nathan Pane was rich, wealthy beyond all dreams of avarice even, but I couldn't imagine abandoning all of the money he'd sunk into the resort.

"You know him almost as well as I do. The man's got a capricious spirit, so I wouldn't put anything past him. The longer this investigation drags on, the better the chances are that he's going to just give up on the whole property." She lowered her voice, and then asked, "Please tell me that you and Maddy are looking into this, too."

"It's too soon to say just yet what we'll be doing," I waffled, not at all certain that I was ready to admit what we were going to do for the chief of police.

"You *have* to," she said as she took my hands in hers. "I'm desperate here. This is all I've got, everything I've ever wanted in the world, and I can't let one killer take it from me. Please, I'm begging you; help me."

It wouldn't hurt to promise her something that I already planned on doing, and I was sure that Maddy wouldn't mind me committing her to the investigation as well. In a very real way, I had already done just that with the police chief. "We'll do what we can to track down the murderer, but I can't make any promises. You know that, don't you?"

"I understand," she said, the relief clear in her voice. "Thank you."

I was afraid that Gina was going to get her hopes up, and I hated the idea of disappointing her. "You need to understand that we can't give you any guarantees," I said.

Gina's smile faded slightly. "I know, but I feel better just knowing that you're doing whatever you can."

She hugged me, and as she broke away from me, one of her staff was suddenly at her elbow. "I'm sorry to interrupt, but we have a mass exodus at the checkout desk, and Haley is being overwhelmed. I was in the business center on my break, and then all of sudden it was like there was an explosion of people."

"Thanks for letting me know. Go back to your station, and I'll take care of it myself," Gina said, and I saw her wipe a tear from the corner of her eye.

She squeezed my hand briefly, and then headed toward the front. I was glad I'd been able to give her at least a modicum of comfort. I just hoped that Maddy and I would be able to get her results.

Bob and David approached me quickly the moment Gina left, and I readied myself for their questions.

"Did Maddy actually go into that interview with Hurley without me?" Bob asked. "What was she thinking? For that matter, what were you doing? I should have been in there to represent both of you."

"Take it easy, Counselor," I said. Lowering my voice, I added, "Kevin asked us for our help, and I agreed, but you have to promise to keep it quiet."

Bob and David both looked visibly relieved when they heard that Kevin Hurley had enlisted our assistance. I hated to take that feeling of comfort from them, but I had to do it. "That doesn't mean that we're off his suspect list, though. He wants us to, in his words, 'keep our eyes and ears open' and tell him if we learn anything new."

"He's got a lot of nerve asking you both to do that," David said.

"It's okay. After all, it's not like we weren't going to do it, anyway."

"You're actually thinking about helping him?" Bob asked. "Do you have any idea how dangerous that could be for the two of you?"

"We'll be careful, and besides, it's not like we haven't done this before."

"I still don't like it," Bob said.

I shrugged, and then turned to David. "Do you have anything you want to add?"

He held up his hands in instant surrender. "I'm

not foolish enough to believe that I have any right to tell you what you can and cannot do. I just hope you'll be careful, and if there's anything I can do to help, you'll ask."

I kissed him, and then added one to Bob's cheek as well.

David protested, "Hey, I supported you and he didn't. Why did he get a kiss, too?"

"We know that you both care about us," I said, "and we appreciate it."

"But you're going to do what you want to anyway, right?" Bob asked a little wryly.

"Absolutely," I replied with a smile.

"Hey, did I just see you kissing my fiancé?" Maddy asked with a grin as she approached us.

"You did," I admitted.

She turned and kissed David's cheek, and then said, "Well then, turnabout's fair play."

"I'm not complaining," David said with a grin, and Bob found a smile deep within himself. "I give up. You two are impossible; you know that, don't you?"

"We do our best," Maddy said. She looked at me, and then added, "Kevin brought me up to speed. Should we get started snooping right now?"

"You're going to start digging into this immediately?" Bob asked.

"There's no time like the present," I said, "and besides, the quicker we figure out who killed Luigi, the faster we can get back to the contest."

"Do you honestly think they're still going to continue it after what happened this afternoon?" David asked me.

"It's a done deal," Maddy said. "The chief got a

call when I was in there being interrogated. Jack Acre is taking over as CEO of the company, and he's decided to dedicate the rest of the competition to his boss's memory. We're still on."

"So let me get this straight. You're going to try to solve a murder *and* win the grand prize?" David asked.

"I don't see any reason why we can't do both," I said.

He just shook his head. "All I can say is good luck." As he started to leave, he turned to Bob and asked, "Are you coming?"

"I might as well," Bob replied. "It's clear that I'm not needed here."

Maddy stopped him, spun him around, and planted a solid kiss on his lips.

"What was that for?" Bob asked as they finally broke apart.

"I just wanted to show you that you might not be needed in our investigation, but you're always wanted. Is that something you can live with?"

Bob dabbed at his lips with his pristine handkerchief. "I suppose I can find a way to manage it," he said with a grin.

"Good. Now you two go on and take off. My sister and I have some sleuthing to do."

Chapter 8

"Where should we get started?" I asked Maddy. "It's all well and good to say that we're going to help Kevin solve this murder, but we have so many suspects that I'm not sure where we should begin. Did he tell you how Luigi died?"

Maddy shuddered a little. "Choking to death on a pizza jammed down your throat cannot be a pleasant way to go. I hope it wasn't one of ours," she added.

"How could it be? We threw our slices away after that round was over, didn't we?"

"I honestly don't remember, but Eleanor, if someone could stoop to murder, how hard would it be for them to grab a piece of pizza from the trash even if we did throw it away?"

"You've got a point," I said. There'd been something pressing on my mind the second I realized that Luigi had been murdered at the hotel, and I wanted to ask Maddy before we went any further with our investigation. "Maddy, I was wondering if I could ask you for a favor."

Maddy looked surprised by the request. "Just name it, and if I can grant it, it's yours."

I felt a little like an idiot asking, but I went ahead anyway. "As much as I love having a luxury suite all to myself, is there any chance we could share yours? There are two bedrooms in each suite, and I'd feel a lot safer knowing that you were right there with me in the other room."

Maddy grinned. "I was thinking the exact same thing, but I felt kind of silly asking you about it. Do you want to move into my room, or should I come over and join you?"

"I'll be happy to move. Thanks, Sis."

"You bet," she said. "Tell you what. Why don't we do it now and get it out of the way? That way we can focus on who we should talk to first while you pack."

"It's a deal," I said.

It didn't take me long to grab my things, and as much as I'd enjoyed staying in such an elegant suite by myself, I'd meant what I'd said. Having Maddy nearby was more important than having a place like that alone. I would have shared a single bed with her if it meant that she'd be near, but in truth, I wasn't really sacrificing much at all. One room was still plenty big enough for the two of us, and I doubted we'd be bumping into each other too much while sharing the space.

Once I was settled into Maddy's other bedroom, I immediately felt better. As I put the last pair of socks away, I turned to her and said, "I'm ready to get started if you are. Should we just start knocking on doors again like we did before, or should we try a more subtle approach this time?"

"As hard as it's going to be for you to believe, I think we should go for subtle, at least for now," Maddy said. "While you were unpacking, I called Gina and asked her if any of the contestants were currently in the restaurant. She told me that the Charlotte team had just gotten there, so I asked her to save us a table beside them. What do you say to a little dining and sleuthing at the same time?"

"It sounds as though we're taking advantage of Gina's good nature by eating in the restaurant every chance we get," I said with a grin.

"Hey, she asked us for our help, and we still have those Golden Tickets whether we're snooping or not, right?"

"Right," I admitted.

"Believe me, when I asked her, she sounded as though we were doing her a huge favor, and in a way, she was right. After all, we're putting both our necks on the line here. Why shouldn't we be rewarded for the chances we're taking?"

"When you put it that way, I have a hard time refuting it," I said.

"Good, that's what I like to hear. So, let's go grill a few fish, shall we?"

"Lead on," I said.

When we got to the dining room, it took me a second to spot our competitors. They were deep in a discussion with Luigi's brother, Frank Vincent. We sat down as quietly as we could near them, hoping they didn't notice us. I doubted that Maddy and I were really all that stealthy, but their conversation was so earnest, we probably hadn't had to be very sneaky to escape their attention. "I don't care what arrangements or agreements you may or may not have had with my brother before he was murdered. As far as I'm concerned, the deal's off," Frank said. "Honestly, what did you think was going to happen?"

"We didn't kill him," Kenny said. "Why would we? Anna and I had every reason in the world to want him to finish judging this contest by himself."

"Leave me out of it. I didn't have anything to do with any of this," Anna said strongly. "I just found out about what Kenny was up to an hour ago."

Frank looked toward her with a new softness in his eyes. "I believe you," he said.

"But you don't believe *me*. Is that what you're saying?" Kenny asked.

Frank's glance grew cold again as he looked back at Kenny. "Do you honestly think that my brother didn't tell me about the conversation the two of you had yesterday afternoon?"

Was that who we'd heard Luigi threatening upstairs? It was too much to believe that it was just a coincidence.

"Kenny, you need to drop this," Anna said.

Kenny shot a look of anger in her direction. "Anna, if I want your opinion, I'll ask you for it, but not until then. Understand?"

"Sorry," Anna said softly, but the look she gave him once he turned to Frank told me that if her boss ever turned up dead, we wouldn't have to look far for a suspect.

He told Frank, "You're going to make this right."

"I wouldn't if I could, but it's out of my hands anyway. Jack Acre is in charge now. I had a little influence with George, but I don't have any with Jack. As a matter of fact, it wouldn't surprise me if he fired me as soon as the competition is over."

"What about keeping you on out of loyalty to your brother?" Anna asked.

"What do you think? George never showed any to the rest of us, and I'm sure he would have been shocked to think that any of his employees had any for him once he was gone."

"So that's it, then," Kenny said with disgust. "We're on our own now."

"You could still win this fair and square if you put your mind to it," Frank said.

"Yeah, like that's going to happen."

"You never know," Frank said as his phone rang. He took the call. "Yes, sir. I understand. I'll be right there." After Frank hung up, he said, "That was my new boss. I'm sorry, but I've got to go."

"Put in a good word for us when you see him," Kenny said.

Frank just laughed. "I'm not sure that would be in your best interest."

After he was gone, Anna said, "Kenny, I'm not about to take that kind of behavior from you. You can't treat me that way."

Kenny looked surprised by her outburst. "I don't know why not; I always have in the past. If you don't like it, you can always quit."

"It's closer to coming true than you might think," she said.

"You can posture all you want to, but I'm not too worried about that ever happening." He looked past her and made eye contact with me. There was real anger in his voice as he asked me, "How long have you two been sitting there?"

"We just got here a few seconds ago," I said.

"Were you eavesdropping on our private conversation?" Kenny asked pointedly.

"Why do you ask? Did we miss something juicy?" Maddy asked him with a smile.

Kenny just shook his head and threw his napkin down on the table. "I've suddenly lost my appetite. Come on, Anna. We're leaving."

His assistant made no move to leave, though. "I'm staying."

"I told you that we're going," Kenny said, much more forcefully this time.

"Go if you want. I'm hungry," she answered, not budging an inch.

Kenny stood, and then walked away without another word.

Anna looked at us and said, "I'm sorry about that. Kenny gets really testy when he's hungry."

"Then I totally understand why he'd storm out of a restaurant before he's eaten. That makes perfect sense," Maddy said with a smile. "Judging by the way he acts, he must be hungry all of the time."

Anna grinned at my sister's response. "Why am I making excuses for the man? He deserves whatever he gets." She looked around, and then added, "This is just awful, isn't it?"

"I don't know," Maddy said as she studied the room. "I think it's all pretty grand if you ask me."

"I wasn't talking about the restaurant. I meant the murder," Anna explained, not getting my sister's humor at all.

"Ignore her, Anna. She's just teasing you," I said. "We both knew what you were talking about." This was the perfect opportunity to see just how much she knew, and how much of it she was willing to share with us. "That was a rather intense conversation you both were having with Frank Vincent a few minutes ago, wasn't it?"

Anna shrugged. "I knew you were sitting there longer than you claimed, but I wasn't about to say anything to Kenny. It turns out that my boss is just a big fat crook. I had no idea that he'd bribed Luigi. To be honest with you, I want nothing more to do with the man, but it appears that we're stuck here, at least for now, so I really don't have much choice."

"Why's that?" Maddy asked, though we both knew the answer to her question.

"We tried to leave, but the police chief wouldn't let us. He said that we were all suspects in the murder, and that we couldn't go home for at least three days. I'm going to stick it out with Kenny while we're here, but after that, I'm gone." She added quietly, "I'd appreciate it if you didn't tell him that I said that. I want to see the look on his face when I actually quit."

Kevin hadn't given us any kind of deadline, but I imagined it was the most he could stretch things before folks got fed up and left anyway. What else could he do, lock everyone up?

"We'd never rob you of that," Maddy said with a wicked grin. "As a matter of fact, if it's not too much trouble, let me know when you plan to tell him so I can see it myself."

"I'll try," Anna said, lighting up just a little.

"Does the police chief have a reason to suspect

the two of you of murder?" I asked, hating to break the joy of the moment. "If Kenny bribed Luigi, something might have happened between them. Did they have some kind of falling-out?"

"Like I said, I don't know anything about that," Anna said quickly. "I just do what I'm told. Kenny is the one pulling all of the strings."

"Do you know exactly what kind of deal he had with Luigi?" I asked. "Was it some kind of trade-off, or did Kenny pay him off with cash?"

"You know everything that I do about it. I can't believe how careless Kenny was, talking that way in a crowded restaurant. He's usually much more discreet."

"Well, they weren't exactly trying to keep their voices down, were they?" I asked. "Are you sure there's nothing else you can tell us that might help?"

"Are you two investigating the murder?" Anna asked.

"Let's just say that we're asking a few questions here and there," I answered quickly before my sister could acknowledge what we were really up to.

After a few seconds, Anna leaned toward us and said, "All I know for sure is that he and Kenny cooked something up together, but I don't have *any* of the details. I don't think that there's anything written down about it anywhere, either." She let out a sigh, and then said, "I'm afraid that I'm not going to be of any help to you at all. I don't have any proof of any of it other than my suspicions."

It was interesting to learn that Tina Lance was closer to the truth than I'd realized when I'd first heard her claim. "Anna, could you try to get us something more concrete?" I asked. I lowered my voice, and then said, "Anything you could do to help us would be great."

"I'm not sure if I can," she said with a shrug. "Knowing Kenny, he could do a lot worse than just fire me, if you know what I mean."

"But you're going to quit working for him soon anyway, right?" Maddy asked.

"Hang on," I said to my sister. "We don't want her to take any chances on our account." I turned back to Anna and explained. "We understand your position, but if you stumble across anything, keep us in mind."

"I can't make any promises, but I'll try," she said.

I was watching her eyes, and they suddenly widened. I checked the source of her sudden anxiety, and I saw Kenny standing in the doorway. He was gesturing to her to join him, and he didn't look as though he was going to take no for an answer.

Maddy said softly, "You don't have to go just because he wants you to; you know that, don't you?"

"At the moment, I really don't have much choice," Anna said. As she started to leave, she turned back to us and asked, "Please don't say anything to anyone about what I said before; I'm begging you."

I didn't want to make her any promises that I might not be able to keep, but she was honestly afraid. "We won't breathe a word of any of it if we have any choice in the matter."

It didn't seem to ease her fears any.

She hesitated a moment more, and then Kenny barked out loudly, "Anna."

She left us quickly, and Kenny shot us a look of triumph just before they left the restaurant together.

"Is she really afraid for her life?" Maddy asked once they were gone.

"She didn't actually come out and say it," I reminded my sister.

"Did she have to? We need to get her away from that man."

I understood my sister's sentiment, but we had a job to do. "Maddy, she's a grown woman. She can do whatever she wants to do."

My sister studied me for a second as our server approached, and then asked, "When did you get so cold, Sis?"

I frowned, and then said, "I'm not, but we have to watch our step. We're in the thick of this too, remember?"

"It's not likely I'll forget," Maddy said as the young woman reached us.

"We'll do what we can for her, but we can't let it hurt our investigation." I hated coming off sounding so cruel, but I meant it. Maddy and I were trying to find a killer. If we could help Anna get away from Kenny we would, but it couldn't be our top priority.

"May I start you off with beverages and an appetizer?" the waitress asked once she was at our table.

"You may," Maddy said. "We'll start with the artichoke and spinach dip, and a pair of Cokes."

"Very good," she said, and then quickly left us.

"When did you start ordering for the two of us?" I asked my sister with a smile. I was happy that the earlier frost was out of her voice now.

"You can choose your own entree, but I want that dip, and I wasn't about to order it just for me. Is there a problem with the soda?"

"No, actually, that all sounds good to me," I said. "I'm not finished talking about Anna yet, though."

Maddy waved a hand in the air as though shooing away a pesky fly. "It's okay. I get it. You're all about the crime-busting these days."

"If you believe that that's true, then you don't get me at all anymore," I insisted. "I don't want anything to happen to Anna either, but Kevin's not letting anyone go anywhere at the moment, remember? Besides, Kenny needs Anna by his side if he's going to have the slightest chance of winning this competition, especially now that it's going to be a fair fight. She couldn't be any safer than if she were in protective custody. Anyway, we can keep an eye on her, but we can't protect her around the clock."

"You're right about all of that," Maddy said as she pushed her menu aside and looked at me. "I'm sorry. I'm frustrated by the situation, but I know that I shouldn't be taking it out on you. I guess I just hate the idea that we're involved in another murder. What is it about us, Eleanor? We seem to attract this kind of behavior no matter what we do these days."

"I'd prefer to think of it as though we're dragged into these random incidents against our will," I said. "Otherwise, I'd have to believe that there's something we're doing to cause all of this, and that's something I just can't bring myself to accept."

"I agree; it's not a pleasant thought to consider."

Our server brought our drinks and the dip, and then took the order for our entrees.

Once she was gone, Maddy took her first bite of the dip, and then let out a contented sigh. "This is truly amazing."

I tried some, and found that it was as delicious as

she'd described. "You know what? We should make this."

Maddy laughed. "Are you kidding? Do you know what we'd have to charge our customers for this kind of appetizer?"

"I didn't mean that we should put it on the Slice's menu," I explained. "I was saying we should try to make it at my house sometime."

"I can't imagine how much trouble it would be," she said. "Besides, if we really want it, we can always just come here and order it."

I had to laugh. "As long as you're buying, I'm game."

Maddy grinned at me. "Don't worry about that. After all, I'm engaged to an attorney, remember?"

"So we'll let Bob buy."

"Why not? He derives a great deal of pleasure in showering me with the things that I want. Who am I to deny him of that experience?"

"Wow, from the way you put it, you're practically a humanitarian."

"I do what I can, however little it might be," she said with a smile.

We had nearly finished the dip, and Maddy was debating about ordering more, when our entrees came. I had a wonderful salmon dish, while my sister had brisket that disintegrated the second her fork even got near it.

It felt funny signing the check with only our room number, but Gina had been serious about comping our meals, and I wasn't going to say no. Like Maddy, I didn't want to hurt anyone's feelings, especially when it all turned out so nicely for us.

"I don't know about you," I said as we walked out

into the lobby, "but I'm too full to just go back to our room yet. Do you have any interest in walking around the grounds a little first?"

"It's awfully chilly out, and besides, aren't you worried that there's a murderer on the loose?" she asked.

"No more than usual," I said. "We can't let fear keep us from living our lives."

"You've got a point," she answered. "Sure, why not? Let's grab our jackets first though, okay?"

"I know it's technically winter, but it was still pretty balmy outside the last time I checked," I said. "Let's at least try it without our coats first."

"Admit it, Eleanor. You're just afraid that if we go back to our room, we'll go in hibernation mode, aren't you?"

"The thought crossed my mind," I said. "Come on, we're made of tough stock. Let's brave the elements."

We walked outside, and I felt as though we were almost in daylight instead of the surrounding darkness of the hour. The parking area for the resort was well lit, and it was easy to see everything to the edge of the property, though the light dropped off dramatically as it was absorbed into the thicket of surrounding trees.

I was admiring the layout when Maddy grabbed my arm and whispered, "Eleanor, look over there."

"Where?" I asked. I tracked her gesture, and that's when I spotted three men standing on the edge of the light, one of them just barely out of the shadows.

"Who is that with the twins?" I asked as I spotted our competitors from Raleigh.

"I'm not sure," Maddy said. "I can't get a clear look at him."

I kept looking, but whoever the man was, he was keeping in the shadows, almost as though it was intentional. One of the twins handed him a thick padded envelope, and the next second, the man in the shadows took it and was gone.

"Let's go after him," I said as I started toward them.

"I'll take the shadow man, and you take the twins," Maddy said, clearly eager for the hunt.

"No, it's not safe. We'll brace the twins together," I said. "Besides, the man they were talking to is probably long gone."

"Are we certain that it was a man?" Maddy asked as we hurried toward the twins.

I thought about what I'd seen, and how much my mind had filled in, and I finally admitted, "I can't say without a doubt one way or the other. Can you?"

Maddy shook her head. "No, I never got a real good look. What are we going to say to these two?" Maddy asked as we neared them.

"I don't know about you, but I feel like the direct approach," I said.

As we walked up to the men, who were still in deep conversation, I said loudly, "Who were you just talking to, and why were you giving him an envelope? Is there a chance that you were paying someone off, gentlemen?"

They looked startled to see us. One said quickly, "What are you two up to, and what in the world are you doing out in the cold without jackets?"

"We don't owe you any explanations, and we

know what you were up to the second we walked outside," Maddy said.

"You only *think* you know what you saw," one twin said as he stepped closer to us. "You need to drop this if you know what's good for you."

"Is that a threat?" I asked.

He seemed to consider his answer carefully, and then he just shook his head. "Think of it more like a friendly warning."

I looked at Maddy. "Did he just seem all that friendly to you?"

"I thought he was a little icy myself," Maddy replied.

"We've had enough of your comedy routine to last us a lifetime," the other twin said, and they started back toward the hotel.

We followed them closely, and they finally stopped and faced us. "Where do you think you're going?"

"We're cold," I said, pretending to shiver. "Going inside suddenly sounds like a good idea to both of us right now. Would you guys care to join us by the fireplace? We can have a nice friendly chat about what just happened before we all go talk to the chief of police together."

For once I wasn't bluffing, but they weren't buying it anyway. "We'll pass. Right, Reggie?" he asked as he glanced at his twin.

"Right, Todd," the other said.

"Wow, I didn't even see your lips move that time," Maddy said. "How do you even tell each other apart?"

They each considered commenting on her sarcasm, but decided to remain silent as they headed for the elevator.

"Should we keep following them?" Maddy asked me.

I thought about it, but I doubted that we'd be able to do much good. Chances were good that they'd just lock themselves in their room, especially if they knew that we were on their tails. "No, they know that we saw them, and what they did, even though we don't really know what they were up to. Right now, that's the best we can do. Let their imaginations fill in the rest." I rubbed my hands together, and realized that I had gotten cold outside. "Let's check out the fireplace after all. I could use a little radiant heat right about now. How about you?"

"It sounds great to me," she said.

The fireplace was exposed on two sides, so Maddy and I found soft, comfy chairs on one side and settled in. The crackling of the wood as it burned, the earthy smell of the fire, and the weaving of the flames calmed me enough to almost put me to sleep.

I was more exhausted than I'd realized.

The next thing I knew, Maddy was shaking me awake. I started to protest when she put a finger to my lips. Instead of fighting her off, I nodded, pulled her hand gently away, and then looked to see what she'd found so fascinating that she'd had to rouse me from a welcome little nap.

When I saw Jeff and Sandy from Asheville on the other side of the fireplace nestled together on a couch, I realized that we might just learn a little more tonight about who might have wanted to see Laughing Luigi dead.

Chapter 9

"We've got to tell the police chief everything we know," Sandy said as she stared into her husband's eyes. "It's going to look a thousand times worse to the cops if they find out what happened on their own, Jeff."

"What makes you think they'll learn anything at all?" her husband asked. "If we don't tell them, who does that leave? Luigi can't say a word anymore, and if we don't talk, it dies with us. Sandy, this isn't the time or the place for your ethical theories. We could be in some big trouble here if this cop Hurley finds out what really happened."

"Luigi could have told someone here at the competition, though. Somebody could have heard us," she said plaintively.

"If they had, don't you think they would have come forward by now? If we just keep our cool and don't say a word about it, we'll be fine."

"I suppose so," Sandy said, though she was clearly unconvinced.

I was hoping they'd say something a little more revealing when the restaurant maître d' approached them. "Excuse me, but your table is ready. If you'll follow me, please."

As they left, I asked Maddy, "What do we do now? Should we follow them back into the restaurant and see if they say anything else about what happened here with Luigi?"

"And do what? If I have to eat another bite right now, I'll explode."

"We could have coffee," I suggested, though it wasn't the drink of preference for either one of us.

"I guess so," Maddy said. "What makes you think that we're going to get lucky twice, though? Chances are they aren't going to discuss anything else juicier than the weather."

I shrugged as I stood and stretched. "One thing's certain, Sis. We won't learn anything new if we just sit here."

Maddy nodded. "You've got a point. Let's see if we can slip the maître d' something for putting us close to their table."

"Fine, go ahead and try." Maddy was a little more worldly about giving someone money for preferential treatment. I'd always been at a loss as to why I should pay someone extra just for doing their job, which explained why I was kept waiting for tables while my sister breezed past me and laughed. "I'll just wait for you right over here."

I found the concierge's desk near the checkout, both of which were currently unmanned, and started looking at a local open map.

I was still picking out my house on it when a woman's voice behind me asked, "May I help you?"

"Thanks, but I'm just looking for my house," I said as I glanced around at the concierge.

The woman looked a little puzzled by my response. "Have you misplaced it, by any chance?"

"No, of course not. It's where it's always been. I was just curious, that's all."

"So then you don't need directions on how to get there?" she asked.

"No need to worry about me. I could find the place with my eyes closed," I said, and then rethought the phrase. "Well, probably not with my eyes closed. Chances are I'd never make it out of the parking lot if I couldn't see where I was going."

The concierge was clearly at a loss as to how to deal with me. I hadn't meant to sound so confusing, but then I realized that it had certainly come out that way.

"Eleanor," Maddy said to me before I could explain myself any further to the woman.

"It was nice chatting with you," I said.

"Of course." The woman looked genuinely relieved that I was moving on, at least away from her desk.

I looked at my sister and asked, "So where are we sitting?"

"We aren't," Maddy admitted reluctantly. "The restaurant is jammed, and short of calling Gina and getting someone else removed from their table, we aren't going to be getting anywhere near them."

"We're *not* calling Gina," I said firmly.

"I *know* that," she answered. "Sorry I struck out."

"Are you kidding? I'm just glad to finally find out that you're as human as the rest of us."

Maddy frowned. "You don't have to look so happy about it."

I hugged my sister as I said, "Perfection is over-rated, if you ask me."

"I feel the same way about you. So what should we do now? Do we head off to bed so we can rest up for tomorrow, or dig around a little more?"

"You can go ahead if you're tired, but I'm not done snooping yet," I said. "We don't have a whole lot of time, so we'd better keep after this till we drop."

"Hey, I like the new you. Where did that come from?"

I shook my head. "Believe me, I'd rather just make pizza and let the rest of the world take care of itself, but we're involved in this whether we like it or not, so we need to dig into Luigi's murder while we've got our suspects all here in one place. I've got a hunch that if this murder is unsolved by the time everyone splits up, we'll never know who killed the man."

"Great. I'm still at a loss where we should go next, though."

"Why don't we see if Kevin's cleared the green-room yet? I don't know about you, but I'd like to see the place where Luigi was murdered for myself."

"Lead on," she said, and I headed for the auditorium, and the place where Luigi, aka George Vincent, took his last breath.

*   *   *

The door to the greenroom was locked, though there was no police tape across it. Did that mean that Kevin was finished with it?

"What do we do now?" Maddy asked. "Should we try to break in?"

"Do you even know how?" I asked my sister with a smile.

She grabbed a credit card from her wallet and held it up. "No, but I've read about it in enough books, and I've always wanted to try it. Stand back and give me some room to work."

"Before you break your card," I said as I put a hand on her arm, "I've got a better idea. Why don't we call Gina and have her unlock it for us?"

"What fun is that?" Maddy asked as she put her credit card away.

"Well, the way I figure it, we've had enough fun for one day, don't you think?" I got my phone out of my pocket and dialed Gina's direct number. It was nice having such direct ties with the complex's manager. It had to save us a lot of energy and effort not running around in circles trying to make things happen, and at the moment, time was the one thing we didn't have a lot of.

I was thrilled when Gina answered on the first ring. I didn't want to give my sister any excuse to try that credit card trick. Knowing her, it would probably end up breaking and we'd still be on the wrong side of the door.

"Go," Gina answered, instead of saying hello.

"Where exactly am I supposed to go?" I asked.

"Who is this? The number's blocked on my phone."

"It's Eleanor. Did I call at a bad time?"

"No, you're fine," Gina said, her voice instantly relaxing. "I had to step away from the property for a few minutes, and my telephone won't stop ringing. Is there anything I can do for you, Eleanor?"

"If you're not around, I can ask you later." I hated to interrupt her rare time away from Tree-Line.

"Nonsense. I've always got time for you. All you have to do is ask."

"This should only take a second. Do you happen to know if the police department has already released the greenroom space where Luigi was killed?"

"I haven't heard. Let me make a quick call and get back to you."

She hung up before I could even thank her for her time.

I turned to Maddy and said, "I don't envy her the job she's got. She must always be on the clock. When we finish our pizzas, the time we have left is all ours."

"I don't know," Maddy said. "I think it might be fun sometimes to be in charge of so many people."

"You're welcome to it," I said. "I have enough on my hands as it is with three people on my staff. She must have dozens working here."

"Do you honestly think there's that many?"

"There's no doubt in my mind. Besides the front desk and the restaurant staff, I can't imagine how many maids she has on her payroll."

"Don't forget security," Maddy said.

"There's that group, too. What made you think of them?"

She pointed behind me. A big beefy man in his late forties with gray hair was approaching, and from his blazer with the resort logo on it and the way he carried himself, I had a hunch that we were about to meet the head of the department.

"We have every right to be here," I said quickly before he could throw us out. "I just called Gina, your manager, and she's trying to find out if we can get in the greenroom."

The big man smiled, and though he might have been trying to make it look nonthreatening, I wasn't certain that he could do it on his best day, let alone when a murder happened right under his nose and on his watch that afternoon. "That's why I'm here. I've been instructed to let you in, and do anything else I can in my power to help."

"Wow, that's a dangerous offer," Maddy said as she stepped toward him. "I'm Maddy Spencer, and this is my sister, Eleanor Swift."

"I know who you ladies are, by reputation, if nothing else."

"I hope it's not all bad," I said with a slight smile.

"On the contrary, my boss speaks very highly of you both. I'm Hank White, by the way." Before he unlocked the door, he said, "I meant what I said. I'd like to offer any help I can in solving this case."

I was about to ask him how he knew we were digging into the murder when I realized that Gina had to have told him. "We're strictly amateurs," I said. "You should offer any help you can give to the police."

"I did, but they weren't interested," Hank said matter-of-factly. "I used to be a cop a long time ago, so I might be of some assistance."

"That's great," I said. "Let me ask you something. Who had access to this room today? Do you know?"

"Well, as you know, each contestant got a key card that was set to this lock," he said as he swiped his electronic key through the slot. It didn't work the first time he slid it through, so he tried it again as he said, "You're really the only ones who had access."

"Besides you, the other senior staff, and the caterers, you mean," I said.

"Point taken," Hank said as he stopped what he was doing and shot me with his finger. "It wasn't as secure as I would have hoped after the fact, but then again, no one considered the possibility that someone might be murdered inside."

"Are there any security cameras around here?" I asked as I looked around the auditorium.

"That's a good question," Maddy said as she patted my back. There wasn't a trace of condescension in it.

"I agree, but I'm sorry to say that the answer is no. Our security cameras are in the lobby, sections of the parking lot, the main hallways, and the restaurant entrance. They were set up in case we were ever robbed, more than anything else. I lobbied for more cameras throughout the property, but that budget was cut so they could fill the atrium with trees and lights."

"You have to admit that they are quite lovely," Maddy said.

"They are, but they don't make my job any easier," he responded.

"So, have you been able to come up with any suspects?" Maddy asked. "I know that you must have been thinking about it."

"Maddy, I don't know that that's a fair question to ask him," I said.

"It's fair enough," Hank said. "Unfortunately, as far as I've been able to tell from what I've learned so far, it could have just as easily been any of you."

I wasn't sure I liked the idea of being investigated by so many different people, but there wasn't much I could do about it at the moment. Besides, Maddy and I knew that we were innocent, so that helped.

"That's fair enough," I said as he finally opened the door, and Maddy and I walked inside. The green-room had changed quite a bit since the last time I'd seen it. The tables and chairs were now positioned in different places, and all of the food and beverages had been removed. In fact, besides the little bit of furniture that was still there, the room was nearly stripped down to the walls and the carpet. Had Kevin taken everything with him as evidence? I was going to have a hard time finding any clues, given the state of the place, and then I noticed the carpet.

Were those bloodstains? I knelt down and got a closer look. A section of the carpeting had been cut out, for testing no doubt, but there was enough of the stain still there.

Maddy put a hand on my shoulder. "That's kind of creepy, staring at bloodstains like that," she said.

"They aren't bloodstains," Hank and I said at the same time.

"My, did you two work that out ahead of time?" Maddy asked.

"No, it's pizza sauce," I said. I started to wet my finger and dip it in when Hank said, "I wouldn't do that if I were you."

"Why not? He wasn't poisoned, was he?"

Hank was about to say something when I heard

another voice behind him. "As a matter of fact, yeah, it turns out that he was."

It was Kevin Hurley, and evidently he was in the mood to share again.

"They need you at the front desk," Kevin told Hank, who nodded toward us, and then hurried away. For a big man, he was pretty light on his feet, and I wondered how he'd do in a fight. I had a hunch that he wouldn't have any trouble dealing with the average rowdy guest at the complex.

"You're not a big fan of his, are you?" I asked Kevin after Hank was gone.

"What makes you say that?"

"Come on, you were just about bristling when you found him here with us," Maddy answered for me. "It doesn't take a detective to figure that out."

"Let's just say that Hank and I have had our differences in the past," Kevin said, "and leave it at that. Now, what *are* you two doing here?"

"Looking for clues, remember? I kind of thought that was the plan all along," I said.

Kevin bit his lip for a second. "I was under the impression that you'd be talking to your fellow contestants and leave looking for clues up to me and my department."

"Why can't we do both?" I asked.

He shrugged. "I was just hoping for more information about your fellow contestants by now, that's all."

"Well, tell me how Luigi was poisoned, and then I'll tell you what we've found."

Kevin must have been desperate for new information, because he didn't even try to fight me on it.

"I've been able to confirm that George Vincent, aka Laughing Luigi, was poisoned. There was a portable crime lab in Charlotte working another case, and they were nice enough to come up here and lend me a hand. That's the only reason we got the results of the tox screen so quickly."

"What was the poison, and how was it administered?" I asked.

Kevin frowned, and I could tell that he wanted to keep it from us, but ultimately he decided to answer my question. "The poison was doused on a slice of pizza, but not the same one we found in Luigi's mouth. That was jammed in a few minutes later after he died. The killer must have delivered the pizza, watched Luigi take a fatal bite, and then rammed another piece in before he left. That tells me that this was personal. It can't be easy to stand by and watch a man die from poisoning without a whole lot of hate in you. As to what poison the killer used, it turns out that it was some kind of common industrial cleaner—some pretty nasty stuff—and I'm guessing that all of you had access to it in your restaurants. We even found some in one of the cleaning supply closets nearby, so anyone could have done it. Now, that's enough questions from you before I get some answers myself. What did you find out?"

I looked at Maddy, who nodded. We'd agreed not to hold anything back from Kevin, given the nature of this particular investigation. It was an odd set of circumstances that had us working so closely together, but I wasn't about to violate the faith he'd put in the two of us. "We saw the Raleigh twins give what looked like a pack of money to someone in the shadows in the parking lot about an hour ago."

"Did you see who it was, or is there any logical reason that you'd have to believe that it was really cash?"

"No," I admitted. "But even you have to admit that it looked awfully suspicious."

"Go on," he ordered. "What else did you find out?"

"Well, it appears that Tina Lance, that food reporter from Charlotte, was right. We heard Kenny and Anna from the Charlotte team talking to Frank Vincent in the restaurant earlier. Kenny was upset that the contest was no longer rigged because of Luigi's murder, and he wasn't mincing words about it."

"Was Anna in on this as well?" the chief asked.

"I don't think so. Do you, Maddy?"

"Not a chance," my sister said.

"And you're going by what, forming your opinion?"

"I just don't think she was involved," Maddy said. "I can't give you any real reasons that you'd buy, but it's what I believe."

"I'm not about to laugh at women's intuition, or any other kind someone might have," the police chief said. "I'm a firm believer that hunches are how our subconscious communicates with us sometimes. Where did you leave things with her?"

"She didn't know anything concrete, but she's promised to keep an eye out for whatever might look suspicious," Maddy said.

"I don't like so many civilians taking these kinds of chances," Kevin said with a frown.

"We're all being careful. You don't have to worry about any of us."

He just laughed ruefully. "If it makes you feel

better saying it, go right on believing it. Surely that's all you uncovered. It hasn't been that long since we last spoke."

"You might want to talk to Jeff and Sandy from Asheville," I admitted, though it pained me to do it. "It's pretty clear they have something they want to tell you, but you're probably going to have to drag it out of them."

"Any idea about what it might be concerning?"

"All I can say for sure is that it has to be about Luigi. Sorry, we tried to find out more," I said, "but that's all we could get."

Kevin finished his last note in his booklet, and then looked at us in turn. "You've both done phenomenally well today. If I could, I'd put you on the short-term payroll."

"Forget the money. I want my own badge," Maddy said with a grin.

Kevin laughed dryly. "Not on your life. Now go ahead. You can ask me three more questions tonight."

"That *is* pizza sauce, right?" I asked as I pointed to the stain.

"It is. We're going to analyze all of the sauces of the pizzas submitted since that was really the only thing you were allowed to use that's unique to each pizzeria, but we're pretty sure which pizza it came off of."

"Fair enough," I said. "Have you managed to eliminate any suspects yet?"

"We're working on it. What's your suspect list look like?"

"It's shorter than yours, I know that."

"How can you tell?"

"Neither one of our names are on it," Maddy said, laughing.

"I meant besides the two of you."

It was a fair question. "So far, we've got Kenny and Anna from Charlotte, the twins from Raleigh, Jeff and Sandy from Asheville, Jack Acre, Frank Vincent, and a woman named Mrs. Ford, whoever she might be."

Kevin opened his notebook, flipped through several pages, and then read from it, "Helen Ford, owner of Flippin' Great Pizza in Greensboro. She was here at the complex until the afternoon session started, checked out, and headed for home."

"Wow, that's thorough," I said. "How do you know that she's still not in Timber Ridge? Just because she's not staying here doesn't mean that she actually left."

"Good point. She received a speeding ticket just outside Hickory at four thirty-nine. She didn't have time to dose the pizza and drive that far, either up or back. She's in the clear."

"Thanks. It's nice to be able to actually pare ours down," I said.

"You've still got a pretty long list. Do you have motives for all of them yet?"

"We have a few," I admitted, "but we aren't ready to share them just yet. We're still digging into it, and you know better than anyone that these things take time."

"Fair enough," the police chief said as he started for the door.

"By the way, just out of curiosity, which pizza had the poison on it? After all, we're entitled to one more question, aren't we?" I asked, almost as an afterthought as we all started to leave the greenroom.

"Actually, that's one of the reasons I was looking for the two of you. I hate to have to tell you this, but the doctored slice *and* the one jammed down Luigi's throat after he was dead were both slices from one of your pizzas."

That was just about the worst thing he could have said to us. When word got out around town, and I knew that it would, sooner rather than later, a great many fingers would be pointing in our direction.

"We almost ate some of that pizza ourselves," Maddy said loudly.

"Well then, all I can say is that you might have dodged a bullet by skipping it," Kevin said.

"You do know that we're not that stupid, right?" I asked. "If we were going to poison Luigi, we never would have used any of our own slices."

"Unless you were trying to be too clever to mislead me," the police chief said.

"You don't believe that for one second, do you?" I asked him.

He shook his head. "No, not really. Just be careful, okay? It's pretty clear that someone's trying to set you up and pin this murder on you."

"Like pulling our power cord, only a thousand times worse," Maddy said.

"What's this about a cord?" the police chief asked, clearly interested in her comment.

"I'm sure it's nothing," I explained. "The cord to our oven was pulled out of the outlet during the first round."

"It was no accident," Maddy insisted. "Somebody wanted us to fail."

The chief just shook his head. "No offense, but

killing your chances to win a contest and killing the sponsor are two entirely different things."

"I couldn't agree with you more," I said. "That's why I didn't mention it."

Kevin thought for a few seconds, and then said, "If anything like that happens again, even if it doesn't seem related directly to the murder investigation, let me know about it, okay?"

"Why?" I asked, curious about why it would matter to him.

"Somebody wanted to get rid of Luigi, and they succeeded admirably. If they perceive the two of you as a threat, either in the contest or to their freedom, they might take action again."

"Don't worry about us. We're already watching our backs," I said. I thought about telling him that I'd moved into Maddy's room so we could watch over each other, but I didn't want him to think that I was overreacting. He might ask us to stop our investigation, and that was something neither Maddy nor I was willing to do. "Thanks for the updates, Chief."

"Thank you. Now if you two ladies will excuse me, I've got a few more interviews to carry out before my night's over."

"Is there any chance that we can tag along with you?" Maddy asked.

"What do you think?" Kevin asked her with a grin.

"Hey, it never hurts for a girl to ask."

I smiled. "Just ignore her. Good hunting tonight."

"You, too. And I meant what I said. Don't go splitting up and heading off digging on your own. Together, you two make a pretty formidable team."

"Hey, we're not all that shabby when we're apart," Maddy said.

"No, but sometimes the whole is greater than the components that make it up."

I whistled. "Wow, a police chief *and* a philosopher."

"Tonight it's a 'buy one, get one free' sale."

After he was gone, Maddy said, "You didn't tell him about our new roommate arrangement. Is there any reason in particular why you decided to hold that back?"

"I felt silly saying it after assuring him that we could take care of ourselves. I didn't want to send any mixed messages. Was I wrong not to tell him?"

"Honestly, I don't even want Gina to know," Maddy said.

That was an odd comment from her. "Why not?"

"The fewer people who know what we're up to, the better. If we tell Gina, the room will open up again, and then her entire staff will know where we are. Let's just keep this between the two of us for now."

"Do you honestly believe that someone on her staff might be the murderer?" I asked.

"I wouldn't say it's all that likely, but I'm not sure there's any reason to tempt fate by spreading the news that we're both in the same room. We can tell Bob and David, but no one else should know."

"Heck, let's keep them in the dark, too," I said. "It should be on a need-to-know basis, and I don't think it should matter to either one of them."

"And what they don't know won't hurt them," Maddy crowed. "I like the way you think, Sis. I didn't know you had it in you."

"Honest to goodness, I think I might have been hanging around too much with you lately," I said with a smile.

"I knew there was a reason you were getting so much cooler to spend time with," she said. "That begs the question, though. What do we do next?"

"I'll let you know as soon as I think of it."

Chapter 10

In ten minutes, I had an idea for another avenue of inquiry, but we couldn't pursue it until the next day. "I might just have something," I told Maddy as we headed back to the lobby through the auditorium.

"What is it? You've certainly got my attention, because I haven't been able to come up with anything on my own."

"It means getting up early tomorrow. I want to talk to the maids who work on our floor before they get started. If anyone's got scuttlebutt around here, it's got to be them. Think about how much they must know about all of us after cleaning our rooms. Can you imagine what they must find just taking out the trash every day?"

"Why is this line of questioning suddenly making me so uncomfortable?" she asked.

"You don't have a problem talking with the cleaning crews, do you?"

Maddy shook her head. "Are you kidding? I admire them now more than ever. I'm just afraid what they might have learned dealing with my trash cans even after just one night."

"Hopefully no one's asked them about the two of us, so our secrets should be safe with them," I replied. "That covers part of tomorrow morning, but it still leaves us with an hour tonight, even if we plan to get to sleep at a decent hour. Since the competition doesn't start until tomorrow morning, we'll have plenty of time to snoop before then if we get up early enough, but I hate to let an opportunity just pass us by. Who would you like to talk to next?"

"That depends," she answered.

"On what?"

"If I believed for one second that there was the slightest chance either one of them would tell us the truth. I'm not ashamed to admit that I don't trust the Raleigh twins. There was nothing innocent about that exchange of something we saw earlier, and I'd love to get to the bottom of it."

"Do you really think they were paying someone off?" I asked.

"I do, though I can't prove it."

"I'd love to find more out about the man in the shadows," I admitted.

"Me, too, but I doubt the twins will tell us anything useful, and we can't just go around accusing people of taking gifts from the twins without any reason to suspect them."

"Why not?" I asked with a smile.

"Just come out and ask him about it? I'm assuming we're both talking about Jack Acre, right? As the new sole judge, isn't he the next logical choice in line? If the twins found out what Kenny had done with Luigi, what would keep them from trying to replicate it with Jack, since he's running things now?"

"From what we've learned about the duo so far, it makes perfect sense that they'd try to bribe Acre," I agreed. "I've been thinking, do we really *have* to admit that we didn't get all that good a look at him this evening?"

"No, I suppose not. It might backfire on us, though. After all, now that he's suddenly the judge we have to please, we need to watch our step, since this contest has never even made an effort to be fair by making it all blind taste-testing."

"Why is that, do you suppose?" Maddy asked. "Wouldn't that have at least smacked more of fairness than the way they're running this thing now?"

"If the contest was never meant to be anything but crooked, they'll need to know which way to throw it, wouldn't they?"

She nodded. "I wish that we'd asked for a blind-tasting provision in the contract you signed before we agreed to do this."

"You're not second-guessing me, are you?" I asked.

"Not a chance. If you hadn't signed just about anything Luigi put in front of you, I would have been furious with you. This was just too good an opportunity to pass up."

"Even if it's still rigged?"

Maddy shrugged. "Hey, like the man said, even if they're cheating, it's still the only game in town."

"I have a feeling the only two people winning tomorrow are Greg and Josh," I said. "We probably should have gone skiing with them and dropped out of this competition from the start."

She hugged my briefly. "Well, that's spilled milk now. Let's go tackle Jack and see what he has to say for himself."

"Do you have a second?" I asked Jack Acre as he opened his hotel room door.

"That depends. Is this about the contest?" Jack asked. His trousers were wrinkled, I could see through the open door that his suit jacket was draped over a chair, and his shoes were haphazardly slung near the bed. It was clear that he'd had a long evening so far, and it probably wasn't going to get any shorter for him, either. "I don't feel comfortable discussing anything with the two of you while the other contestants are absent."

"I understand," I said. "This will only take a second. My sister and I were just wondering what the twins gave you earlier in the parking lot."

Acre took a second to react, and then his puzzled face quickly shifted into an angry one. "What are you talking about?"

"This evening. The envelope in the parking lot with the twins from Raleigh. We saw the entire thing," Maddy said.

"I don't know what you think you saw, but I can assure you that I've been too busy trying to take over for Luigi to have time to meet with anyone who doesn't work for me."

"You mean the dough company, right?" I asked.

"Of course that's what I meant. Now I must insist that you go. This conversation is entirely inappropriate."

"Don't worry. We're leaving," Maddy said, and she let us be forced out into the hallway.

"What was that all about?" I asked her. "You gave up awfully fast in there. Are you really afraid that we might not win if we get him mad?"

"You're kidding, right? Tell me that you saw it, too," she said excitedly as we moved back down the hall.

"See what? You've lost me." Whatever Maddy had noticed I'd missed completely. That was just one reason the two of us made such a good team. It was tough to get something past both of us when we were working together.

"His shoes," Maddy explained. "The soles were as slick as a skating rink."

"Did you happen to see any dirt on them?" I asked.

"No," she admitted, "but I've got a feeling that if we go over to where the mystery man was standing when we saw him talking to the twins, we might be able to check the prints and see if it was really him."

"Good spot. We'll do that first thing tomorrow morning," I said, proud that my sister had spotted something that I'd missed.

"Eleanor, we can't wait until then," Maddy said.

"Well, the parking lot may be bright, but we're

going to have a tough time seeing anything at all in the shadows."

"That's why we're calling Hank White. I'm willing to bet that he owns a serious flashlight with the job he has. What do you say? Are you up for it?"

"Let me give him a call," I said. At first he didn't pick up, and when he finally did, he was a little out of breath.

"Is this a bad time?" I asked. Why did my calls lately always seem to interrupt someone?

"No, I'm good. What's up?"

"Maddy and I need a big flashlight, the industrial-strength kind that doubles as a club. Can you help us out?"

"Absolutely. I've got one in my trunk. Do you mind if I ask what it's for?"

What could it hurt to tell him? "We want to check out an area in the far parking lot. We saw something there a while ago, and we want to see if we can find any evidence of what happened."

"It sounds intriguing," he said. "You can count me in."

That was a little awkward. "Actually, we don't need an escort. We just need your flashlight."

"Then it's your lucky day. You're getting two for the price of one. Give me three minutes and I'll meet you in the lobby."

"Okay," I said, and then hung up.

Maddy asked, "What was that all about? Why on earth does it take that long to ask someone for a flashlight?" She paused, and then added with a frown, "Don't tell me. He wants to come with us, doesn't he?"

I nodded. "Gina must have asked him to keep an eye on us, and I couldn't just say no. You don't mind, do you?"

"Why not? The more, the merrier," Maddy said.

Two minutes later we were in the lobby, but there was no sign of Hank yet. How long did it take him to retrieve his flashlight from his vehicle? Or maybe he'd decided to go look around a little by himself.

The only problem with that was that I hadn't told him what we were looking for. He'd have to check with us before he started nosing around, and then we'd all go hunting for footprints together.

Sure enough, I looked outside and saw him heading straight for us in the bright lights of the parking area. "Come on, Maddy, let's go meet him out there. Clearly he didn't wait for us."

She whistled softly. "What good did he possibly think that he could do? He doesn't even know what he's looking for."

"True," I said as we got closer. A crazy thought just struck me. "What if Hank's somehow involved in this whole thing?"

"The murder?" she asked. "Why would he want to kill Luigi?"

"I don't know, but we know for a fact that his key was coded into that room," I said.

"Don't forget. Ours was, too," my sister reminded me. "But that doesn't mean that we killed Luigi, even if our pizza was used as a murder weapon."

When we got close enough to him, I asked Hank, "Why didn't you wait for us?"

"That's near where my car is parked. Besides, I figured if I looked around a little myself, I might be able to keep you two out of trouble," he admitted.

"Good luck with that," Maddy said. "Better men than you have tried and failed before, and I'm sure they will again."

"Well, it would have helped to know exactly what I was looking for," Hank said. "I've just been wandering around, but I didn't see anything that looked out of place to me."

"That's funny, because you were closer than you ever realized," I said. "May I?" I asked as I held my hand out for the flashlight.

"Be my guest," he said.

I took the light and walked over to the edge of the parking lot where we'd seen the twins talking to the stranger. Shining the light down into the dirt, I saw that someone had taken a broken tree branch and had obscured the footprints that must have been there at one point.

"We're too late. They beat us to it," I told Maddy.

"Do you think he saw us, or is he just really careful about covering his tracks, no pun intended?"

"It looks like this is fresh," I said as I knelt down beside the dirt, "But I'm really no judge. Hank, what do you think?"

He took the flashlight from me, and then leaned down so he could get a better look at the dirt from a horizontal angle. Touching it lightly with his index finger, he studied the dirt deposited there, and then his fingertip. "It's fresh, all right. Whoever did this didn't act until twenty or thirty minutes ago, unless I miss my guess."

"What were you, a buffalo tracker in another life?" Maddy asked him with a smile.

"I was the next best thing. I was a Boy Scout growing up, and before I was a cop, I was in the military police. You'd be amazed the kinds of things they all taught me along the way."

"I'll take your word for it," Maddy said as she turned back and looked at me. "What do we do now?"

I got the flashlight, and then searched the surrounding ground. It took me a few minutes, but I finally found the tree branch I was looking for.

Holding one end up, I said, "This was cut with a knife, and the sap's still oozing a little."

"As rough as that bark is, there's absolutely no chance of getting any fingerprints off it," Hank said.

"Or any evidence of a crime at all, for that matter," Maddy added. "What are we looking at, when it comes down to it? Someone rubbed a branch across the dirt. It's not exactly the caper of the century."

"No, but it tells us that whoever did this was being pretty careful. I have a hunch that he was covering up more than a meeting with the twins."

"I don't mean to be nosy, but would you two mind telling me what's going on?" Hank asked.

What could it hurt, now that he knew what we were doing? Once we brought Hank up to speed on that particular angle of our investigation, he said, "That's curious, isn't it? My only question is how can we be sure that this had something to do with the contest or the murder? I know it sounds crazy, but it could just be a coincidence."

"Think about it. If it was all aboveboard, why did they make their exchange in the exact space where no one could see them?" I asked.

"That's a good point. We should go talk to the twins."

"I think the police chief already beat us to it," Maddy said.

"That's all well and good, but I want to confront them with this directly," Hank said, pounding the heavy light in his hand. "Are you ladies interested in coming with me?"

It was clear that Hank was in full-on cop-mode, but I wasn't about to let him take the investigation away from us. "Slow down. Remember, Maddy and I are running things. You can come along as backup, but only if you promise to behave yourself."

"What if I think of something you forget to ask?" Hank asked.

"Then say something to one of us, but we're in charge. Understood?"

He shrugged. "Sure, that's fine. What should I do, stand behind you and try to look intimidating?"

"I'm not sure how hard you have to try to look that way," I said with a smile to take away some of the sting.

"Fine. Let's go."

He stopped at the desk, no doubt to check in, but I heard him ask what room the twins were staying in. I tugged his sleeve as the clerk checked the computer. "We already know where they're staying. They're just down the hall from us."

"Sorry. Old habits die hard."

We all got into the elevator, and as we rode up to our floor, Maddy asked softly, "Do you have any idea about how we should handle this?"

"I think Hank is right. Let's just come right out and ask them what they were doing out there this evening."

Maddy said, "Just remember. They've already declined to tell us once."

"But I wasn't with you then," Hank said.

"Why not? What have we got to lose?" I asked.

We got off the elevator and walked down to the room we'd seen the twins exiting earlier. Once we were all standing there in front of the door, I knocked firmly.

When one twin answered, he didn't look all that pleased to see any of us standing there. He was wearing his own brown robe, and it had a *T* embossed on it, so I knew that it was Todd, unless the brothers had exchanged robes. He frowned at us for a full five seconds, which felt like a lifetime, before he asked, "What is it? Don't you two ever spend time in your own rooms? And who's the goon you brought with you this time?"

"I'm the head of Security here at the complex," Hank said.

I waved a hand at Hank behind my back to remind him he was supposed to be quiet, but when I answered Todd, I knew that I wasn't about to tell him that Maddy and I were bunking together ourselves. "Listen, we all know that we saw what happened in the parking lot. What was in the envelope that you handed to Jack Acre? Was it a bribe so you'll win the competition?"

Todd was about to answer when Hank took a step forward toward him. He was almost in the room now.

"Don't bother lying to us," he said coldly. "We want the truth."

Todd studied him for a second, and then called

back over his shoulder to his brother, "Reggie, you need to come here right now."

His brother was dressed identically, with the exception of the *R* on his robe instead of a *T*. "What do they want?" he asked as he looked at Hank, and then us. I wasn't happy about the Security head trying to take charge, but I couldn't exactly drag him back into the hallway without looking like a complete idiot.

"They think we were paying Jack Acre off so we could win the contest," Todd said simply. "Do you want to explain the truth to them, or should I?"

"What exactly did you see?" Reggie asked us. I noticed that he addressed it to Hank as well as to us, but it was only natural, since the man was head of Security at the complex and happened to currently be blocking their only way out.

"It is clear that an envelope exchanged hands in that parking lot," Hank said. "We want to know what was in it."

So much for Hank following my instructions.

"It was Jack Acre, wasn't it?" I asked firmly, shooting Hank a warning look as I did. The second it sunk in why I was upset, he looked apologetic and even took a step back into the hallway so he wasn't such a looming presence.

"Wrong. It was nobody you'd know," Reggie said.

"Tell us who it was then, and we'll leave you alone," Maddy replied.

"If you have to know, we owed a man some money, and he was pretty insistent on being paid back immediately."

"Is he from Timber Ridge?" I asked.

"No, he's from Raleigh, just like we are," Todd explained. "Why would we know anybody in this smudge of a town?"

"And you're telling me that he drove all this way just to collect?" I asked.

Todd smiled without warmth. "Believe me, he would have come a lot farther than he did if he had to in order to get paid."

Hank spoke up again, forgetting again that I was in charge. I still was, wasn't I? At that point, I couldn't really be sure anymore. Hank said, "What's his name and contact information so we can confirm your story?"

"Hank," I said abruptly. "We've *got* this."

He shrugged once in my direction, as though I'd annoyed him this time with my presence, but kept his gaze on the twins.

"I don't care who wants to know this guy's name, because I'm not going to tell you," Reggie said, "and neither is my brother. Trust me when I tell you that he can do a lot worse things to us than anybody in Timber Ridge could ever dream of."

"Where'd you get the money all of a sudden to pay him off?" Maddy asked.

"What?" Reggie asked. "Why is that any of your business?"

"It just stands to reason," Maddy said. "If you couldn't pay him off in Raleigh but you can now, where did the money suddenly come from?"

"Listen, I've tried to indulge you three, but you have no right to question us, and my brother and I don't have to answer anything else. Now go away."

With that, he slammed the door in our faces.

I turned to look at Hank critically. "What happened to the strong and silent type you were supposed to emulate? You just couldn't keep your mouth shut, could you?" I was angry at him, but even madder at myself for letting him step in and take over.

"I can't help it," he said plaintively. "Old instincts just kicked in, and I couldn't stop myself."

"Well, you'll just have to forgive me if we don't invite you along on any more interviews," I said.

Maddy asked Hank, "What's your professional opinion based on your extensive experience? Were they lying to us just now?"

Hank thought it over for ten seconds, and then replied, "I can't say for sure. I'm not a walking polygraph."

"No, but every cop I've ever known—retired or otherwise—has had a sixth sense about that kind of thing," she explained. "What does your gut tell you?"

I could see Hank mulling it over again, and finally he said, "There was money in the envelope, I'm pretty sure about that, but I can't say if they were paying someone back, or trying to fix the competition."

"Good," I said. "At least that's something."

"Listen, I really am sorry about stepping on your toes back there. Give me another chance. I'll prove I can keep my comments and questions to myself."

"It won't be necessary, at least for tonight," I said.

"You're not finished questioning suspects, are

you?" Hank asked, clearly disappointed with my answer.

"Listen, we appreciate your enthusiasm and all, but it's late, and we have a big day tomorrow," Maddy explained. "We'll walk you to the elevator."

"It's not necessary," he said.

"Oh, but we insist."

I wasn't sure why she was making a point about seeing him get on, but I knew better than to disagree with her. After Hank was on the elevator and the doors closed, we watched the numbers until they showed that he'd gone directly to the hotel's lobby with no stops along the way.

"What was that all about?" I asked.

"I don't want anyone to know that you're staying with me in my suite," she said simply.

"Even the head of Security for the entire complex?"

"Well, now's not the time to start making exceptions," Maddy said as she moved to her suite and unlocked the door.

"Is there a chance that you don't trust him?" I asked once we were safely inside.

"Right now, you're the only one I trust in the entire place. Gina is close to being in the clear, but I'm not even willing to vouch for her at this point."

I laughed and hugged my sister. "Thanks for letting me make the cutoff."

"I wouldn't have, but neither one of us had time to kill Luigi without the other one knowing about it. In essence, we're great as each other's alibis."

"Why don't I feel so warm and fuzzy anymore?" I asked.

"Who knows? It pays to be paranoid, Sis, and neither one of us should forget it."

"Got it. Do you want to shower first, or should I?" I asked.

"No, you go for it. I'm going to call Bob and bring him up to date on what we've been doing. It will also give me a chance to see if he's learned anything digging around on the outside of all of this."

"Just don't stay up talking too late," I said. "We still have two pizzas to make tomorrow, besides trying to solve Luigi's murder on the side."

"Hey, you know me; I thrive on multitasking. Do you have any ideas about how we should tackle the deep dish competition tomorrow?"

"Well, given the fact that Jack Acre is our new judge, it's not going to be a simple concoction again. At least I've had some experience in the past making deep dish. I'm not sure our competitors have ever even tried to make one."

"So, that gives us a leg up at this stage," she said.

"I wouldn't say that, but at least we won't be at a complete disadvantage. Don't forget, we're in a dead heat right now, so it's anybody's game. With Luigi gone, we still actually stand a chance of winning."

"I've got faith in us. Good night, Eleanor."

" 'Night," I said, and then grabbed a quick shower. It felt luxurious, and after I got out, I glanced toward Maddy's bedroom door, but it was closed. I could hear voices, so she was most likely still talking to Bob. I thought about calling David, but our relationship wasn't at the point where we checked in with each other every night before we called it a night and went to bed. Maybe someday, but just not yet. I thought about Joe as I drifted off to sleep. He would have hated staying at the hotel, no matter how nice the accommodations were. He was, down to his very core, a homebody, and after we'd finished rehabbing our Craftsman-style cottage, he'd been loathe to spend even a single night away from it. My thoughts were comforting as I fell asleep thinking of the only two men I'd ever really loved, and how lucky I was to have had both of them in my life.

All in all, it wasn't a bad way to end the day.

Chapter 11

The next morning came much too early, in my opinion. I'd forgotten to set the bedside alarm or ask for a wake-up call, but my phone was set to ring every day when it was time to get up. I could have probably slept a little longer, but as I awoke, I smelled something wonderful coming from the common lounge area of our suite.

Maddy was reading the paper and nibbling on breakfast when I walked out in my robe and jammies. "Good morning, sleepyhead. I was just about to come in and wake you."

"When did you order all of this?" I asked as I grabbed my covered plate. It was a western omelet, made just the way I liked it. There were strawberries and fresh orange juice on the tray as well, both my morning favorites.

"I called it in last night after I hung up with Bob. You don't mind me ordering for you, do you?"

"Are you kidding? I love it." I took my first bite and let the explosion of cheese, egg, ham, and green pepper fill my mouth. "This is amazing."

"I'd expect nothing less from the staff here," Maddy said as she took another bite of her eggs Benedict.

After polishing off another forkful, I asked my sister, "Was Bob able to come up with anything for us yesterday?"

"He had a little luck, but mostly he was frustrated by his lack of progress. I tried to tell him that we seasoned investigators were used to the process, but he didn't buy it."

"What was he able to find out?"

Maddy took a sip of her grapefruit juice, and then said, "Well, Tina Lance is the real deal. She worked on several notable newspapers throughout the South before coming to Charlotte, and she's more than just the food critic for her little paper. She owns the majority of it as well, and is its managing editor."

"That just makes sense. We figured she must be legit after we confirmed that the contest was rigged from the start," I said.

"Regardless, it made Bob all kinds of happy when he told me on the phone."

"Was he able to come up with anything else?" I asked.

"There's one thing that's pretty huge, actually. Evidently Luigi was carrying a pretty large insurance policy on his life," Maddy said.

That got my attention. "How much?"

"It's around a million bucks, after all is said and done," she answered.

"And who gets the money? Does it go to his brother, or is someone else getting it?"

"Bob is still working on that. He's having trouble getting anything more specific out of the insurance company without pushing them too hard."

"He shouldn't take any chances with his reputation on our account," I said.

"That's the exact same thing that I told him," Maddy said, and then finished her breakfast and pushed the tray away. "I had a thought, if you're interested in pursuing another angle."

"I'm listening," I said.

"Do you have any interest in calling Art Young and seeing what he might be able to find out?"

"Seriously? I didn't think you were one of the man's fans." That was an interesting development, since most of the time Maddy tried to keep me away from my friend. She believed that his shady reputation was well earned. Art and I had bonded over the years, much to my sister's—and most of Timber Ridge's—dismay. I knew that our association had cost me some business in the past, but honestly, I didn't care. A friend was a friend, and while I had no proof that he'd ever done anything illegal, I did know that he had plenty of connections on the shadier side of the street.

"I suppose that he might be able to help."

Maddy shrugged. "Bob has hinted to me on several occasions that Luigi may have had some ties to the dark side of Charlotte, and I was just wondering if Art might ask around about him for you."

"They don't have club meetings, you know," I said. "It's not like he'd automatically know what

Luigi was up to." My voice must have gotten a little shrill, and I knew it, but I couldn't seem to stop it. I was more than a little defensive when it came to my friend.

"It was just a thought," she said.

As I ate my breakfast, I considered the idea on its merits. I knew that Art had some connections in Charlotte, but I wasn't all that certain I wanted to exploit our friendship. "Why don't we put it on the back burner for now and see what happens today?"

"That sounds like an excellent plan," my sister said, dismissing it as though the subject had never come up in the first place. "So, are we sleuthing with the time we have right now, or are we going to focus on making pizza?"

I glanced at the clock and saw that we had almost an hour before the morning competition was set to resume. "Why don't we do a little of both? After we get ready, we can corner one of the maids and then head downstairs to the auditorium to see if we can find any of our competition to grill before the contest starts up again."

"That sounds perfect," Maddy said. "I'm calling dibs on the shower first."

I laughed. "You're welcome to it. I haven't even touched my strawberries yet."

"Don't eat too much, Eleanor. You know it's good to be just a little hungry when you're making pizza."

"Oh, there's plenty of time between now and then to get hungry again. Besides, you have no one to blame but yourself," I said with a grin. "Next time, don't order so much food if you want me to be lean and hungry."

Maddy frowned a little, and then said, "Just think.

By midnight, nothing about this contest will matter anymore. Win or lose, the competition will be over, and the grand prize will be awarded. After all is said and done, we can sleep in tomorrow, have a late breakfast, and just enjoy ourselves before we have to check out."

"Don't forget, we still have to find a murderer, and soon," I reminded her.

"Like I said, if we don't have a better idea by this time tomorrow, I have a feeling we'll never solve the case, and neither will the police," Maddy replied.

"Then I suggest we get busy," I said. "Go take that shower so we can get started."

She smiled a little as she saluted me. "Yes, ma'am."

While Maddy was in the shower, the house telephone rang. I finished my bite, and then answered it without giving it another thought.

After I said hello, Hank replied, "Eleanor? Is that you? I could have sworn that I dialed Maddy's room."

"It's just one digit off," I said, not caring to explain why I hadn't stayed in my own room the night before. Then again, how hard would it be for him to find out that I hadn't slept in my own room last night? It might be better just to nip his curiosity in the bud before he started pursuing it. "Maddy and I made a late night of it chatting, so I just crashed here with her. What can I do for you?"

"I was feeling bad about how I behaved last night, and I was hoping that I could make it up to you both. Is there any chance I could tag along with you again today?"

"I hate to disappoint you," I said, "but we're fo-

cusing more on the competition right now than we
are on finding the killer." While it wasn't strictly the
truth, I couldn't have Hank stepping all over our investigation again.

Hank sounded a little sad as he answered, "Of
course. I totally understand. This is a big deal for
you guys, and it should be. I'm just saying, if you
need me, you know how to find me. You have my
personal cell number, right?"

"You gave it to us last night," I reminded him.

"Good. I thought so, but I just wanted to make
sure that you still had it. Don't be afraid to use it
now, okay?"

"We won't."

"One more thing, Eleanor."

"Yes, what is it?" Was this man trying to tell me
something about the case? If he was, I wished that
he'd just spit it out.

With a hint of shyness in his voice, he said,
"Good luck today."

"Thanks. I'm afraid that we're going to need it."

Just as I hung up the phone, Maddy came out of
the bathroom after her shower and asked, "Did I just
hear voices?"

"I don't know," I said with a grin. "Did you?"

"It wasn't all that funny when we were kids,"
Maddy said with an answering smile, "and it hasn't
aged all that well, either."

"Hank White just called," I said. "He wanted to
apologize again for trying to take over our investigation last night."

"He should," Maddy said as she ran a towel
through her blond hair. "He kind of forgot his place,
didn't he?"

"He knows that, and now he wants to make it up to us," I said.

"How does he propose to do that?"

"I'm not sure," I admitted, "but I told him we didn't need him, since we had a pizza contest to win. I know it's not strictly true, but it just seemed easier to me to tell him that. After all, we are still trying to win twenty-five grand."

"You bet we are," Maddy said. "The Slice could use a little sprucing up." She must have realized how that could have sounded to me, because she quickly added, "Not that it's not perfect just the way it is right now."

"You can quit backpedaling," I said as I chuckled a little. "I agree with you. I just don't want to spend too much time thinking about what we *could* do if we win. It's a lot of money, and I don't want to be disappointed if we don't win."

"Look at it this way," Maddy said. "We have a much better shot at winning now that Luigi is out of the picture." She shook her head, and then amended, "That didn't come out right, either. Of course I never would wish that anyone was ever murdered, but it sure sounded like that just then, didn't it?"

"Don't worry about it, Sis. There's nobody here but us gals," I said. "I understood you, but other people might not. We both need to be especially careful about what we say today."

"Got it," she said. "The shower's all yours, and if we're going to talk to the maids on this floor and still have time to do a little more snooping, we'd better get moving."

"I don't know about you, but I can be ready in nine minutes," I said.

"Well then, go to it."

I was ready in eight, though my hair was still a little wet as we walked out the door together. The blow dryer in the bathroom worked wonderfully, but I didn't have the time or the patience for it. Not today. There was too much we still needed to do before the competition was over.

"How's that for prompt timing?" I asked.

"I'll let the damp hair slide," Maddy said, "Mainly because I want to get going. Come on, Eleanor. Let's go do what we do best."

"Making pizza?" I asked.

"Snooping," she replied.

We found four maids clustered down at one end of the hallway beside the linen closet, and from the look of things, they were stocking their carts up with the supplies they'd need before they started cleaning rooms.

As I approached them, their chatter died instantly.

"Excuse me," I asked, "but I'm looking for the maid who cleans the pizza contestants' rooms."

"Is there a problem I can help you with, ma'am?" an older maid with graying hair and a trim figure asked me. Her ID tag said that she was Helen, a name I thought was rather elegant. "I'd be glad to address whatever concerns you might have."

"Oh, we're perfectly happy with our service," I said. "I just need to ask whoever is cleaning those rooms a few questions."

"May I ask what this is about?"

I suddenly realized that I'd gone about this the

wrong way. "I'm sorry. Can we start over? Your boss asked us to look into the murder that happened at the hotel yesterday, and we believe that it might involve some of the folks here for the pizza making competition."

"I'm sorry, but Renee didn't tell me anything about that," Helen said.

"I'm not exactly sure who Renee is. I was talking about Gina Sizemore."

Helen thought about that for a moment, and then said, "If you have something from her stating that we can speak freely with you, that would help tremendously."

"I have her card. Will that do?" I asked, getting it out of my jeans. I'd just transferred it over to the clean pair I was wearing now, but I didn't think that I'd have to use it that quickly.

"I'm sorry," she said as she examined the card and then handed it back to me. "There are a thousand ways you could have gotten this. Please understand; I'm not trying to be rude. We just have to protect ourselves, since all of us need our jobs."

"I get that totally," I said.

"Call her," Maddy said.

"I hate to bother her with this," I replied.

Maddy pressed me a little harder. "Eleanor, this is important, and Gina offered to help us in whatever way that she could. Just make the call, or if you don't want to, I will."

"I'll do it." I dialed Gina's number and got her on the first ring.

"Good morning, Eleanor. How were your accommodations last night?"

"Are you kidding? We enjoyed it so much that my sister and I may never leave."

Gina chuckled for a second, and then asked, "Is there anything I can do for you?"

"I hope so. I'm speaking with a maid on my floor named Helen, and she's understandably reluctant to talk with us about any of your guests without your approval."

"As well she should be," Gina said. "Put her on the phone."

I handed the cell phone to Helen, and after a brief and rather one-sided conversation, she handed the phone back to me.

"Hello?" I asked, but Gina had already hung up. I turned to Helen and asked, "What did she say?"

The maid smiled at me. "I have been instructed to tell you whatever you'd like to know. Should we step into my office for this conversation?"

"You have an office on this floor?" I asked as I looked up and down the hallway for any signs of it.

"Forgive me. It's just our private little joke. The linen closet serves as my office on this floor. There's more room than you might realize, and we won't be bothered by any of the hotel's guests." She turned to the other maids and said, "Elaine, you need to stay. Jessica, you have rooms to clean. Sheila, that goes for you, too. Go."

The dismissed maids were off like a shot, and the four of us walked into the closet together. It was indeed larger than it appeared, and I wondered about the logic of taking up so much real estate for supplies, but knowing Gina, she hadn't wanted anyone to have to wait for anything. It was just one more indication that she was running a class operation here.

There weren't any chairs, but we did have room to move around once we were inside.

Helen said, "I clean most of the rooms in question, but Elaine has the Luigi's employees. After you speak with her, we can go over the rest of the guests in question."

"Hi, Elaine," I said, trying my best to keep my voice open and friendly. I knew that Kevin Hurley and the cops who worked for him had a tendency to be abrupt when they were interviewing people for information, and I also realized that it probably cost them valuable knowledge in the course of their investigations. The police could be intimidating by their very nature, and if there was one thing my sister and I were not, it was scary. At least *we* thought so.

"Hello," she said in a voice so soft that I had to step forward to hear her.

"There's no reason to be afraid of us. What we're discussing will never go any further than this room. We're just looking for information that might help us."

"I understand," she said. "I'm just not sure what I can do to help you."

Helen turned to me and explained, "Elaine isn't intimidated by you, ladies. She has the softest voice of anyone I've ever known, but she's hardworking, dependable, and as honest as the day is long. If you ask her a question, you can believe that she'll answer it as best she can."

Elaine beamed a little at the praise, and I was glad that Maddy had suggested bringing Gina in to vouch for us.

I asked her, "Have you seen anything unusual

about the rooms of Luigi and his two employees since they've been here?"

"Well, Mr. Luigi was very messy. It made it very difficult to clean for him, since I was never sure what I could move and what I couldn't." She paused a moment, and then added, "He kept lists constantly, and his trash can was full of them every morning when I cleaned his room. He liked that particular room for some reason, so I've taken care of his room on his earlier visits, too."

"Did you happen to see what any of the lists were about?" Maddy asked. It was a very good question.

"No, it was just trash to me, you know? It doesn't pay to be too nosy in this job, and after a while, it's easy to ignore most of it and just take care of my work."

"Was there anything else different about the man?" I asked.

"He always slept on top of the comforter," she said. "I could tell his sheets weren't ever touched. It was odd, to say the least."

"Is there anything else you can think of?"

"No, that's about it."

"How about the other two employees?" Maddy asked.

"Well, Mr. Vincent's room is always so clean that it's hard to know that he's even staying with us overnight. There's barely anything to clean by the time I get there; His trash cans are always empty, and the bed's neatly made. I have to admit that it's one of my favorite rooms because of that," she added with a smile.

"Do you think there's any possibility that he is

visiting someone else overnight as a guest, since the room is so pristine?" I asked as delicately as I could.

"I don't think so, but I can't be sure. Mr. Vincent seems like he's all business. He spends a fair amount of time in his room though. There's no doubt in my mind."

That was interesting, but not helpful in solving his brother's murder. "How about Jack Acre?"

Elaine's face clouded up the instant that I mentioned the man's name. "I don't care for him," she said firmly.

Helen looked more surprised than we were by her comment. "Elaine, why would you say that? There must be a reason for you to feel so strongly about him."

The head maid turned to us and said, "This is the first time I've ever known Elaine to complain about any of our guests."

"May I ask why you don't like him?" I prodded her gently.

"He has dirty shoes," was all that she would admit to, and try as we might we couldn't coax her into saying anything else.

"Thank you, Elaine. You may go," Helen said. She leaned forward and whispered something else in her ear, and the younger maid seemed to let go of some of the tension she'd been holding in, and even managed to smile on her way out.

After she was gone, I couldn't help myself. "Excuse my nosiness, but I can't help wondering what you just said to her."

"You are a boss yourself, is that true?" the maid asked me.

"I am," I admitted, "though I normally don't like to think of myself that way."

"Then you know. It is up to us to keep our employees focused and not worrying all of the time. I simply told Elaine that she'd done a good job, and that I'd pass the information on to Renee."

"Not Gina?" Maddy asked.

Helen looked shocked by the very idea of it. "It is not my place to do that. There is an order we follow here, and it works quite well for us."

I nodded my understanding. "Thank you for helping us out," I said.

"What Ms. Sizemore wants she gets, if it is in my power."

I hoped that I inspired that kind of loyalty in my staff, but I'd never want to put it to the test. "If we could go over the three other teams staying here, it would be most helpful."

Maddy glanced at her watch and added, "Feel free to add anything that you think might help, but keep in mind that the contest is due to start again soon."

"The competition must be really exciting," she said. "I slipped away and watched a little of it from the back of the room. You two are very gifted making pizzas."

"We do the best that we can," I admitted. "Have you ever been to our pizza place?"

"I'm sorry to say that I haven't," Helen replied.

"You should come by sometime when you get a chance and we'll give you a pizza on the house."

Did she stiffen slightly at my last comment? "Because I'm just a maid and probably can't afford one on my own?" Helen asked lightly, but there was a definite hint of steel in her voice as she said it.

"No. Because you're being so helpful to us right now," I countered.

"That's because I was ordered to be," she answered.

"Well, as far as I'm concerned, you've gone beyond the call of duty with us. It's entirely up to you, but the offer stands."

"Thank you," she said. "I may take you up on it someday."

"There's just one thing, though."

"What's that?" she asked suspiciously, clearly wondering what was coming next.

"You have to eat back in the kitchen with me. That's where all the maids who come into the Slice have to eat." I knew that it was dicey saying it, but I had to try to tease her out of an assumed affront if she was going to do us any good from here on out. Besides, I didn't want her to think that I was some kind of elitist. It just wasn't, by any stretch of the imagination, who I was, and it was important for me that she knew it.

It was touch-and-go for a few seconds, and then Helen brought out her brightest smile. "Actually, that sounds pretty good to me. Honestly, the company's probably better back there, anyway."

"You can take that to the bank," I answered with a grin. I had dodged a bullet that I hadn't even seen coming. I knew that some folks wore their hearts on their sleeves, but others wore their pride there.

After taking a few moments to consider my original question about my fellow competitors, Helen said, "I'll be as brief as I can. The couple from Asheville is mostly neat, and clearly not used to staying in fine hotels. They had a book open on the nightstand yesterday that I found interesting."

"What was it about?" Maddy asked.

"It was a murder mystery called *Poisonous Peril*. That's an odd coincidence given what happened, wouldn't you say?" She paused, and then added, "They must be fighting, too."

"How could you know that?" I asked. "Did you overhear them arguing about something?" This could be the exact kind of information that I'd been looking for.

"No, but I didn't need to. The trash can by the bed was full of tissues. She'd been crying, that's for sure."

"She has allergies," I said, remembering Sandy's sneezes on stage.

"I still think they've been fighting," Helen said, sticking to her guns.

"What about the twins?" I asked.

"Those boys from Raleigh are heavy drinkers, and they smoke by the window even though it's not allowed. It's foolish of them to try to mask it with air freshener, because I can smell it in a second when I walk in, but they are guests of the management, so there is nothing I can do but have the entire room steam-cleaned once they are gone."

"Why are they sharing the same room?" I asked, curious about that development, even though Maddy and I were doing the same thing.

"It was their request, that's all I know."

"And what about the two contestants from Charlotte?" Maddy asked.

Helen shrugged as she said, "They have separate rooms, but only one bed has been used while they've been here."

I tried to imagine Kenny and Anna together that way, but I just couldn't wrap my mind around it. "Are you sure about that?"

"I'm pretty sure," she said simply. "Just like I know that you two are sharing one room yourselves."

"I thought it might be prudent if we stayed together since there was a murder here," I said. "But how did you know?"

Helen said, "I could make something up and tell you that it is maid's intuition, but this morning the kitchen staff told me that you'd ordered enough food for two people, but had it all delivered to the same place."

"We could have spent the night apart and breakfasted together," Maddy said, clearly amused by Helen's explanation.

"You could have, but then why would you need extra towels as well? The front desk noted that you requested them earlier this morning."

"I didn't. Did you?" I asked as I turned to Maddy.

My sister nodded as she explained, "I didn't even think about that. Yes, while you were in the shower I called downstairs." She turned to Helen and said, "We'd appreciate it if you'd keep that fact under wraps for now. We're trying to present as narrow a target as we can while we're here."

"Completely understandable, given what's happened recently. I'll have a word with Steven, so no one needs to know."

I wasn't sure if Steven was the chef or the room service attendant, but it didn't matter. I knew that

Helen would indeed make sure that our secret was safe.

"Is there anything else I can help you with?" she asked.

"No, nothing I can think of." I took a paper napkin from one of the shelves and jotted my cell phone number down. "If anything comes up, will you call me?"

She tucked it away in her apron. "I will." Almost as an afterthought, she smiled slightly as she added, "I'll be in for that pizza soon, too."

I laughed easily. "I'll be disappointed if you don't." I dug into my pocket for my wallet, but I saw that she was frowning as I did it, so I quickly explained, "Helen, you've done us a real service answering all of our questions so frankly—whether you were ordered to or not—and we want to reward you for it."

"Answers for you are free, so I won't take money for them," she said, and then added with a grin, "However if you're pleased with your maid service at the end of your stay, I'd suggest you might show it at that time by telling the management that you enjoyed your visit here. We are not expecting, nor will we accept, a tip from you, but I appreciate you making the offer. I'm sorry, but that's an order I will not disobey."

I knew that Gina was just trying to make it a nice stay for us, but I couldn't let it go at that. Then again, the last thing I wanted to do was to get Helen in trouble with her big boss. I thought of a solution though, and acted on it instantly. "That's fine, but you'll just have to accept this as my thanks instead."

I hugged her briefly, and was happy when she returned it.

Maddy just laughed at us both. "Don't let her fool you, Helen. She knows that she just got off cheap. My sister is good for more than that."

Helen just smiled. "Do you really think so? I myself consider it payment in full." She got a mischievous look on her face, and then said, "Now you'd both better scat so you won't be late for the contest. I'm pulling for you today."

"Does that mean that you weren't yesterday?" Maddy asked her with a grin.

"Let's just say that the staff on this floor was split on who they were pulling for the night before the contest got started, but we're all behind you now."

"Why the change of heart?" I asked.

"You have Gina's backing, we've met the other contestants up close and personal now, so that's all we need to know. We're all on your side."

"As much as I appreciate hearing it, it's not going to do anything to help us win the contest," I said.

"Don't sell our support short. You'd be amazed by what good wishes and prayers can do," Helen answered.

As Maddy and I turned toward the elevator to go to the auditorium, I found myself hoping that it was true.

My sister pushed the down button again. "Where is that elevator? We're going to be late if it doesn't get here soon."

"We can't wait any longer. Let's take the stairs," I said. "It's not that far."

Maddy wasn't a huge fan of stairs in general if an

elevator was available, but after watching the display stay frozen on the main floor for another full minute, she finally gave in. "Come on. Let's go."

As we hurried down the steps, I put a hand on her shoulder. "Slow down, we've still got plenty of time."

Maddy slowed her pace, and then she said, "It's odd that the elevator chose that moment to get stuck, isn't it?"

I considered it, and then said, "There *are* coincidences in this world, whether we like them or not."

"I'm just saying. Think how bad it would have been if we'd gotten trapped between floors on that thing? The rules are pretty specific. Anybody not at their station at the appointed time is automatically disqualified."

"You could be right at that," I said as we finally got to the main floor door.

I pushed it easily, expecting it to swing open for us, but it wouldn't budge.

It appeared that someone had jammed the door, and we weren't going to make it to the stage in time after all.

Chapter 12

"**P**ush harder," Maddy said as I hit the release latch again.

"I'm shoving the handle as hard as I can," I said. "It's stuck."

"What are we going to do?" she asked. "Even if we go back up to the second floor, we still won't be able to get down the stuck elevator. This is the only way out."

"Start pounding," I said as I banged on the solid metal door with both fists.

"Help!" I shouted, and Maddy soon joined me. Instead of asking for help like I was though, she started screaming, "Fire!"

"What are you doing?" I asked as I caught my breath, but continued to pound.

"I read somewhere that if you're in trouble you should shout 'fire' instead of 'help.' People are more likely to respond."

"By pulling the alarm, maybe," I said. "Keep pounding."

We both hammered at the door, and I was about to give up when I realized something. I stopped, pulled out my cell phone, and called Hank's number.

"Are you on the main floor?" I asked the second he answered.

"Where are you two? They're about to begin."

"The elevator's jammed, and someone's jimmied the door in the stairwell so we can't get out. We're trapped in here."

"I'm on it," he said, and hung up before I could say another word.

In less than a minute, I heard someone working at the door from the other side. After the briefest of pauses, the door swung open suddenly. "Someone jammed a folding chair under the handle," he said. "Go."

"Thanks," I said as Maddy and I took off toward the auditorium.

We broke through the doors and raced for the stage. I was in front, and the second Maddy's back foot hit the stage, the clock ticked down to 00:00. Thank goodness I was two steps ahead of her.

"Cutting it kind of close, weren't you?" Jack Acre asked from the podium. "We were about to disqualify you both."

I looked over at the twins and said, "Don't look so disappointed that we made it."

"What are you talking about?" one of them said.

"You know the answer to that question without even having to ask it," Maddy answered.

"You've both lost your minds," the other twin replied. "I don't know how we ended up being cast as villains in your lives, but honestly, neither one of you is all that interesting to us."

Everything suddenly got quiet, and I looked up to see Jack Acre quietly staring at us. After he knew that he had our attention, he turned to the crowd and said, "Contestants, today's pizza is going to be deep dish, using our new dough formula guaranteed to give you the best, chewiest dough imaginable. I know that the folks from Chicago might disagree, but we think it's the very best."

Clearly someone in back was from the Windy City, or maybe just a fan of the original deep dish pizza. They booed for a few seconds, and there was a smattering of claps spread throughout the room approving of the sentiment.

Acre put the mike close to his mouth and said, "Thank you for your comments and applause, but we ask that you reserve your participation until we announce the winner for this part of the competition." Acre reset the clock to ninety minutes, and then turned to us all and said, "Good luck."

I grabbed the dough from our small refrigerator while Maddy started working on the toppings. The deep dish we preferred making was heavy on green peppers, mushrooms, onions, two kinds of pepperoni, and three kinds of sausage. It was going to be a battle getting everything ready in time, and we didn't have a moment to lose.

I helped her out as the dough warmed up. I wished that Luigi had let us use our own recipes for the dough, since I'd come up with a pretty good one as I'd learned to make these pizzas for one of my eccentric customers, but I supposed that if he'd done that, it would have been too tough promoting his own types of dough to the audience and the rest of the world. Still, it was going to be tight time-wise. I checked the oven, made sure that it was warming up, *and* that it was still plugged in. We didn't want any repeats of what had happened the day before, and I meant to keep an eye on it this time myself. Maddy was the star of this particular show with the deep dish, and I was going to do my best as her support.

"What can I do?" I asked as she feverishly chopped on her board.

"Start the fry pan and cook the sausage blend," she ordered. I did as she asked, and then set it aside to cool. Without asking, I started sautéeing the mushrooms in butter, added the onion and pepper, and then gave everything a quick cook.

"Done. What next?"

"Make the cheese blend," she said, and I took the cheeses we used for our deep dish and began grating it all at a fast pace, though still slow enough not to kill my knuckles. After that was finished, I glanced at the clock. "I have to get the dough ready."

"Go for it; I'm fine," Maddy said.

I knuckled the now-loosened dough into a round, and then made another one as a backup just in case the first one failed. That left one ball in the fridge, but barring a major catastrophe, we should be fine without it. After I had the dough spread out in the pan and had rimmed it all the way around, I reached for the cheese.

"I'm going to start building," I said.

She just nodded, putting the finishing touches on the rest of her toppings.

I added the cheese directly to the crust, then the

cooked sausage and pepperoni. After that, a light dusting of Romano cheese touched everything. I kept building, adding the veggies and mushrooms I'd sautéed before, then the sauce, and finally our own blend of Romano and Parmesan cheese.

"How's it look?" I asked Maddy.

"It couldn't be any prettier," she said.

I slid it into the oven, relieved that it was still on and hot.

"Whew, that was intense," I said as I slid the spare crust back into the fridge. We wouldn't need it after all. I took a moment to look at the other teams, and though the Asheville couple had barely beaten us to the oven, the Charlotte team was lagging, and the Raleigh team appeared to have fallen apart. The twins were arguing about the order of the toppings, and I could see a handful of spectators watching them raptly, as though they were watching a chess match.

They finally agreed on their toppings, and ten seconds after they slid their pizza into the oven, the back doors burst open and Kevin Hurley planted himself in the aisle.

"You all need to leave in a calm and orderly fashion right now," Kevin announced loudly.

"What's going on, Sheriff?" Jack Acre asked from the judge's table.

"It's Chief," Kevin corrected him. "And I don't have time to explain. Let's go, people. Move. Now."

No one in the audience was exactly sure why they were leaving, but that voice didn't leave any room for debate. As people started quickly filing out, Kevin gestured to a few other officers and motioned for them to keep the crowd moving.

Nobody had left the stage yet, though.

"I'm afraid you're all going to have to leave as well," Kevin said as he approached us.

"But what about our pizzas?" I asked. "They'll be ruined if we just leave them."

"I'm afraid we have a more important situation than that at the moment." He motioned to one of the maintenance men in back and said, "Cut the power to the ovens, and then get out of here."

He nodded, and I saw the light go from red to dark on our oven.

Kevin looked at us and said, "Let's go! There's been a bomb threat called in, and we have to assume that it's serious."

I grabbed Maddy and we headed for the exit, but the aisles were still full when the fire alarm went off. If we'd been trapped in that stairway, I don't know what Maddy and I would have done. I had to be sure and thank Hank once this was all over. David and Bob had lagged behind to wait for us, not knowing why we were all leaving but both looking concerned when they heard the fire alarm.

"Is there a fire in the hotel?" David asked when we finally caught up with them.

"No, but it might be a whole lot worse," I said. "Someone called in a bomb threat to the complex."

"I doubt there's really a bomb here," Bob said as he looked around. "There rarely is."

"Do you want to hang around and find out the hard way?" I asked.

"Come on. Let's go," Maddy said, taking her fiancé's hand. "We don't need any heroes today."

"But what about your pizza?" David asked. "I

couldn't believe how great it looked. Eleanor, it was a work of art."

"Thanks, but if we did it once, we can do it again," I said. "It's not even on my top-ten list of things that are important enough to save."

"Where do I rate?" he asked as we finally started making progress as we headed for the doors. "Did I crack the top ten?"

"Barely," I said as I tugged on him as well.

Once we left the auditorium, I saw that many folks were exiting the building, and not just those who had been watching the competition. Gina was there by the main door along with Hank, ushering folks out in as orderly a manner as possible.

"Is there anything we can do to help?" I asked Gina.

"No, we've trained for this. I'm just sorry that we had to use it."

"Don't worry," I said, "I'm sure the complex will be fine."

"This can all be rebuilt," Gina said. "But I won't be able to forgive myself if anyone's hurt. Hank has his staff checking every room for anyone dragging his feet, but I hate to leave any part of my staff in the hotel any longer than I have to."

I didn't have any encouraging words for her, since she was right on the money. If there *was* a bomb on the premises, it was hard to say how much damage it might do.

I just hoped that everybody got out in time.

It felt like forever, but just a bit over two hours later Kevin came outside and announced, "We've swept every building in the complex, and it's all clean. You can return inside now in an orderly fashion. Sorry for the trouble."

There were shouts from the crowd wanting more information, but clearly the police chief wasn't going to be giving any out. I doubted he knew anything more than what he'd already told us, anyway.

I started toward Gina, but she was already inundated with guests demanding to check out immediately. The hotel was going to lose a fortune because of somebody's stupid prank, but there was nothing that could be done about it now. I hoped that Kevin caught the idiot who called the threat in, and not just because of my ruined pizza. Flogging was too good for them, if you asked me.

"What does this do to the contest?" David asked as we all walked back inside.

"Well, we happened to overstock our veggies and toppings, so we should be fine. I can't say the same for the other competitors, though. I imagine they'll most likely just have to delay the competition."

I was wrong, though.

Jack Acre met us at the foot of the stage and waited until all eight of the contestants were back together. Once we were, he said, "Okay, gang, sorry for the interruption, but we're pressing on. If you're low on any of your supplies, let me know; the restaurant has agreed to provide whatever you need."

"We're actually going to continue?" Sandy asked. "What about the bomb threat?"

"You heard the man. They searched everything and didn't find a thing. We need to keep moving forward, but if anyone is afraid for their lives and wants to drop out of the competition, I completely under-stand."

It was clear that no one had the least bit of interest in quitting, though, not when we were all halfway to the final prize.

When Acre saw that there were no takers, he smiled and said, "We've already disposed of your first attempts, so the clock will be restarted and you'll have the same ninety minutes that you had before. Again, good luck."

"We're going to need it," I told Maddy as we took the stage. "How on earth are we going to duplicate that last pizza?"

"We aren't," my sister said. "We're going to make it better. Don't you always say that practice makes perfect? Well, it's time to put that to the test. Are you game?"

"I was born ready, and you know it," I said.

"I wasn't there, remember? That's on account of you being so much older than me, you know."

"Older, wiser, and better looking to boot," I said with a grin as I got the dough out of the fridge and started helping Maddy replicate what we'd made to perfection earlier. She was right, though. It was time to try hard to top what we'd done before, and if I could, I meant to do it.

The next attempt was no better, but most likely not much worse than our first try at a deep dish pizza for the contest. If any of the other competitors had been rattled by the bomb scare, they didn't show it. We all produced pizzas within the allotted time frame, and we waited breathlessly for Jack Acre to announce the results after he'd tasted each of our slices. He kept fiddling with his clipboard, going back and forth between two of the pizzas on the judging table, but we couldn't see from where we stood who was being scrutinized so carefully. I was beginning to wonder if he was ever going to make up his mind when he finally stood and addressed the crowd.

"Ladies and gentlemen, let me make one announcement before the results for this round are delivered. Because of our earlier unavoidable delay, we will now hold the last event at five o'clock, with the formal announcement of the overall winners to follow its conclusion." There were a few murmurs from the crowd, but Jack didn't acknowledge them. "Now, as to the entries I've just sampled. I was amazed that this leg of the competition was so close that it was almost impossible to judge. Tied for second place, we have the teams from Asheville and Charlotte, and tied for the top spot is Raleigh and the local folks from right here in Timber Ridge. The scores are so close that whoever wins the final judging will be our grand prize winner and will leave here twenty-five-thousand-dollars richer."

The crowd applauded, but no one on the stage was all that happy with the final results. While I was thrilled that we'd tied with Raleigh for the best deep dish pizza, knowing that the contest was anyone's to win or lose stole a great deal of the satisfaction from it for me. It was almost as though nothing we'd done so far had meant anything.

"What's going on?" Maddy asked me as the crowd started to stand. "Could our pizzas have really been all that close?"

"I'm wondering if this wasn't planned all along

so that the suspense would build until the grand finale," I admitted. "Tell me that doesn't sound like something that Luigi would do."

Maddy shook her head. "I wish I could, but I can't. You know what that means though, don't you?"

"The fix might still be in," I said, having just come to the same conclusion myself ten seconds earlier.

"So, we might have done all this for naught?"

"It seems that way to me," I said, "but we can't give up now. We still have a shot. I believe that in my heart."

The Raleigh twins must have picked up on part of our conversation, but clearly not the gist of what we'd been discussing. "What's the matter, ladies? Don't be upset that you didn't win this stage outright. We saw your pizza. Jack Acre was being charitable giving you a share of our glory."

"I guess we'll all find out this evening who is really the best," I said.

"We already know the answer to that one," one twin said as he and his brother walked off the stage, strutting as though they already knew the outcome. As a matter of fact, they might. If that had really been Jack Acre we'd seen in the parking lot accepting what might be cash from the Raleigh twins, none of the rest of us stood a chance. However, I knew that a lot could happen before the final judging tonight.

"Come on, Sis," Maddy said as she tugged on my arm. "Our fans await."

I looked down in the audience and saw that both David and Bob were smiling broadly at us. There were other folks from Timber Ridge in the milling crowd as well, but it was particularly nice seeing the two of them there waiting on us.

We were about to join them when Kevin Hurley walked up on stage. "Eleanor, do you have a minute?"

"Sure. What's up?"

"We need to talk," he said as he looked around.

"What's going on?" Maddy asked me.

"The chief wants to talk to me," I reported as I signaled for the men to stay where they were and wait for us.

"Us, you mean, right?"

"This doesn't directly concern you, Maddy," Kevin said.

"Does it involve my sister, the competition, or finding the murderer?" she asked.

Kevin reluctantly nodded.

"Then I'm involved, no matter how you cut it."

I looked at Kevin and said, "You know she's not going anywhere, and the second you tell me, I'm going to share whatever you tell me with her."

"Fine, have it however you want." He pulled something from his pocket, and I saw that it was a clear plastic evidence bag. There was a slip of paper on it, but I couldn't make out what it said immediately. As he handed me the bag, I looked closer and saw that the paper had my name on it, and the number to the room I was no longer using. The letters and numbers were printed in block style, something I knew would make the note nearly impossible to identify.

"What does this mean?" I asked as I handed the

evidence bag to Maddy so she could look at it as well.

"I found it in the hallway outside the contestants' rooms when we were clearing the area because of the bomb threat."

"Was that a part of your search, too?" I asked. I had a sudden suspicion about the threat, and before I could consider whether it was wise or not to say it out loud, I asked Kevin, "There really *was* a bomb threat today, right?"

"What are you talking about?" Kevin asked darkly.

I should have stopped right there, but I didn't. "It suddenly seems awfully convenient to have a bomb threat so you can search everyone's rooms without their consent."

He looked at me long and hard before he spoke. "Eleanor, I didn't do it, nor would I even consider it. There are lines that can't be crossed, and that's one of them."

"I apologize," I said as quickly and as sincerely as I could muster. "I wasn't accusing you of anything. I guess the stress I'm under right now is making me see villains around every corner."

"It's understandable," Kevin said. Fortunately he'd chosen to be gracious about it. I'd better watch my mouth if I wanted him to keep us in the loop about the murder investigation. That crack was something that Maddy would say, but I never should have said a word of it aloud.

His voice softened for a second as he added, "I'm one of the good guys. That's something you should remember."

"I will," I said. "I really am sorry." It was time to change the subject. "What do you think that note really means?"

"If I had to guess, I'd say that someone came looking for your room while you were in the competition."

"Why would they do that?" I asked as Maddy handed the bagged note back to the police chief.

"To spy on you, or set a trap," Kevin said. "Either way, they weren't going to do you any favors tracking you down like that." He lowered his voice, though the stage was nearly empty and added, "You're going to stay with Maddy again tonight, right?"

I hadn't told him that, at least not outright, but he must have figured it out on his own without any hints from me. "Right," I said.

"Good. Well, that's all I wanted to talk to you about. For what it's worth, I hope you win the grand prize this evening."

"Thanks; we're doing our best," I said.

"Tell him about what happened in the stairwell earlier," Maddy prodded me.

"What's this about? Did someone attack you?"

"Not directly," I explained. "The elevator was stuck on the first floor, so Maddy and I took the stairs. Once we were down there, the door was jammed and we couldn't get out."

"Why didn't you call me?" he asked, clearly unhappy with our behavior.

"Hank was nearby, and he let us out. Someone had shoved a chair under the handle. I don't think it's because of the murder, though. If I had to guess, I'd say that one of our competitors wanted us to miss the deadline and be disqualified."

"The next time anything like that happens, you need to call me, not hotel security."

Was he a little hurt that we'd called Hank and not him? "It won't happen, but if it does, we'll call you."

"Good. Watch your backs, ladies, at all times."

After Kevin was gone, I looked around for our two fellas, but they weren't there.

"Where do you suppose Bob and David went?" I asked Maddy.

"I don't know," she said as she plucked out her telephone. "I'll call Bob and see."

I could hear her fiancé's voice on the other end of the phone, and after a brief conversation, Maddy hung up. "They're already in the restaurant. Gina's reserved tables for all of us again."

"She's really spoiling us, isn't she?" I asked as we started off to join them.

"Hey, I'm not about to complain. Do you think that Kevin was right?" she asked me as we walked off the stage and past the seats.

"About what?"

"The note," Maddy said, a little impatient with me. "Is somebody gunning for you?"

"Who knows?" I asked lightly.

"You seem awfully cavalier about it, that's all," Maddy said.

"What can I do, go to your room and hide until the competition is over? We have too many questions to ask too many people yet, and I won't let someone force me to hide in the corner. In a way, this note is real progress."

"How do you figure that?" Maddy asked.

"Well, we surely must have gotten under somebody's skin with our questions to make them come looking for me."

"Sis, we can't take this lightly. We both need to keep watching our backs until we catch this murderer—us or Kevin and his squad."

"Frankly, I don't care who nabs him," I said sincerely, "as long as he's nabbed."

"Or she," Maddy amended.

"Or she," I agreed. "It's the same to me either way."

Chapter 13

We fought through a crowd of folks waiting to get into the restaurant, and there were a few grumbles as we moved through them. "Excuse us, but we're meeting people who are already here," I said.

"Important people," Maddy added.

As we found our way to Bob and David, I asked her, "Why on earth did you say that?"

"Don't you think these two are important?" Maddy asked innocently as we joined them at the table.

How else could I answer that loaded question? "Of course I do."

"You do what?" David asked as he stood and grabbed my chair. I appreciated the gesture, unlike some of my contemporaries. If a man wanted to get a door for me or let me go through first, I didn't feel right robbing him of the gesture. It made me happy that he thought enough of me to be considerate, and he got to feel a little chivalrous, too. What was wrong when both parties got something out of a noble and innocent gesture?

Bob had followed suit with Maddy, and we ordered quickly. We had a contest to get back to, after all.

While we were waiting on our food, Bob said, "I'm happy to report that I've been able to acquire some information for you two after all."

"Don't keep it to yourself then," Maddy said. "Spill."

"I have to tell you first that while I didn't break any rules in seeking this out, I'm not at all certain that I want the world to know what I did to get this information. It's more a matter of timing right now than anything else, but I'd appreciate your discretion."

"You didn't have to do anything risky for us," Maddy said as she touched her fiancé's arm warmly.

"I wanted to help, so I pulled some strings to get some timely information. Would you like to know what I discovered?"

"We'd love to," I said.

Bob nodded. "The papers were just filed, so technically I'm cleared in telling you this. It turns out that Luigi, or George Vincent, to be exact, wasn't expecting to go quietly into the night when he died. He must have had enough enemies to make him paranoid, based on the way he prepared for this eventuality. We might as well keep calling him Luigi, since that's how everyone knew him. Anyway, Luigi left strict instructions with his attorney about what to do

with his company in case he ever came to an un-
timely end, and who should run it in his absence."

"Does Jack Acre take control of everything?"
Maddy asked.

"That's the interesting part. Until last week, he
would have taken over the helm, but Luigi changed
the provisions less than six days ago. His brother,
Frank Vincent, is the new CEO."

"Where does that leave Jack Acre?" I asked.

"He will continue on at the company at Frank's
discretion," Bob replied.

"Ouch! That's going to leave a mark," I said.

"I wonder why he changed his mind?" David
asked.

"Knowing Luigi, it could have been a real slight
on Acre's part, or even an imagined one," I said. "I
wonder if either one of those men knew about the
change Luigi made."

"That's not even the most important question,"
Bob replied. "I can't help but be curious if they
know even now. I imagine Luigi's attorney will be
contacting Frank any minute, but is someone going
to tell Mr. Acre what's about to transpire?"

I saw the man himself sitting at a table alone at
one side of the restaurant going over some notes,
probably prepping his speech for the last phase of
the contest.

"If he doesn't know, I want to tell him," I said as I
started to get up.

David frowned. "You're not going to kick the
man when he's down, are you?"

"Of course she's not, at least not without me,"
Maddy said.

"Nobody's kicking anyone," I said. "I just want to see how he reacts when he hears about Luigi's change."

"What are you expecting him to do?" Bob asked me.

"If he's surprised, then I'm guessing that he could have killed his boss so he could take over the company, but if it's no shock to him, I think we might just have to let him off the hook. Why kill the man if he knew that he wasn't going to get the job he coveted?"

"It's sound reasoning, I suppose," Bob said.

"Go on, Eleanor," Maddy added. "We don't want it to look like we're ganging up on him. Besides, we can see his reaction from here."

I stood, and then walked over to Jack Acre. He looked up as I approached, and I tried to smile for him. It was the least I could do, since his world was about to tumble in on him.

"Do you have a second, Jack?" I asked.

"Eleanor, how clear must I be?" he asked with ire in his voice. "I can't be seen talking to you in public since I'm the sole arbiter of this competition."

"Are you sure about that?" I asked.

He looked puzzled by my response. "What are you talking about?"

"Just in case no one's told you, Luigi's attorney just filed the paperwork. Frank Vincent is taking over your company."

Acre didn't even bat an eye at the news. "That's nonsense. Just two weeks ago Luigi assured me that I was his successor, not some bumbling fool in Production."

"I'm sorry to have to be the one to tell you this,

but he changed the amendment last week," I said. "You honestly didn't know?"

Jack frowned for a moment. "If this is a joke, you need to drop it now. It's not funny at all."

"I'm not joking. I'm truly sorry."

Jack Acre stood abruptly, gathered his things together, and then said, "We'll just see about that," as he stormed out of the restaurant.

I went back to our table, where I found all three of my companions looking at me.

Bob said flatly, "He didn't know."

"There's no way that wasn't news to him," Maddy agreed.

"David?" I asked.

"I agree with them. Sorry about the earlier crack. I should have known better than think that you just wanted to tell him to be spiteful."

I touched his cheek gently. "That's okay. I've been known to have a mean streak every now and then if I'm provoked."

"I'll be sure to keep that in mind," he said.

"You should be safe," I answered. "I wonder where he went, though."

"I'm guessing that he took off in search of an attorney of his own, the second he realizes that you were telling the truth."

"I honestly can't see him working for Frank," Maddy said.

"Don't be so sure," David chimed in. "If he could stand working for Luigi, he'll probably be able to find a way to work for the man's brother. You really stirred up the pot there, didn't you?"

"It's what we do," I admitted. "Half the time Maddy and I are looking for cracks in people's armor so we can exploit them." I paused, and then added, "I know that it doesn't sound all that altruistic when I put it that way, but we've gotten results doing it in the past."

"Hey, don't apologize for anything. We both know that we've helped the police bring killers to justice in the past," Maddy said. "Don't take that too lightly."

"I don't," I said, "but that doesn't mean that I enjoy some of the ill feelings we generate in the process."

"Collateral damage can't be helped sometimes," Maddy said. "It's just a part of it, whether we like it or not."

I was about to reply when our food arrived. It was a welcome break in the serious nature of our conversation. "Let's eat, shall we? We don't have a great deal of time until the final stage of the competition."

"I can't believe they've gone this far with it," Bob said.

"I imagine Luigi would have wanted it that way," I answered. "He always did enjoy being in the spotlight, and his murder has accomplished that, if nothing else."

After we finished eating, Bob's phone rang. He glanced at the number, and then said, "Hang on. This is the call I've been waiting for."

He covered his mouth so we couldn't follow what he was saying, but the attorney was smiling when he hung up.

"Did you just get a fat retainer?" Maddy asked.

"No, as a matter of fact, I've got one more piece of information for you. Guess who's the beneficiary of Luigi's insurance policy?"

"I'm guessing that it's not Jack Acre," I said.

Bob smiled again. "No, he left it all to his brother."

"We figured that much," Maddy said, "but thanks for confirming it. How were you able to find out so quickly?"

"It turns out that Frank himself just asked that the insurance be paid out as soon as possible. From what I was able to gather, he wasn't pleased when the adjuster told him they wouldn't be sending out any checks until the police found out who murdered his brother."

"Wow, that was quick," I said.

Bob nodded in agreement as he explained, "It also proves that Frank knew that he'd be receiving a million dollars if his brother died. Getting control of the company may have come as a surprise to him, but he clearly was expecting a rather substantial inheritance. That means that he had a very strong motive to see his brother dead, as far as I'm concerned."

"Thanks for digging this all out," I said. "We can't tell you how much we appreciate it."

"Maybe not, but I can show you," Maddy said.

Bob looked around the restaurant. "Right here? Now?"

She had to laugh, and the rest of us joined in as she said, "Later, somewhere a little more private."

"Excellent," Bob said.

"Are you two going to stay for the grand finale?" I asked.

"We wouldn't miss it for the world," David said. "We both cleared our schedules so we could be here all day, and into the night, if it runs that long."

"You both certainly got your money's worth

today," I said as I squeezed David's hand. "I appreciate you being here."

"Eleanor, whether you win, lose, or draw, I'm on your side," he said.

"As much as I appreciate the sentiment, I'm kind of hoping for win," I said with a smile.

Maddy slapped me on the back. "That's the spirit. We haven't even come up with a strategy for this evening's pizza. What feels lucky to you?"

I thought about it, and then said, "I know that it might be counterintuitive, but I think we should make our basic garbage pizza with a regular crust."

Maddy's eyebrows arched. "Really? Not another deep dish specialty? We tied for first with that one, remember."

"It's good, but it takes me too far out of my comfort zone," I said.

Maddy considered it, and then nodded. "Then let's make our garbage pizza and take our chances."

I nodded, and then glanced at the clock. "We don't have much time left, and we need to raid the pantry here for supplies before we continue. I know we have a lot of supplies still on hand, but what if theirs are better? Maddy, we both know that we need this playing field as level as we can manage. I still can't believe how generous Gina is being."

Bob said, "She feels as though she owes you a debt that she won't ever be able to repay. I completely understand that."

"I get it, too," I said, "but what about everyone else? Why is she helping them out?"

"If you ask me, I have a feeling she's charging Luigi's company dearly for the privilege," David said, grinning.

"I hope she is," I said. "As a matter of fact, if she's not doing it already, I'll mention it to her the next time I see her." I stood, and the rest of the table stood with me. "Guys, we hate to just desert you two like this, but remember, either one of you is free to call me if you get into too much trouble; I've always got bail money."

"Hey, that's my line," Bob said, and it was true. He often made the offer to Maddy and me, and I wasn't always certain that he was kidding. For that matter, I didn't know if he knew himself. That was just the nature of the sisterhood that Maddy and I shared.

After we left them, we found Gina at the main desk. She looked worried and more than a little frazzled, but she still tried to give us both a smile as we approached.

"How goes the great exodus?" I asked. "Did you lose many guests?"

"Just under a dozen," she said. "It's really not as bad as I was expecting, to be honest with you."

I'd just been kidding about anyone actually checking out. "Really? Did they think you could do something about a random false bomb threat?"

"Eleanor, you'd be amazed by what people feel they can hold me responsible for. What can I do for you ladies? I understand it all comes down to this next pizza. There's no pressure there, right?"

"None at all," I lied. "Is the offer still good to raid your pantry for supplies?"

"You bet it is," she said. "I need a break from this desk, so why don't I go with you?" She called to a young man in the business center beside the front desk and said, "Timothy, take over the front desk for me. You know the drill, right?"

"I've got it all under control, boss. No worries."

"How I wish that were true," she said.

As we walked the short distance to the restaurant, I asked Gina, "Before I forget, I wanted to ask you something. You're charging Luigi's to let us raid your pantry, right?"

"Oh, yes. We negotiated the fee ahead of time, and Luigi was so enamored with this place that he didn't even blink an eye when I quoted a price to him."

"Why *did* he choose to hold his competition here?" I asked. "Not that it's not beautiful and all, but he could have done it easier in one of the larger cities in the state."

"That's true, but he was trying to get on my uncle's good side, so that's why he booked the contest here at Tree-Line. He clearly didn't know my uncle Nathan, though. I'm his closest family left in the world, and I don't have a clue why he does some of the things he does. I'm determined to make this place a success, so I appreciated the extra publicity." She hesitated, and then added, "At least I did at the time."

"Don't worry. You'll get through this," I said as I patted her shoulder lightly.

"Let's hope so," Gina said. We walked through the dining room, nodded toward Bob and David as we passed them, and then we all headed into the kitchen. The guys were sitting there enjoying their coffee at a leisurely pace, but we were on the clock, and time was quickly ticking away.

The kitchen was a flurry of activity, but the chef

stopped the moment that he saw Gina there. She smiled at him as she explained, "Demetri, I need you to give these two ladies anything they need. Understood?"

"Yes, ma'am. I will take excellent care of them."

"That's good to hear. Carry on."

He went back to his staff to continue shouting orders, and Gina told me, "Why don't you make a list and he'll have it delivered to the auditorium in time for the final stage?"

"We really appreciate you going to so much trouble just for us," Maddy said.

"I would do it gladly without any reimbursement on my own, but it's even sweeter that I'm making Luigi, or I should say his company, foot the bill."

"Excellent," I said as I turned to my sister. "Maddy, would you mind making a list for Demetri? You know what we can use better than I do."

"I'd be glad to," she said, taking a pen and some paper from her purse. In seconds, she started to write, and I had to wonder what kind of exotic choices she might be making for our final pizza. "Keep it simple, okay?" I told her.

"No worries, Sis."

Gina touched my arm lightly. "Eleanor, I was wondering if I could ask you a favor while Maddy's working on that. Don't feel obligated to say yes, but it would mean a great deal to me if you could help me out with something."

We stepped out of the way in the kitchen so we could talk without being run over by someone with a knife or carrying anything sizzling. "You know that I'll do whatever I can. Just name it."

"It's about Paul."

I was surprised to hear her mention him, since I knew that they'd been an item in college. Gina had dumped him in search of greener pastures, and he still resented the way she'd dropped him. "What about him?"

"Listen, I know that I messed up with him royally, but I'd love to get another chance. If I asked him to dinner out here, do you think he'd come?"

"No," I said.

Before I could finish my thought, she said, "Of course not. And who could blame him? What was I thinking? Thanks anyway."

She turned to go, but I grabbed her arm before she could get away. "What I was going to say was that it would have to be a meal earlier than dinner. Don't forget, Paul has to get up in the dark, so he's usually asleep by seven-thirty or eight at night. Why don't you ask him out for a late lunch instead? He closes the pastry shop around three most days."

She looked at me curiously as she said, "You seem to know a lot about him. Is he dating anyone special right now?"

I shrugged as I answered, "Maddy and I tried to fix him up a few times, but it never seemed to work out."

Gina looked fretful. "I don't know if I should even try. I'm afraid I ruined it with him forever, and to be honest with you, I'm almost too scared to ask."

"Do you want some free advice, worth every cent it costs you?" I asked.

"From you? Always."

"The way I feel about it is that you'll never know unless you try," I said.

"Would you talk to him for me?" Gina asked

softly. "Rejection might not feel so horrid if it happens secondhand."

I took her hands in mine and said, "Gina, I'll do it if you really want me to, but think about it first. Paul likes strong women, and he admires brave ones as well. In my opinion, you have a much better shot if you approach him yourself and lay it all out like you just did with me."

"Did you two ever date?" she asked.

I laughed loudly enough to cause some of the staff to look over in my direction. "Me and Paul? No. No way. We're friends. Just friends. That's it. He's young enough to be my, my, I don't know, little brother maybe? We are allies in life, nothing more."

"Sorry, I didn't mean to touch a nerve."

I smiled broadly at her. "I'm the one who should apologize. I don't know why I just reacted that way. It took me forever to let someone back in my life, and David's the first man I've even looked at since my husband died. Paul was there for me all along through some of my roughest times, but as a friend. He's like family to Maddy and me."

"I can see that," Gina said.

I didn't let it go, though. There was a point that I needed to make, something she had to understand if she decided to go down that particular road again. "I want to be certain that you know exactly what I'm saying. Paul is like family to Maddy and me, and neither one of us would appreciate it if you broke his heart again. It nearly killed him the last time, from what he's told us. Don't do this unless you're willing to see it through to the end." I was serious, too. I might be overstepping my bounds, but I meant every word of it.

"Eleanor, I've grown up a great deal since college. That wasn't when I changed though, and we both know it. When my brother died and my uncle was nearly murdered, I learned pretty quickly to put things in perspective. The fire just cemented the change within me. Paul was perfect for me, but I was too stupid to realize it at the time. If he gives me the chance, I won't make that mistake again."

"Then you should call him," I said.

"Now?" she asked as she glanced at her watch.

"I didn't mean this very second," I said.

"No, you're right. I need to do it right now. Otherwise I'll just overanalyze it and end up chickening out." She hugged me, and then said, "Thank you for everything."

"Hey, don't give me too much credit. He could still say no."

"If he does, I'll be sad, but at least I'll know that I tried. And in the end, isn't that all that really counts?"

"It is if you go by me."

Maddy handed the chef her list, and then walked me out of the kitchen. Once we were out of earshot, she asked me, "What was that all about?"

"Gina, you mean?"

"Of course that's who I mean. She just hugged you like you were the last life jacket on the *Titanic*."

"She wants to date Paul again," I said.

Maddy frowned. "That's a bad idea, Eleanor. Remember how he told us that she was the only woman he's ever really loved his entire life? She broke his heart. Can he take it if it happens again?"

"He can't live his life in bubble wrap," I said. "If he's still interested in her despite everything that happened between them in the past, I say he should go for it."

Maddy grinned at me. "My, my, my. My big sister has really grown up, hasn't she?"

"I didn't realize that I hadn't already," I said.

"Come on, you know what I mean. I love the changes I've been seeing in you since you let David into your life. I've got a hunch that the pep talk you just gave Gina was based on personal experience, or am I mistaken?"

I had to laugh. "I'd love to be able to tell you that you were wrong, but this one time, you're not. Okay, maybe I was a little too enthusiastic about the idea of them giving it another go, but we both know how lonely Paul is. If he can give Gina a second chance, who knows what might happen?"

"You, my dear sweet sister, are nothing more than a hopeless romantic," Maddy said once we were in the lobby.

"What can I say? I'm just like my little sister," I said proudly.

"What do you mean?"

"Maddy, no one walks down the aisle as many times as you have without truly believing in love. You've got the biggest heart of anyone I've ever known."

"It's a fact. I'm every bit as wonderful as you say I am," she said melodramatically, and then we both erupted in laughter. A few older guests were enjoying the fire in the hearth, and one of them looked at us with disapproval. I saluted her, and then walked my sister back into the auditorium. I was the one who owed Gina a debt of thanks. I'd been wound up pretty tightly thinking about the contest's stakes tonight, but her question about Paul had allowed me to put things in perspective a little. Could we use that money at the Slice for improvements, and maybe even a rainy day fund? Absolutely. But if we didn't win, life would go on in my little pizza place, and I'd be as happy as I made up my mind to be.

And that really was all that mattered in the end.

Chapter 14

Sandy from Asheville approached me the second Maddy and I walked up on the stage to join our fellow competitors. "I'm sorry to bother you, Eleanor, but have you seen Jeff?"

"Your husband? No, I didn't know that he was missing. When's the last time you saw him?"

She bit her thumbnail as she said, "We split up half an hour ago so he could make a few telephone calls about our pizzeria, but he should have been here ten minutes ago."

"Don't worry. I'm sure he's fine," Maddy said. "Sorry, I didn't mean to eavesdrop, but we *are* all here jammed up here together like eggs in an omelet. How far off can he go? The next time that door opens, I'm willing to bet he walks right through."

"I hope you're right," Sandy said as her gaze darted to the back entrances.

The door opened, and I think that we all held our

breaths a little, but it wasn't Jeff, and I could feel the air go out of us.

"If he doesn't make it, you know that you'll be disqualified," one of the Raleigh twins said. "And unlike her, I fully intended to eavesdrop. Sorry, but those are the rules."

I looked around, but I didn't see the other part of the matching set from Raleigh. "I wouldn't be too smug about it. After all, your brother's not here, either. Doesn't that worry you in the least?"

"He can take of himself. He'll be here on time; there's no need to worry about him."

"If neither one of them show up, it's going to be down to the two of us," Kenny said. Anna was by his side, but it was clear that she wasn't happy to be there.

"I have faith in them both," I said. "This is too important to just skip for no reason at all."

"Who said they didn't have their reasons?" Kenny asked wickedly.

"What did you do to them?" I asked strongly, getting up in his face. His attitude smacked too much of knowledge that he might have done something to delay them himself. The same disqualification had nearly happened to us, so I was probably more than a little sensitive about it, but I couldn't help wondering if the police dusted that chair that had blocked us in the stairwell for prints if Kenny's might not be on it.

"Back off, train wreck," Kenny said, his lips forming two thin lines.

"I want the truth. Are you the one who rigged the elevator and locked us in the stairwell?" I asked.

Did Kenny flinch when I mentioned what had

happened to us? I was fairly sure that he had, but what I couldn't tell for sure was whether it was from a guilty conscience or not.

Maddy joined me, and we presented a united front against him. She smiled with sweet false sincerity as she said, "If I find out you had anything to do with what happened to us, I'll make certain you pay for it, one way or another."

"That's a threat! You can't threaten me!" He whirled around and looked at Anna. "You heard that, right? You'll be able to testify about what she just said to me."

"I'm sorry; I don't know what you're talking about. I'm a little preoccupied with something else. What did she say?" A ghost of a smile slipped past her lips, and then it was gone just as quickly as it had surfaced.

Kenny looked at his assistant in amazement, and then he turned to the twin from Raleigh and Sandy. "Surely *you* both heard it."

It was an odd request for reinforcements, especially since Kenny had so recently admitted to rooting for both of their teams to be disqualified from the competition.

Sandy shook her head, and the twin added, "I have more important things on my mind than trying to follow your petty little conversation."

"I guess it's just your word against ours, then," I said.

Maddy grinned. "Don't you just love it when it works out that way?"

I could tell that Kenny was about to respond when the back doors opened again with three minutes left. Sandy visibly deflated as the twin with us smiled as the other walked in, a little breathless and flushed. There was bright red lipstick on his cheek, but if he knew about its presence, he didn't seem to mind.

The twin who'd been with us tapped his watch, and his brother just smiled. That was the only exchange between them as they reunited on the stage.

"Where is he?" Sandy asked again, the worry thick in her voice. Finally, she threw her apron down on the stage and said, "I'm going to go find my husband. I don't care about this stupid contest anymore."

I blocked her way. If I could keep her from doing something foolish, even if it cost me a win here tonight, I was going to try to do it. "Think about it, Sandy. What if Jeff shows up on time and you're out searching the complex for him? You need to wait at least until that clock hits zero before you go searching for him." I glanced up at the clock and saw that there were only ninety seconds left. Her husband was cutting it close—there was no doubt about it— and I had to believe that something dire was holding him up. "Just give him the ninety seconds, and then you can go with a clear conscience," I said.

"Okay, I guess I can do that, but when that thing hits zero, I'm out of here."

"You don't have any choice then, remember?" Kenny asked, getting a little of his steam back. "If you don't leave willingly, they'll have you escorted off the stage."

"You're not helping," I told Kenny.

"I wasn't trying to," he said with a wicked grin.

With five clicks left on the clock, Jeff rushed into the auditorium.

"He has to be on stage for it to count," Kenny said. "He'll never make it."

Jeff must have heard him, or else he spied the clock himself, because he raced for the stage, launching himself in the air with one second left. Just as his left hand touched down on the stage in front of us all, the clock hit zero.

"He didn't make it!" Kenny shrieked with joy. "He's disqualified."

"That's not true. He made it at the last second," I said, and Maddy and Sandy backed me up.

"No way," he said as he looked around. "Where's Jack Acre? He needs to make a ruling on this right now."

Instead of Jack though, Frank Vincent walked out onto the stage from the back of the room with a nervous smile on his face.

"Where's Jack?" Kenny asked, the insistence thick in his voice. "We need a ruling here."

"I'm afraid that Jack won't be able to make it tonight," Frank said.

"If he's not here, then who's going to be our judge?"

Frank smiled again, and even looked a touch embarrassed as he admitted, "That would be me. It turns out that I'm the new CEO of Luigi's, not Jack. Now, if you'll all take your places at your stations, we can get started with the grand finale."

I looked in the fridge, but it was practically empty. "Frank, we'd love to get started, but none of our supplies have arrived from the kitchen yet." For one split second I worried that someone else had stolen them, but after checking, each team reported the same thing.

Frank turned to one of the men with him on stage and said calmly, "Steve, go see what the holdup is, okay?"

"Your brother wouldn't have put up with this kind of sloppiness, and neither would Jack Acre." Kenny must have lost his mind talking to the final arbiter of the contest like that, snapping under the pressure.

I wasn't sure how Frank was going to react to the personal nature of the attack, but he took a moment, caught his breath, and then smiled at Kenny, though there wasn't an ounce of warmth in it. "My late brother—and Jack Acre, too, for that matter—had their own style of running things, and I have mine. I find that people respond better to kindness than fear." He hesitated, and then added, "But if you believe that anything about this contest is unfair in any way, you're free to withdraw your team from consideration." It was as though he were channeling his brother for just a moment, and my worries about Frank having the backbone to run the company were gone.

Anna didn't even try to hide her smile now as she nodded happily toward Frank. He took a second to grin back at her, and I had to wonder if there might not be something going on between them. I had a hunch that Helen had been wrong about her, just as she'd mistaken Sandy's allergy attacks for tears.

"Thanks for the offer, but we'll stay and bake with the rest of them, and we'll win this thing fair and square."

Frank laughed a little at that, and then said, "How refreshing a change that would be for all of us."

At that moment, I realized that he knew the contest had been rigged before, at least once. If the Raleigh twins had paid off Jack Acre as Maddy and I suspected, two different teams had tried to influence the outcome of this competition. At least now I firmly believed that we were all on a level playing field. No matter what happened from here on out, I truly felt as though we'd be judged on the merits of our pizzas, and not the favors any of us had managed to curry along the way.

The back doors opened again, and three staff members from the kitchen came in wheeling large carts in front of them. As they took the ramp on the right side of the stage, Frank looked at us all and grinned. "See? We'll be ready to commence in no time."

We each got our selections based on the lists we'd provided, and it was finally time to begin. This was it.

Frank was a little nervous as he took the microphone, and his voice cracked a bit at first, but he soon found his way, and after a moment, he even began to look comfortable with the mike in his hand. "Ladies and gentlemen, allow me to introduce myself. I am Frank Vincent, the new CEO of Laughing Luigi's Pizza Dough. It's been a traumatic time for us these past few days, and I mourn the loss of my brother, our company founder, but he, more than anyone else, would have urged us to go on. If you would, I'd like to ask everyone to bow your heads in a moment of silence for George Vincent, or as you all knew him, Laughing Luigi."

We were all dead silent, and I could hear the heat kick on above us from normally whisper-silent vents. The effect was stunning in its simplicity, finer than any spoken eulogy.

After a suitable interim, Frank lifted his head and

said, "After tonight's contest is finished, we'll all break up for an hour so the results can be tabulated and the final winner chosen. We're going to set up a cocktail party here in the meantime, and that takes a little time, so if you'll bear with us, we'll announce the winner then."

I wasn't happy about the last-minute change since the check was supposed to be awarded the moment the winner was announced, but I took some satisfaction from the fact that no one else seemed all that thrilled about the delay, either. On the plus side, it would give all of the contestants a chance to get cleaned up before the big announcement. I didn't know about anyone else, but if I won, I didn't want my picture in the newspaper to be of the outfit I currently had on. Frank was going to be better at this than I gave him credit for.

He reset the clock to ninety minutes, and then said, "Begin. Remember, this is the pizza chef's choice, so wow me."

I turned to Maddy, smiled, and asked, "Are you ready?"

"All the way, Sis. Let's win this puppy."

We worked in happy tandem, not needing words to communicate on something we made individually just about every day we were in the kitchen at the Slice. I realized that I'd be glad to get back to my old stomping grounds soon and forget all about competitions, and more important, murder, though I wasn't all that eager to make pizzas again anytime soon.

After the dough was the perfect temperature—something I'd become used to determining given the flurry of my recent pizza making using Luigi's products—I knuckled it into the pan, pressing it firmly all around and making a nice crust ridge. The sauce was next, the last of our own blend, which I carefully ladled out over the dough in a counterclockwise pattern. I wasn't sure why I did it that way, but it was a habit long ingrained in me. While I'd been waiting for the dough to reach the proper consistency and temperature, I'd grated our special blend of cheeses, and it was ready to be added now. I let it fall like snowflakes, covering the pizza in a pleasing pattern. My part was over for the moment as I gently slid the pizza to Maddy, where she waited to add her own artistry to the pie.

After my sister had arranged the toppings on top of the cheese, I took it from her and slid it into the oven. I set the timer just in case, but I wasn't about to rely on that to tell me when it was done.

As I shut the oven door, I said, "And that's that."

"We did the best we could," Maddy said with a tired smile. "No matter what happens now, we can both hold our heads up high."

I started to help her clean up our workstation, but she said, "I can handle this. You watch the pizza. That's your only responsibility."

"Okay," I said. After all, we could be baking a pizza worth twenty-five grand, and that was worth the extra attention.

I was almost ready to pull the pizza from the oven to test it when I felt someone tap me on the shoulder.

It was Sandy from Asheville.

"Do you have a second?" she asked.

"Maybe sixty of them," I said, though I kept watching the cheese and toppings for just the right shades and hues.

"I just wanted to wish you two the best of luck," she said. "You've worked really hard to make this happen, and if you hadn't helped me keep my cool this evening, Jeff and I wouldn't even be in the competition right now."

"Thanks. Good luck to you, too."

As Sandy left us, one of the twins asked loudly, "Hey, Asheville, aren't you going to wish us luck, too?"

"We all know that you don't think you need it," Sandy replied. "You must have been shocked when Frank took over the judging for the last stage. How much did it cost you to buy Jack Acre off?"

"What are you talking about? Have you been smelling too much pizza sauce lately?" he asked.

Sandy shook her head. "Give it up. I happened to be looking out my window when you gave Jack Acre an envelope full of money. You didn't think anyone saw you do it, did you?"

The twin bit his lower lip so hard I thought it might bleed when his brother tried to shut her down by saying, "You don't know what you're talking about."

"Yes, she does. We saw it, too," I said. While it wasn't technically true that we'd been able to identify Jack Acre as the other person in the transaction, I was going to back Sandy up all of the way. Frank Vincent had been standing close by during this exchange, but it was obvious we'd all forgotten about him until he spoke. "Is this true?" he asked both the Raleigh twins. "If it is, you are in serious trouble."

"They're either honestly mistaken, or they're knowingly lying," one twin said.

"Be very careful about what you say right now," Frank said.

"We aren't about to let some little hippy from Asheville taint our good names," the other twin said as he approached her menacingly. Jeff moved forward to block him, but I was even quicker, and stood between Sandy and the threat to her. "Why don't you pick on somebody your own size?"

"You?" he asked with utter disdain. "Please, you aren't even worthy of being on the same stage as the rest of us, and we all know it."

There may have been a part of me that would have agreed with him before the contest had begun, but now I knew better. "I might not sell as many pies as the rest of you, but I've proven that I belong here just as much as you do."

"That's enough!" Frank Vincent snapped. "Everyone, go back to your stations this instant."

One of the twins started to say something else when Frank cut him off. "If any of you leave your work areas again, or so much as address another contestant during the remainder of this competition, you will be disqualified and escorted off the stage immediately. Don't think I'm bluffing either. Do you understand?"

We all nodded, and I headed back to Maddy, who had a worried expression on her face.

"What's wrong?" I asked.

And at that moment, I realized that I'd been so wrapped up in the exchange that I had completely forgotten about my pizza. The timer reminded me of it just as I smelled that stage of a pie's life where it was already too late to pull it out in time. Most folks might not be able to tell the difference, but it was amazing what thirty seconds could do to a pizza that was already done.

I reached in with an oven mitt and pulled the pizza out, sliding it out of the pan just as it hit the cooling rack.

Maddy leaned over, looked at it for a moment, and then she said, "It looks nice."

"It is, but it's not perfect, is it?" I asked, furious with myself for wasting this opportunity to show the world that I knew what I was doing.

"Hey, I should have pulled it while you were defending Sandy," my sister said.

"No. I won't let you do that, Maddy. It was my responsibility, not yours. I'm just sorry that I let you down."

Maddy hugged me. "Eleanor, you could never do that."

I felt better, even though I knew that it wasn't true. I cut the pizza, slid it into the warming station, and waited.

Within four minutes, everyone else's pizzas were ready as well.

It was time for the final judging, but I didn't need to hear the results to know that we weren't going to win. If the twins—or even Sandy—had staged that confrontation as a way of distracting me, it had worked beautifully.

Frank tasted each slice and seemed to savor every bite. When he got to ours, I shook my head and dropped my chin slightly. Maddy put her arm around me without saying a word. That was okay. She didn't need to.

After Frank was finished, he approached the podium. "I'm pleased to report that each of these four pizzas is worthy of the grand prize. We should give the contestants a round of applause for all of their hard work and craftsmanship in constructing their pizzas over the past two days."

The applause felt great, and I suddenly realized that Maddy was right. No matter what, we'd held our own with some very talented pizza makers.

"Now, we'll reconvene here in one hour for the cocktail party where I will announce the winners and hand out the check."

David was the first one to greet me as I stepped off the stage. He pulled me to one side, wrapped me in his arms, and gave me a heartfelt kiss. "I'm so proud of you."

"Thanks, but I overcooked the last pizza. We can't win."

"I'm not talking about the competition," David said. "We all saw how you stepped in to protect Sandy from being pummeled by that twin. You didn't even hesitate, did you?"

"I couldn't just stand there and watch him bully her," I said.

"Neither could her husband, but you beat him to it, didn't you? Five years from now no one is going to remember who won this contest, but I'm willing to wager that not a soul who saw it will be able to forget how you defended Sandy the way you did."

Bob and Maddy joined us in our little alcove just off the stage. "Are you two celebrating already, or can anyone join you?"

"You two are always welcome," I said.

Bob looked up at the stage. "Do you think there's any of your pizza left? I'd love a slice of it, myself. Yours was by far the best-looking pie."

"It's not our best effort," I said. "And besides, aren't you worried about tasting a tainted pizza?"

He pretended to consider it, and then nodded his head gravely. "For one of your slices, I'm willing to take the chance."

I hugged him, and then my sister gave him a kiss.

David grinned. "Man, I knew that I should have said that."

Maddy and I both laughed, and then we hugged him as well.

Once we were all free again, Bob asked, "I suppose you both want to shower and change before the cocktail party."

"You'd better believe it," I said.

"Good. That will give David and me time to grab some dessert from the restaurant. Are you two hungry?"

"I don't think I could eat a thing," I confessed, and Maddy agreed with my sentiment.

"Then we'll meet you back here in an hour, okay?"

"That's perfect," Maddy said. "You always know just what to say and do around me."

"Believe me, it only comes from the experience of a great deal of trial and error," he replied.

Chapter 15

Maddy and I took the elevator to our floor. When the doors opened, I glanced up and down the hallway to see if anyone was watching me. After I saw that the coast was clear, I ducked into my sister's room the second she opened the door.

"Why are you acting like a character from a Cold War spy movie? Was someone following us?" Maddy asked as she bolted the door behind us.

"Not that I was aware of, but we can't take any chances. I still don't want anyone to know that I'm staying with you."

"Now you're afraid when there's nothing there but shadows?" Maddy asked with a laugh. "I thought you were going to deck that twin on stage when he tried to intimidate Sandy. What were you thinking?"

"That nobody was going to get away with that kind of behavior while I was around," I admitted.

"Thankfully, it didn't come to blows. I'm just glad that Frank finally decided to step in and stop it."

"All in all, I think that he's got a pretty firm hand on things. Am I the only one surprised by how well he's taken to his new role?"

"No, I noticed it, too," I said. "We can talk about it after we both take our showers and change."

"You bet we will," she said. "You can have the bathroom first this time."

"That's gracious of you, and I accept," I said with a smile.

After we'd both showered and changed into the nicest clothes we'd brought with us, Maddy and I still had some time to chat as we applied our makeup and finished getting ready. There was something on my mind, but I hadn't spoken it aloud yet. "Do you think that Frank could have really killed his own brother for control of Luigi's?" I asked her.

"I have to admit that I've been wondering the same thing," Maddy said. "Does that part really even matter? If Frank knew about the million bucks he was getting when Luigi died, I would think that might be reason enough for some people. Remind me never to be worth more to you dead than alive."

"I just can't see him as a murderer," I admitted.

Maddy shrugged. "If you would have asked me before, I would have said no way myself, but we're certainly starting to see a different side of the man, aren't we?"

"I don't know how anyone could kill their sibling for personal gain," I said.

Maddy laughed as she replied, "As your only sibling, I have to say that I heartily approve of your attitude."

"You know what I meant," I said, smiling in return.

"I'd love to know if Frank had any idea that his brother left so much to him," Maddy said.

"Knowing Luigi, I kind of doubt it. The man always struck me as someone who wasn't big on keeping folks around him informed about what he was up to. I have no problem imagining that he'd drastically changed how his company was going to be run after he was gone without bothering to tell anyone else about it."

My sister nodded. "You're right; I can completely see that happening. We don't have much choice but to keep Frank on our list, do we?"

"Unless he can convince us or the police that he wasn't involved in the murder, he has to be near the top of everyone's suspect list." I couldn't believe how hard a time we were having eliminating people, but how easy new possibilities seemed to keep popping up. "We still have way too many potential candidates, don't we?"

"Why don't you write them all down so we can discuss each one while we're waiting?" Maddy asked.

"That's not a bad idea." I took some of the stationery and the pen that the hotel complex provided, and started writing. "Let's see. First up, we should start with the contestants," I said as I listed the pizza makers from Asheville, Raleigh, and Charlotte.

"And we've also got Frank Vincent and Jack Acre from the company," Maddy added.

"Anyone else?" I asked.

"Since Kevin gave us Mrs. Ford's alibi, she's excluded, no matter how she felt about him. I can't think of anyone else off the top of my head," she said.

"That gives us eight suspects then, if we don't count ourselves."

"Well, I know I didn't do it," Maddy said with the whisper of a smile.

"And neither did I. Okay, eight is our working number. Now, why don't we look at what we have for motives?" As I went down the list, I said, "Jeff and Sandy had problems with Luigi making a pretty aggressive pass at her."

"I know, but was that enough to kill someone over?" Maddy asked.

"Jeff is a pretty jealous guy, and if Sandy thought she was protecting her marriage, she might kill him herself. I have a pretty good hunch that she wanted to tell Kevin about the altercation they had with Luigi, but Jeff must have persuaded her not to mention it." Those two believed that their bond of matrimony was the most important thing in the world, and though I didn't want to think about it, if they felt their marriage was being threatened by someone outside, either scenario could happen.

"How about Kenny and Anna?" Maddy asked.

"Kenny could have killed Luigi for reneging on their arrangement if everything Tina Lance told us was completely true. Remember, we've got some confirmation of that story, too."

"What about Anna?"

"You saw her backing Luigi into the corner after the cocktail party," I said. "I'd love to know what they were talking about."

"If we have any hope of finding out, we're going to have to come right out and ask her," Maddy said.

"Do we even need much of a motive for the Raleigh twins? They could have done it just out of spite."

"I've been thinking about that, and I've got a feeling that they could have gotten rid of Luigi if they thought that Jack Acre was next in line to take over the company and the competition. Why not? If they're as desperate for money as they told us they were, they might do it if they thought they would have better luck buying Acre off."

"How do we know for sure that they needed money?" Maddy asked.

"Think about it. Their alibi for having an envelope full of cash was so that they could pay off a bookie. Who comes up with an excuse like that off the top of their head?"

"People do worse things for less, don't they?"

I looked at my list, and then said, "That leaves Frank Vincent and Jack Acre. Either one could have killed Luigi because of greed since they both thought they'd profit from his death, so they both have to stay on our list, too."

"So let me get this straight. In two days of hard work, extensive questioning, and an enormous amount of legwork, we haven't been able to eliminate a single suspect," Maddy said. "Does that about sum it up?"

"Sadly, yes," I said. "That doesn't mean that we should just stop trying to solve the murder, though. I'd love to compare notes with Kevin."

"Call him," Maddy suggested.

"Seriously?"

"Why not? We're ready for the party, and we still have eighteen minutes before it gets started. Why don't you invite him up here and we can tell him what we've uncovered, and then ask him to do the same? What's the worst thing that could happen? If he refuses, we're no worse off than we were before."

"Okay, it's just crazy enough to work," I said as I dialed Kevin's cell number.

He answered on the second ring. "Hurley."

"This is Eleanor Swift. Are you at Tree-Line?"

"As a matter of fact, I am."

"Do you have a few minutes to come upstairs to Maddy's room? We'd like to share what we've uncovered so far." There was a knock on the door, and as Maddy went to answer it, I asked, "What do you think?"

"It's a great idea," Kevin said as she opened the door and Maddy let him in. "I was just thinking the same thing. What have you two got?"

I handed Kevin my list. "We can fill in any gaps you might see on some of these entries," I said.

He nodded as he scanned my notes. "This is good," he said as he tapped the paper. "You two are getting better at this."

"Was that an actual compliment?" Maddy asked with a smile.

"Don't get too swelled with pride," he added. "I didn't say it was great, just that it's getting better than it was."

"Hey, you just told us we were improving and you can't take it back," Maddy said with a grin. "We'll take any compliment that comes our way. Thanks."

Kevin shook his head, and I could see him trying to hide a smile with his hand. "I didn't find out about these instructions Luigi left about who runs the company until Frank took the stage tonight. When did you two find out?"

"Not long before you did," I admitted. "We were going to tell you, but we had the competition and all to worry about." It was stretching things a little, but mostly it was true.

"That's fine. I get it; it's why you're here." He looked at my notes again, and then added, "I can work with this. May I take it with me?"

It appeared that Maddy was about to protest when I cut her off before she could speak. "Absolutely. Now that we've shared our information, can you strike any names off that list, just so we won't keep hounding people who are innocent?"

He considered it, and then said, "That's fair enough. Can I borrow that pen of yours for a second?" I knew that he always carried a notebook and pen with him, but he must have reserved that for his official police business.

I handed mine to him, and the police chief put the paper on the desk and crossed through one name. Well, sort of, because he attached a question mark to the end of his strike. I looked at the list to see which suspect he'd eliminated, and then I asked, "Why one of the twins and not the other, and how can you tell?"

"I admit I'm guessing as to which one has an alibi, because I can't tell them apart any more than anyone else can. All I know is that one of them was seen hitting on a waitress when Luigi was murdered."

"But we don't know which one it was," Maddy said.

"No, and I'm not certain we ever will. As alibis go, it's pretty clever if they planned it that way. Talk about reasonable doubt."

"It's not much, is it?" I asked.

"You know how this goes. You just keep digging, and see what you can find out."

There was a knock on the door, and I saw Kevin's hand go straight to his handgun.

"Should I see who it is first before you start shooting?" Maddy asked.

"Check, but don't open it until you tell me."

Maddy looked in through the peephole, and then turned to us. "It's Anna from Charlotte."

"I'll be just inside the bathroom," Kevin said.

"Should I go, too?" I asked. "After all, this is Maddy's room."

"You have every right to be here. Stay," Kevin said as Anna knocked on the door again.

He ducked into the bathroom, and Maddy opened the door.

"Hey, Anna. What can I do for you?"

"Do you know where your sister is?" she asked, and then spotted me. "Good, you're here. I've been looking all over for you."

"Should I leave you two alone and give you some privacy?" Maddy asked, though I knew she had no intention of actually doing it.

"No, honestly, I was hoping to find you both together."

"What's this about?" I asked.

She looked at me firmly as she said, "I know you're trying to find George's—I mean Luigi's—killer, and I want to help."

"What makes you think that?" I asked her.

"It wasn't all that hard to figure out. You've both been asking a lot of questions around the complex," she said. "Word gets around pretty quickly."

"I hate to bring this up, but you know that you're on our suspect list right along with your boss, don't you?" I asked.

"He's not my boss anymore, as a matter of fact," she said. "I just quit."

"That's going to make it hard on you, especially after you've been sleeping with him," Maddy piped up.

"What? Where did you hear that? Whoever told you that is lying," she said as her head pivoted quickly toward my sister.

I had to stop Maddy before she revealed the name of our source. It wouldn't help Gina, or Helen, to bandy their names about. "We overheard something at the first cocktail party," I said quickly.

"No doubt spread by Kenny himself. I wouldn't dream of letting that man touch me. Besides, I'm engaged."

"Congratulations," I said. "Is it anyone that we might know?"

"Actually, it's Frank Vincent," she said, blushing slightly.

"Isn't that a conflict of interest if he's judging the contest?" Maddy asked, though I was thinking it as well.

Anna smiled. "Oh, we're not going to win. That's already been settled."

"Does Kenny know yet?" I asked.

"He doesn't have a clue," she admitted, "and Frank and I would appreciate it if you didn't say anything to him about it, or to anyone, actually."

"Just out of curiosity, how long have you two been a 'we'?" I asked.

"Six months," she said proudly. "I've been pregnant for the last eight weeks, and this was the weekend we'd decided to tell George about our engagement."

"Is that what you were arguing with him about when we saw you two together after the cocktail party?"

She nodded. "He thought that I was trapping Frank into marriage. I told him that we didn't need his blessing or his money, but he just laughed at me."

"That must have made you furious," I said softly.

"I was angry, but I wasn't mad enough to kill him," she said.

"So you say," Maddy added.

"It doesn't really matter, though. We have an alibi," she said.

"Did anyone ask you for one yet?" I asked loudly, knowing that Kevin could hear me anyway.

"A deputy came by our room yesterday, but we didn't answer. We were otherwise engaged."

" '*Our*' room?" I asked.

"I have a room here for the competition, but I've been staying with Frank since we got here," she admitted. That explained Helen's report that Anna hadn't been sleeping in her own bed. The maid had just gotten the wrong room number where Anna had ended up.

"So, no one has asked you for your alibi," I repeated, louder this time so Kevin could hear it in the bathroom.

"No, but if they do, they can check with the front desk clerk when George was murdered. We left the contest, came straight into the lobby, and then spent the rest of the time sitting by the fireplace discussing our plans. There wasn't the time, or the opportunity, for either one of us to kill George. We weren't happy that he didn't embrace the idea of our upcoming marriage, but it wasn't reason enough to kill for it."

"What if he threatened to fire your fiancé once he heard the news? That might be reason enough," Maddy said.

Anna shook her head. "It wasn't anything like that. George would have warmed up to the idea sooner or later."

"I notice that you call him George now that he's gone," I said.

"I have a hard time bringing myself to call him Luigi after Frank asked me to use his real name," she admitted. "So, is there anything we can do to help?"

"No, not right offhand," I said. "We'll let you know if we think of something. By the way, congratulations again, on everything."

"Thanks so much," she said. "I doubt I could be any happier. Well, that's not true. I'm sorry that Frank lost his brother, but he'll have a new family soon enough."

Maddy showed her out, and once she was gone, Kevin came out of the bathroom. "If you two will excuse me, I've got a deputy to fire for incompetence. He was supposed to question two of my suspects, but clearly he didn't."

"Don't be so hard on him," I said. "I figure it was important enough for you to ask them yourself, but you didn't get around to it, either. That's not a slam on you. There hasn't been enough time to do everything you've had to take care of."

"That's true, and there *have* been distractions all

the way around. I can't deny that. Maybe I'll just chew him out a little."

"Much more satisfying," Maddy said. "At least we can cross two names off our list. Whoever poisoned George—I can't call him that, it's got to be Luigi. Anyway, since they had to poison Luigi after everyone else was gone, there's no way Frank and Anna could have done it."

"Maybe," Kevin said as he pulled out his cell phone. After a brief conversation, he hung up and then turned to us and said, "I was in luck. The same clerk is on duty right now. He confirms what Anna just told you. They're in the clear."

"Are you telling me that he watched them both the entire time?" I asked. "I find that a little hard to believe."

"It was a slow time at the front desk, and he didn't have anything else to do. He was pretty emphatic about it."

"Then we can finally cross two names off that list," I said.

"It appears so," Kevin said as he did the honors. "That still leaves us with a pretty long list of suspects, and I can't keep them all here indefinitely. We'd better ramp things up."

"We couldn't agree with you more," I said.

After Kevin was gone, I looked at Maddy. "So, are you ready to step on a few more toes?"

"I was born ready to do that," she answered with a smile.

We were leaving Maddy's room and walking toward the elevator when I heard footsteps behind us.

Bracing myself, I whirled around, ready to face any attacker who came my way.

Chapter 16

"Hey, take it easy. I'm on your side, remember?" Hank White said as he held up his hands, his palms thrust out toward us.

"You startled me," I said, lowering my hands. I wasn't sure what I'd planned to do, but that didn't matter now. "What's go-ing on?"

"I still feel bad about the way I acted before," he said.

"I told you, it's fine," I said.

"Yeah, but I need to redeem myself. How would an alibi for two of your suspects do to make up for how I behaved?"

"I'd say we'd be even," I said. "What have you got?"

"Just an alibi for the team from Asheville," he said with a grin. "Interested?"

"You bet we are," I said. "Should we go back into Maddy's room and talk about it?"

"No, we have to go to my office."

I glanced at my watch. "Hank, I hate to say it, but we don't have a lot of time."

"Don't worry; you'll get to the party in plenty of time. I've got everything cued up, so it won't take long," he said.

"Then what are we waiting for? Let's go, Sis," Maddy said.

We followed Hank to the elevator, and once we were inside, I noticed that it went all the way to the basement with the special key he inserted in the panel. "Why are we going down to the basement?"

"The secondary staff offices are all downstairs," he explained. "Gina's the only one who has space in guest quarters, and her office is behind the check-in desk and across from the business center. She didn't exactly get prime real estate."

Once the doors on the bottom level slid open, we all stepped out into the hallway together. It was clear that Gina hadn't spent much money decorating the corridors downstairs. Concrete floors and exposed cinderblock walls were painted the same generic beige, and I wondered if they'd bought their paint by the tractor trailer load.

"It's just down here," Hank said as he led the way.

He ushered us into his office and then hit a few buttons on his computer before turning the screen toward us. It was a surveillance tape facing the cashier's station in the restaurant, and as the time swept past, it showed Jeff and Sandy eating a meal at a nearby table, and then spending the rest of the time in deep conversation.

"The time line is pretty clear. It alibis them both," Hank said. "Anyway, I thought you should know."

"Have you told the police yet?" I asked.

Hank looked a little guilty. "I should have, and I know it, but I wanted to make things right with the two of you first."

I stood as I said, "Thanks, but you don't want to get any closer to Kevin Hurley's bad side than you already are. The second we're out of the elevator, call him, and do yourself a favor. Don't tell him that you showed this to us first."

"I know he's not a big fan of mine, so I'll tread lightly," Hank said.

"You never know. He might just come around after he sees this," I said. "Come on, Maddy. Let's go."

"Right behind you, Sis."

After we were back upstairs, I spotted Kevin by the front desk talking a little more to the clerk there. As his telephone rang, Maddy and I ducked into the auditorium. Neither one of us wanted to be anywhere around when Kevin heard about the Asheville couple's alibi.

The party hadn't started yet, but several people were inside milling around.

Maddy said softly, "We have three suspects left on our list, right?"

"As of right now, that's what it boils down to," I said.

"So, who do we tackle first? The mysterious twin, Jack Acre, or Kenny from Charlotte? We can split up if you'd like so we can get more questioning in."

I didn't like the thought of that, even in such a crowded environment. "No, we stick to the plan and we stay together," I said as I looked up. "Bob and

David are headed our way. What are we going to say to them?"

"Leave that to me," Maddy said as she walked toward both men. I was about to join her when Frank Vincent touched my arm. "Eleanor, do you have a second?" he asked.

"I do," I answered.

Frank pulled me aside and said, "I just spoke with Anna. She told me what she'd done."

"Don't be mad at her," I said. "She was just trying to help."

"Why would I be mad?" Frank asked with a spreading grin. "I want to tell the world, but Anna says the timing is bad. I know that I shouldn't be so happy with George being gone not that long ago, but I can't help it. I'm finally getting the family I always wanted."

"I understand your brother didn't share your joy about the news," I said. "That must have made it harder on you."

"Do I wish things had gone better? Of course I do. But there's nothing I can do about it now. What's done is done, you know?"

"I do," I said.

"We appreciate you keeping the lid on this, at least until tomorrow. That's when we're making the announcement at our corporate headquarters in Charlotte."

"Will Jack Acre be there for it?" I asked as I looked around the room.

"He will, and he'll be here tonight as well, if he wants to keep his job."

"You're not going to fire him?" I asked. I'd seen the

way Jack had treated Frank earlier, and I doubted that anyone could blame him for firing the man the second he took full control of the company.

"Why would I do that? He's really quite excellent at what he does." Frank paused, and then added, "I might make him squirm a little at first, but as long as he can keep doing his job, he's safe with me."

"That's awfully magnanimous of you," I said.

"Not really. It just makes good business sense."

One of Frank's employees approached and said, "Excuse me, sir, but I need a moment."

"Of course," he said, and then turned back to me. "Sorry, but duty calls."

"Absolutely."

After he was gone, Maddy rejoined me, without our boyfriends. "What was that all about?" she asked.

"He wanted to thank us for our discretion," I said.

"Was that it?"

"Yes, why do you ask?"

"It just took a little longer than he needed to ask for a simple favor," Maddy explained.

"We chatted about a few other things, too," I admitted. "I was surprised to hear that he's planning to keep Jack Acre on his staff."

"I figured he would," Maddy said. "From what I hear, good marketing and sales people are important to any business."

"Not so much ours, though," I answered.

"There you're wrong. All four of us are in Marketing and Sales for A Slice of Delight."

"Just don't tell Greg and Josh that," I said. "They'll expect a raise."

"Don't worry; the secret is safe with me."

"How did you get rid of Bob and David so fast?" I asked as I found them at the bar.

"They know this investigation is important to us, so they've agreed to step aside."

"That's hard to believe they gave up without a fight," I said as I looked over at them.

"Well, I had to promise them our full attention once this is finished, but I don't think that's going to be too hard to keep, do you?"

"I don't know about *full* attention," I said.

"Just do the best that you can. I'm sure that David will be happy no matter what." She stopped, and then gestured to one corner. "There's a twin, and miracle of miracles, he's alone. Let's go grill him."

"After you," I said, knowing how difficult it was to get one of them apart from the other. But I had one problem. How should we question him? If he was the one with the alibi, then our questions wouldn't apply, but if he wasn't the one hitting on a waitress, how would we know that he was telling the truth? There was only one way to find out, and that was by asking the man, and seeing what he had to say for himself.

"So, are you the twin with the alibi, or the one who's a suspect in Luigi's murder?" Maddy asked the twin as soon as we got close to him.

"You've completely lost your mind, haven't you?" he asked.

"If you won't answer my question, I'm going to assume that you're the murder suspect. Otherwise why would you not want to tell me?"

"My brother and I both have alibis for the time when Luigi was poisoned," he said.

"It's funny that the police don't know about them both. They just told us that one of you is in the clear, but the other one is a legitimate suspect," I said. I wasn't about to let Maddy have all of the fun, and if I could bring the twins down a notch or two, I was going to do it. They might be arrogant about their chances in the contest, but let them both scoff at the prospect of one of them being a murder suspect.

"I don't know what to say," the twin said. "I was on tape with one of the waitresses, but my brother has an alibi of his own."

The problem with that was we weren't able to tell them apart by looking at them, and neither could Kevin. If I could prove irrefutably that one of them was in the clear, it would let the police focus on the other one exclusively. "Then you must be Todd," I said, taking a stab at it. After all, I had a fifty-fifty chance of being right.

"*What*? No, I'm Reggie," he said. "*I* was the one with Stella when Luigi was murdered."

"Prove it," Maddy said.

"Why should I bother proving anything to the two of you?"

"Put it this way," Maddy said. "If you don't, you're *both* going to be locked up on suspicion of murder."

"I was with Stella. You can ask her if you don't believe me. Here she comes," Reggie said as he pointed over my shoulder.

One of the women I'd seen working in the restaurant earlier started toward us, but I wanted to cut her off before this twin could signal her. Maybe I was being too paranoid, but it was the only way I knew how to confirm what he'd just told us.

I marched toward her and asked, "You're Stella, right? I'm a friend of your boss. You know that, right?"

"It's okay that I came," the waitress said defensively. "I got it approved by my supervisor, and my shift was over an hour ago."

"Everything's fine. I just need to know exactly who it is that you are here to meet."

"Him," she said as she looked toward the twin and pointed.

"Look at me," I snapped, and the girl's gaze came right back to me. I'd have to apologize for being so abrupt when this was all over, but for now, I needed the truth. "What did he tell you his name was?" I asked.

"He said it was Reggie," she explained. "He didn't lie to me, did he?"

"Everything is fine. He is indeed Reggie," I said, relaxing a little.

"Good. May I go now?"

"Sure thing," I said.

Maddy came over and smiled at me. "That was pretty slick, Sis. You cut her off like a Pro Bowl Safety." One of Maddy's ex-husbands had been a sports nut, and some of it had rubbed off on her; at least the metaphors and similes of the game had. "So, is he the one she was with?"

"He is," I said. "I need to tell Kevin about it right now."

As I grabbed my phone, Maddy asked, "Are you sure you want to do that? He's bound to have talked to Hank by now."

"Great. That will give him a chance to share some news with us, too." I dialed his number, and after he answered, I said, "The twin without an alibi is Todd."

"How do you know that?"

"I asked the waitress for the man's name she'd been with, and she said that he told her he was Reggie Blackwell."

"Could he have lied to her?" Kevin asked.

"Absolutely, but why would he? The alibi clears just one of them. There really wasn't any reason for either one of them to incriminate their brother."

"I'll buy that. Good work. You can cross the Asheville couple off our list, too," he said proudly.

"Why is that?" I asked.

"I got an outside confirmation that they were on a surveillance tape the entire time that was open to poison Luigi."

"That's good work," I said, maybe pouring it on a little too thick.

"It was just dumb luck," he admitted. "So, then there were three. I'm heading over to the party. You did a good job finding out which twin I'm after."

"Maddy helped, too," I said.

"When I compliment one of you, you should know that it's for you both. You'll just have to share it with her yourself, okay?"

"Don't worry; she already knows," I said, and hung up.

"We need to talk to the errant twin, Jack Acre, and Kenny from Charlotte," I told Maddy as I put my telephone away.

"Do you have any order in particular in mind, because I doubt any of them are all that eager to talk to us again."

"If all else fails, we can get Frank to make Jack cooperate," I said.

"But will he tell us the truth?"

"That I can't say," I admitted. "Todd from Raleigh isn't going to want to chat, so I'm hoping that Kevin will tackle him himself."

"And that leaves Kenny." She scanned the room, and pointed to the man, who was at that moment waiting in line for a drink. "Let's go tackle him."

"Sounds good to me," I said as we cut through the crowd toward our prey.

"Kenny, there you are," I said as we approached.

"Go away," he said defiantly. "You heard Frank earlier. I don't want to take a chance of being disqualified."

"Relax. The contest is over," I said. "The winner has already been chosen, remember?"

"Then I don't want you two to jinx me," he argued. "This thing is in the bag."

"For the winner," Maddy said smugly.

It got Kenny suspicious immediately. "What are you talking about? What have you heard?"

"Not a thing. I'm just going by my gut," Maddy said.

Kenny was clearly relieved that my sister didn't share any hard proof that she was right. "You don't think you two actually have a chance, do you?"

I didn't want Maddy angering him too much. If he stormed off, we'd never get the chance to talk to him. "Our chances are every bit as good as yours," I said, knowing that while he wasn't going to win, our inferior offering was not a grand prize winner, either. "We just wanted to come by and wish you good luck."

"I don't need luck," he said smugly. "I rely on good pizza instead." He looked around the room, and then asked absently, "Have either one of you seen Anna, by any chance?"

"I thought she quit working for you," I said.

Kenny shook his head. "Don't worry about it. She quits every other month. She never means it, though, and I always take her back."

"Things might be different this time," Maddy said.

"Why would they be? You didn't hire her, did you?" he asked me.

"No, of course not."

"What's the matter? Don't you think she's good enough to work at your little pizza joint?" Kenny said, defending his former employee.

"No, I'm sure she's great. We just can't afford her. We barely get by with the two of us and a couple of part-time college students."

"I have eleven people on my staff," he said proudly.

"Technically, that would be ten," Maddy said, and I frowned at her, shaking my head slightly. She picked up on it, and added quickly, "But you could be right. It might be eleven again soon."

"It will. Trust me."

"Kenny, we've been chatting with the other contestants about their alibis," I said. "Just about everyone is covered. Where were you when Luigi was poisoned?"

"How could I possibly know that?" he asked. "Do the police even have a time of death yet?"

"They've got something better. Luigi couldn't have eaten that pizza before everyone else left the auditorium. From then until the time he was found, there was a two-hour gap."

"Yes, I know all about it."

"So, where were you?"

Kenny looked at me angrily, then at Maddy, and then back to me. "Are you kidding me? I was in my room."

"Alone?" I asked.

"Of course I was alone. I watched a movie on the pay-per-view, though. There was a thriller on that I hadn't seen yet. That covers me for the entire two hours."

"Really?" I asked. "Just because the movie was playing on your television doesn't mean that you were there watching it."

"Ask me anything you want about it," he said smugly. "I can lay out the plot of the movie point by point if I have to."

Maddy laughed. "No doubt you'll have all of the answers to our questions too, except one, that is."

"What is it?"

"How can you prove that was actually the first time that you watched it?"

He didn't have an answer for that.

I touched his shirt lightly as I said, "All it will take is one person spotting you not in your room during those two hours, and you're dead. You know that, don't you?"

"I may have gone out into the hallway to the machine to get some ice once," Kenny reluctantly admitted.

"So then you lied about watching the entire movie," Maddy said.

"No, I watched it all. I paused it; that's all," he said.

"I'm sure they can check that as well with their records," I replied. I had no idea if they could even do that, but I wanted to put as much heat on Kenny as I could.

"Let them," he said. "Computers foul up all of the time. I've never trusted them myself." He looked over my shoulder, and then smiled gently. "What did I say? I told you that Anna would come."

When I turned to look, I saw his former assistant walk in, her hand clasped tightly in Frank's.

"They look pretty cozy," Maddy said.

"They've dated a few times in the past, but that's all over," he said.

"I wonder if they know that?" I asked, but Kenny never heard me as he started toward them.

"Come on," Maddy said. "Let's go."

"Where are we headed now? Frank has to be about ready to start."

"That's where I want to be. I want to see Kenny's face when Frank shoots him down."

"Have I ever told you that you have a mean streak sometimes, Maddy?"

"Oh, yes," she said. "Are you coming or not?"

"I'm right behind you." Honestly, it was something I wanted to see for myself.

When we got close to them, I heard Frank tell Kenny, "We'll talk about it after the announcement, but not until then."

"It's a fair question, Frank. You can't just steal my best employee."

"He can't steal something that's willingly given," Anna said.

"I expected more from you," Kenny answered as he looked at her.

"Life's full of disappointments though, isn't it? I'd work on getting over it if I were you, Kenny."

"What is that supposed to mean?"

Frank was tired of the games. "I'm sorry, but I shouldn't delay the announcement any longer. It's time."

The new CEO of Laughing Luigi's Pizza Dough wouldn't meet our gazes, and if there was any doubt in my mind that we'd lost the contest before, I knew at that moment that it was all over for us now.

It appeared that someone else was going to be going home with that big check. I just hoped it wasn't the twins. If it meant losing to the Asheville couple, I could live with it, but not to the duo from Raleigh. I took some satisfaction over the fact that we weren't going to come in last, knowing that the Charlotte team had been disqualified, but I would have loved to come in second, even though there was no prize attached to it.

Chapter 17

As Frank mounted the stage, Bob and David rejoined us. Maddy had promised them earlier that they could.

"Are you nervous?" David asked me softly as he took my hand in his.

"Not at all," I said.

"Really? If it were me, I'd be scared to death," he answered.

"That's because I know that we already lost the competition," I said, feeling a certain sense of calmness sweep over me as I spoke the words aloud.

"Frank already told you that?" he asked, unhappy about the new development.

"He didn't have to, David. We submitted an inferior pie. We don't deserve to win."

He took that in for a few moments, and then asked, "Is there any chance that you're just being too hard on yourself?"

"Unfortunately, no. It's okay, though. We proved that we could hang with these big-time pros. It's all the satisfaction I need."

"But the money would have been nice, right?" he asked with a grin. I loved this new and improved version of David. In the past, he would have tiptoed around me until he could judge the waters, but these days he said what was on his mind without much of any filter at all.

"Oh, yes, I won't deny it," I said as I kissed him lightly on the cheek.

"And you just kissed me why exactly?"

"Are you complaining?" I asked with a grin.

"No, ma'am. I just want to know what I did so I can repeat the experiment later."

I laughed and squeezed his hand as Maddy and Bob approached us. She shot her eyebrows skyward, and I winked back. The silent question she'd just asked me was *May we join you?* and my wink had answered *yes*. I doubted anyone else had even noticed the exchange. No wonder some folks thought we were a little creepy with the way that we could read each other's minds.

"Good luck," Maddy told me.

"Here's hoping for second place," I said, showing her my crossed fingers.

My sister laughed. "To be honest with you, I'd consider that a victory."

Frank tapped the microphone on the stage and said, "We have the results, and at least one check to present this evening."

"What does he mean by that?" Maddy asked me softly.

"Maybe there were two winners," I said.

"A tie? Really? I'll be as mad as a wet cat if we come in third."

"Shh," a woman next to Maddy said.

"Really?" my sister said, staring into the woman's eyes as she snapped, "Are you sure that you want to do that?"

The woman must have seen something in Maddy's fierce gaze, because she suddenly found something more interesting on the other side of the room.

Frank must have caught it, because he smiled for a moment before he continued. "In fourth place, with a valiant effort, is the team from . . ." He dragged it out as long as he could, and then finally said, "Charlotte."

"That's just wrong," Kenny said angrily. "There's no way we lost this competition to these clowns."

Most folks probably didn't hear all of it over the applause, but our group was close enough to catch it in its entirety. I smiled at Kenny as he glared at me and I clapped heartily at the news. Maddy joined me, and our applause was the last to die in the room. We'd known it was coming, but it was still sweet seeing the expression on Kenny's face when he realized that he'd lost.

"In third place, but just barely, is the team from . . ."

These pauses were killing me now, and all of the other contestants, too. Frank seemed to be enjoying himself though, and I was beginning to wonder if the newly found power had gone straight to his head. Finally, he finished, "Raleigh."

The twins stared at each other for a split second, and then, without a word, they stormed out of the room together without a single look back. So much for being gracious losers. The applause for them was still going on as they left.

"That leaves just two teams still in the competition," Frank said. "Would both groups please join me on stage?"

He was killing me, pure and simple.

"Do we really have to go up there?" I asked Maddy.

"Come on; let's take our bow for coming in second and then fade away into the background as he's giving the Asheville team the check."

Maddy and I approached the stage with Jeff and Sandy. If we did manage to squeeze out a victory, it would be sweet indeed, but if we had to lose, I was at least happy that it was going to be to the couple from Asheville.

"Good luck," Sandy said as we mounted the steps together. Though the auditorium had been cleared of all the chairs that had been set out for the audience, the kitchens we'd all used on stage hadn't been touched.

"You, too," I said.

We took our places and stood on either side of Frank, and after the crowd settled down, he announced, "We've made a last-minute change to the rules that we hope everyone will be all right with once they hear what we've done."

There were murmurs from the crowd, but not from the stage. It didn't surprise me at all. Frank was turning out to be that kind of guy.

"The contest was originally conceived by my brother as a winner-take-all scenario, but given the difficulties placed on the contestants during this trying time and the way they've overcome a great many obstacles, we've decided to award a cash prize of one thousand dollars and a year's supply of Laughing Luigi's Pizza Dough to the first runner-up."

Maddy and I may have clapped the loudest at this news.

Frank continued. "Don't worry, folks. First place will still pay out twenty-five-thousand dollars, just to be fair. Without further ado, I'm proud to announce that the winner of this competition—as well as the twenty-five-thousand dollars—is the team from Asheville." As he said it, Frank pulled a large check out of an oversized envelope and handed it to the winning team.

I was so stunned that he hadn't drawn the final announcement out as well that it took me a second for it to register who had actually won. I had figured all along that we wouldn't be winning the whole thing, but having a thousand dollars as a consolation prize was a great deal more than I'd been expecting. I'd even find something to do with all that pizza dough, too. It was hard to tell who was more excited by the announcement—Jeff and Sandy, or Maddy and me. I kept expecting confetti to drop from the ceiling, but after the applause finally died down, Frank said, "That's it. Thanks for coming, and enjoy the party."

As music started to play in the background, the Asheville couple came over and offered their hands to us. "Congratulations. It was a close race all the way to the very end."

I laughed. "That's nice of you to say, but we all know that our pizza in the end just wasn't up to par."

"That's because you were too busy defending me against that horrible man," Sandy said. "I just don't feel right taking this money."

"You could always just endorse it over to us if it will help your conscience," Maddy said with a grin.

"Maddy," I scolded her.

"Hey, I'm just kidding," she said quickly. "We're getting a grand we weren't expecting, so we're all winning as far as I'm concerned.

"Except for the other two teams," Maddy said with a grin.

"That makes it even sweeter, doesn't it?" I asked. "Seriously, congratulations. Do you two know what you're going to do with the money?"

"Oh, yes. We're going to pay off the rest of our mortgage so we can own our pizza shop outright," Jeff said.

"And we're taking a second honeymoon with some of it, too," Sandy added, "mostly because we never got a first one."

"That all sounds perfect," I said as Frank approached the group. He shook Sandy and Jeff's hands again, and then congratulated them once more.

"If you two don't mind, Tina Lance wants a chance to interview you for her paper, and after that, I've set things up with newspapers from Charlotte, Raleigh, and of course, Asheville. What do you say?"

"We'd be happy to do it, of course," Jeff said.

After it was just the three of us left on the stage, Frank said, "I'm truly sorry that your team didn't win."

"Are you kidding? You picked the best pizza,

which is all anyone could ask of you. Thanks for the consolation prize."

"I felt that it was the least that Luigi's could do for you, after all that you've done for us," he said.

"Are you going to keep your brother's nickname even though your founder is gone?" I asked.

"We've been discussing it," Frank said, "but we haven't made a decision yet."

"Who's this 'we' you keep talking about?" Maddy asked with a grin.

"Anna, of course," he replied. "After all, once we're married, she's going to help me run the business."

"I'm sure you'll do both fine," I said.

"With her by my side, how can I fail?"

Anna came on stage, and as she joined us, I said, "Congratulations."

"What did I do? You're the ones who came in second."

"We hear you're going to be a full partner," Maddy replied.

"Oh, we're still discussing that. With a little one on the way, I'm not sure I'll have the time."

"You'll have to find some way to come up with it then," Frank said. "You know that I want you as my equal partner once we're married. If you'd like, we can even set up a crib in one corner of our office."

Anna patted his hand. "Like I said, we're still discussing it." She turned to her fiancé and asked, "Did you give them the check yet?"

"To be honest with you, it completely slipped my mind," Frank said as he reached into his suit jacket and pulled out an envelope. "Sorry it's not gigantic like the other one."

I grinned at him as I took it. "I'm sure that it will cash just fine. Thanks again."

"It was the least we could do," Frank said.

"Not necessarily," Maddy said.

Frank looked quizzically at her, but Anna put her hand on his arm. "It doesn't matter. Frank, there's someone I want you to meet. I invited the CEO of Sammy's Sauces here to have a little chat with you about our companies working together."

"Okay," he said, happy to follow his pregnant fiancée anywhere.

"She's going to be running the business in no time," Maddy said. "I've seen a powerful woman operate like that before."

"Do you mean like in the mirror?" I asked. I looked at the check and asked, "What should we do with this windfall?"

"Let's put it in the bank," Maddy said, something that was completely out of character for her.

"Are you serious?"

"Well, at least until we can decide how we're going to blow it," she expanded with a broad grin.

"That's the sister I know and love," I said as I folded the check and put it in my back pocket. "It's too soon to celebrate our second-place victory, though."

Maddy's smile quickly vanished. "I know. We still have a killer to catch."

"And not much time to do it in," I reminded her.

"Then I suggest we get busy," Maddy answered, and I couldn't have agreed with her more. I searched the auditorium for any of our three suspects, but apparently they'd all already ducked out.

"They aren't going to go out of their way to make this easy on us, are they?" I asked.

"Have they ever in the past?"

"No, that's a good point. So, who do we track down first?"

"Let's start nosing around and see who we come across," Maddy said.

"It sounds like as good a plan as any," I answered, and my sister and I went off searching for our remaining suspects as the evening crept on. The clock was on us now more than ever, and if we were going to do anything, it had to be before noon tomorrow when everyone checked out of the hotel. I just hoped that none of our suspects left early, but then again, they most likely couldn't take the chance of looking guilty by fleeing before it was time to go.

Hopefully that meant that Maddy and I would have a little more time to detect, but it was hours now instead of days.

We found Gina working at the front desk with a worried expression on her face. "What's wrong?" I asked. "Paul didn't turn you down, did he?"

"What? No, as a matter of fact we're having a late lunch on Friday."

"Then why do you look so gloomy?" Maddy asked. "After all, that's great news, isn't it?"

"I just hope I still have a job by then," she said. "I just got off the phone with my uncle, and he told me that if Luigi's murder isn't solved by this time tomorrow, he's going to pull the plug on this entire operation." She looked around the lobby as she added,

"These people have become a second family to me. I don't know how I'm going to tell them that's it's probably going to be all over by this time tomorrow."

"Do us a favor and don't say a word to anyone until you absolutely have to," I said.

Her eyes brightened for a moment. "Does that mean you've discovered who the killer is?"

I lowered my voice as I explained, "No, but the good news is that we've gone from eight suspects to three. That's some serious progress in this kind of situation."

"I appreciate everything that you two have been doing, but it's still not going to be enough. Is Chief Hurley any closer to finding the murderer than you are?"

I hated to have to say it, but I didn't really have any choice. After all, she deserved to know the truth. "I'm sorry. We've been comparing notes all along, and we're stuck on the same three people."

Gina frowned, and then asked quietly, "Is there any chance you could tell me who your suspects are? I might be able to help if I knew who you were considering."

"I can appreciate that, but Maddy and I hate dragging someone's name through the mud if we're wrong," I explained.

"Eleanor, I'm not going to tell anybody. Whatever you tell me is safe with me. Hank found you earlier, didn't he?"

"Yes, why? Did he tell you about the tape?" Maddy asked.

She laughed wryly. "Actually, I was the one who suggested that he study them. He was in his office all day checking every surveillance video we have during the time of the murder on my orders."

It was interesting how the security chief had failed to mention that particular detail.

It was time to make an executive decision. "Okay, we'll share with you what we know, but it would mean a lot to us if you'd keep this to yourself."

"I won't breathe a word of it," she promised.

I looked at Maddy, and she nodded. We were in agreement. It was time to share. "Our last three suspects are Kenny Henderson from the Charlotte team, Jack Acre, and Todd Blackwell from Raleigh."

"Todd? Why is his name on your list? I know for a fact that he couldn't have done it," Gina said.

"Why do you say that? We know that one of the twins was spending the time trying to pick up one of your waitresses in the restaurant, but Reggie said that he was the one, and your waitress confirmed it. He's the only one we have on tape."

"Todd might not have been where a camera could see him, but I know that he was doing something else the entire time when Luigi might have been murdered."

"How could you know that?" Maddy asked. "You weren't with him personally, were you?"

Gina frowned, and then got the implication of my sister's question. "No, no, and ewww. I have better taste than that."

"Then how could you possibly know that he didn't kill Luigi?" I asked.

"He was right over there in our business center," she said as she pointed to the door just off the front desk. "I'm surprised no one told you."

"And he never left that room the entire time?" I asked.

"No, and I can prove it, too."

"How can you be so certain?" Maddy asked her.

"Let me show you," she said as we all walked together to the business center space. "You need my key to get in. We've had some trouble lately, so our sign-in policy is pretty strict. I don't mind someone using our facilities, but one of our guests used the computer for some pretty depraved things, so I have to keep a close eye on it. No one gets in, or out, without signing my sheet. Todd walked in there right after you all left the auditorium, and he didn't sign out until three minutes before you started back up again. He asked me to have something to eat sent in to him, so I contacted the restaurant myself. I was around this desk and in my office across the way from the business center the entire time, and he never left it. I'd swear to it under oath."

"Thanks," I said. "You've really been a help."

"I just wish I could tell you something about the other two, but I'm drawing blanks on both of them," she replied.

"Don't sell yourself short. You've done plenty."

I started to call Kevin Hurley's number when I saw him walk into the hotel complex.

"I was just getting ready to call you," I said as I put my phone away and spoke his name.

"What's up?" he asked as he joined us.

"We've got an alibi for Todd from Raleigh," I said.

"How'd you manage to do that?"

"Gina just told us," I said.

Kevin looked over at the front desk, and then turned back to us. "Stay right here, both of you."

After two minutes, he said, "Come with us," to Maddy and me, and we all followed the police chief back to the business center. Gina swiped her card and unlocked the door for us, and then she sat down at one of the computers there. After tapping several keys, she brought up a log. "See? It's right here. He was signed into the system the entire time."

"But that doesn't prove that he was here. He could have left, and then come back after he poisoned Luigi's pizza. Were you here every second?"

Gina frowned, and then after she considered the question, she admitted, "No, come to think of it, I was gone for about four minutes."

"It's not much time," Kevin said, "but he could have had enough time to poison the pizza and give it to Luigi without being caught."

Gina shook her head.

"What's wrong with my theory?" the police chief asked.

"Do me a favor. Leave the room for one second."

"You aren't keeping secrets from me, are you?" Kevin asked. "If you tell Eleanor and Maddy something, you need to tell me, too."

"Just do it, okay?"

The chief of police wasn't happy about it, but Kevin reluctantly did as she asked.

Once the door clicked behind him, she said, "Watch this."

She gestured for Kevin to rejoin us, but of course, he couldn't get through the door. Gina got up and unlocked it for him, and then she said, "It locks automatically every time anyone comes in or out."

"What if he rigged it somehow?" Kevin asked. "He could have always blocked the door with something so it wouldn't close all the way, and you'd never know it."

"Let me show you something." She turned back to the computer, tapped several more keys, and then she said, "Here's the log for every time the door opened and closed during the period in question when Luigi could have been poisoned. If you study it closely, you'll see that the door was never unlocked for more than the standard six seconds."

"And there's no way around this system?"

"None," she said.

"Okay then, I'll buy it. Thanks for letting us know about it."

"Good luck catching the killer," she said as we all walked out of the business center. "The way I see it, you've got a fifty-fifty chance now."

"Thanks," all three of us said simultaneously.

It was all I could do to stifle my laugh, but when I remembered that my pizza had been used as a murder weapon, the mirth died quickly enough.

"So, now we're down to two," Kevin said as we moved away from Gina.

"Yes, but which one is a killer?"

"I'm going to press both of them," he said with conviction. "Now that our list is manageable, it won't be long before we figure out which one is the murderer. Ladies, you've been a great help to me and the department in this investigation, and I won't forget it, but my staff and I can take it from here."

"You're firing us?" I asked incredulously.

"Don't think of it that way. Just realize that your part in this is over. I'm glad you won second place."

"Does that mean that you didn't want us to win the whole thing?" Maddy asked.

"What? Of course I did. I'm just saying that there's no reason to hang your head coming in second."

"We couldn't agree with you more," I said, "but we're not ready to give up just yet." I turned to Maddy and asked, "Isn't that right?"

"It is," she agreed.

Kevin clearly wasn't all that pleased with our answer, and who could blame him really? Maddy and I were probably the only people he'd ever come across that would have the nerve to refuse to be fired by him. He said calmly, "I can appreciate how you feel, believe me, but like I said, there's nothing left for you to do. I'll interview our suspects again, and unless I miss my guess, one of them will crack by morning."

"If you can even find them," I said.

"What do you mean by that?"

"What makes you think that Kenny and Jack Acre are even still here at the complex?"

"Why wouldn't they be?" Kevin asked. "Running away now would just make them look guilty."

"Which we all believe one of them actually is," Maddy reminded him.

"Don't worry about that. There's no place they can hide that we won't find them. Good night."

"I still think you're making a mistake trying to fire us," I said to him. "We aren't finished with this yet."

"I disagree. Do you understand what I'm telling you?"

"We understand," Maddy said.

He studied her a moment, and then the police chief asked, "But you aren't going to change your behavior, are you?"

She just shrugged.

Kevin said to me, "She's your sister. Can't you do anything with her?"

"Honestly, I wouldn't if I could, since I happen to believe that she's right."

Kevin wanted to say something in response, I could see it in his eyes, but he finally decided not to and just gave up. As he walked away from us, he was on his radio, no doubt putting out an all-points bulletin for Kenny and Jack.

"Where does this leave us?" Maddy asked me as Kevin left.

"Do you honestly think we'll have any more luck finding the two of them than Kevin will? He's got a staff of trained investigators and more resources than we can even imagine. On the other hand, we're just a couple of pizza makers who snoop on the side."

"So, we're just giving up?" Maddy asked.

"I didn't say that. I'm just not sure where we should go from here. You don't happen to have any bright ideas, do you?"

"I wish I did, but I don't have a clue what we can do, either."

"Then let's go back upstairs, change into more comfortable clothing, and then we can keep hunting for our suspects. Who knows? We might actually find one of them first ourselves. Kevin may know criminals, but we know pizza makers, and more important, how they think."

"Do you honestly believe that's going to be an asset in any way?" Maddy asked.

"I don't know, but at the moment, it's the best I can do."

"Then let's go change and keep hunting," she said.

Chapter 18

If felt good getting back into my jeans again. I had never really been a big fan of getting dressed up, which was one of the great reasons to own my very own pizzeria. I could wear whatever I wanted, and no one could tell me otherwise.

After Maddy changed as well, she plopped down on a chair in our sitting room. "Eleanor, until we get a solid idea about what we should do next, I vote we sit right here and see if we can figure out who killed Luigi without running around this complex like a couple of crazy ladies."

I took the couch as I asked, "It's not just because you're tired of standing on your feet all day, is it?"

"No, it can't be that. We do more time than this on a typical day at the Slice," she said.

"Yes, but there's no pressure there. We're in our comfort zone in our own place."

"That's true. This competition was kind of grueling, wasn't it?"

"Hey, we got a grand out of it, and a year's supply of dough. By the way, they're going to deliver the first installment tomorrow at eleven-thirty. I should probably call Greg or Josh and have them meet the delivery man at the Slice."

"Does that mean that we're not going to open tomorrow?" Maddy asked, clearly disappointed by the news.

"I haven't really thought about it. Why, would you like to?"

She just shrugged. "If we'd won the grand prize, I was going to suggest that we take a week off. As it is though, I'm not sure we can afford to lose any more customers than we might have already. We don't want any of them to get used to eating somewhere else, do we?"

"No, I see what you mean," I said. "Okay, we'll check out a little early, and then go straight to the Slice to get ready to open at noon."

"That doesn't give us much time to make fresh dough," Maddy said.

"We could always just use some of the free supply that Luigi's is supplying us with tomorrow. It's really not half-bad once you get used to working with it."

"Actually, I was thinking that we should donate that part of our winnings to a food bank," Maddy said. "I don't know about you, but personally, I don't want to look at another one of Luigi's crusts as long as I live."

"I totally get that. I agree; I'll take fresh, or what

we've frozen or refrigerated, anytime. It shouldn't be a problem, since I've got a good supply built up. If we have to, just in case we can't do it otherwise, we'll use that dough until I can make more." I stretched, and then said, "But that's tomorrow. What are we going to do tonight?"

"We're going to find the killer," Maddy said confidently.

"And how do you propose we do that?"

She thought about it, and then Maddy said, "We're going to do what you suggested before. Kenny's a pizza maker, and Jack Acre has devoted the last five years of his life to it, too. There's got to be a clue hiding somewhere that Kevin can't see."

"The kitchens were still in place on stage at the party. Did you happen to notice that all they moved were the chairs in the audience? Do you suppose there's a clue anywhere there that we might have missed?"

"It's worth looking into," Maddy said as she stood. "Let's go see if Kenny's kitchen is hiding any secrets."

"I'm right behind you," I said.

The auditorium was eerily empty as we walked in. The party remnants had been cleaned up, but the kitchens were still all in place on the stage. I started to hit the main lights when Maddy touched my arm. "Do we really want the entire place lit up? It might not be a bad idea to hide our presence here while we're digging around."

"Okay, I see what you're saying," I said. "I'll just turn on the lights backstage, so it will give us some light to look around without announcing what we're doing to anybody who happens to walk past the auditorium doors."

I carefully walked up the steps to the stage and found the light switches in back. After flipping a few on and off, I finally found the ones that gave us a chance to see without letting everyone know our business.

"What exactly are we looking for?" Maddy asked in a hushed voice.

"Anything that's out of place," I answered.

"Should we search together or split up?"

"We only have one suspect left who was in the competition. Let's check Kenny's work space together."

We looked everywhere in his assigned area of the stage, but if there was a clue hiding anywhere there, we didn't find it.

"Well, that was a complete wash," Maddy said as she idly played with one of the knives on the table where we'd done our own prep work.

"I'm not ready to give up. We're not done searching yet," I said.

"Where should we look next—at our own setup?" she asked, clearly joking.

"Sure, why not? Someone could have stashed something incriminating there to make us look bad, especially since we've been nosing around so much. That's not a bad idea at all."

"I think you're being a tad too paranoid," Maddy said.

"You're probably right, but what's it going to hurt to look?" I asked as I glanced inside our refrigerator. Maddy had been right; there was nothing there.

Hang on a second. Or was there? I pulled out some of the supplies we'd gotten from the restaurant's kitchen at that last second but hadn't actually needed, and there in the back was a prescription bottle.

"What's this?" I asked when I spotted it.

"I don't know; I can't see anything," Maddy answered as she approached our station.

"Hand me one of those paper towels."

She did as I asked, putting the knife down in front of her as she grabbed a few sheets from the roll. I took one, and then I reached in and used it to pull the bottle out of the fridge. "Maddy, you didn't put this in here, did you?"

"Not a chance," she said. "What's the scrip for?"

I took it over to one of the lights and read the label. The bottle was still nearly full, and I wondered what condition Luigi had been taking it for. I read the name of the medication aloud, or at least as close as I could come to pronouncing it, and then I finished with saying, "It says it's for the temporary relief of allergy and allergy-like symptoms," I said.

"You didn't say whose name was on the label, Eleanor. Who does it belong to? Don't tell me. It's Luigi's prescription, right?"

"Well, technically it's made out for George Vincent, but yeah, it belonged to Luigi." Something was odd about that, though. I thought back to the conversation we'd had with Luigi on the stage. "Hang on a second, Maddy," I said. "Do you remember when Sandy sneezed on stage and said it was because of allergies?"

"Yeah. Luigi made it a big point of saying that he'd never had them himself. Why would he lie to us about something as trivial as all that?"

"What if he was using this medication for something else?" I asked. I looked at the label again and asked, "Do you have your Smartphone on you?"

"You know that I never go anywhere without it," Maddy said as she dug it out of her purse.

"Check out this name online, and tell me what else it could have been used for."

She got online on her phone, and after she typed in the word exactly as I spelled it, she read the screen. "No, sorry; it's just for allergies."

"Are there any secondary uses for the medication?" I asked.

Maddy scrolled farther down the screen, and then looked at me in amazement. "What are you, psychic now?"

"Why? What does it say?"

Maddy read from the screen. "This drug can also be used for the temporary relief of a poor sense of smell or taste."

Everything clicked then. "I knew it. Everything fits."

"What are you talking about?"

"Luigi turned down a piece of pizza when he came to the Slice to tell us about the contest, remember? He accepted, but after he checked his pockets, he changed his mind."

"Sure. Why bother eating something if you can't taste it? That must mean that someone took his pills so he couldn't taste the cleaner on the pizza when they tainted it. It was absolutely premeditated."

"Not only that, but it could explain why he scored our pizza so well right before he died. Luigi couldn't taste anybody's entry."

"Now we know how they got him to eat a pizza

that was doused in cleaner. The real question is who would know about his condition?"

Maddy answered, "Well, there's his brother, obviously, but we've already eliminated him as a suspect."

"Who else could know about his condition? How well did he and Kenny really know each other? I'm guessing that it was not as well as someone who worked for him for years. Hey, Luigi sent Jack Acre to get his pills at the cocktail party, remember? He had access to them from the start. Are these even real?"

"I'm guessing that they're just placebos. Jack must have swapped them out when he went to fetch them at the party. The only way Luigi would have eaten that pizza was if he couldn't taste the poison on it, and the only person who had the means and the opportunity was Jack Acre."

"We have to call Kevin Hurley right now," I said.

"I'm afraid there won't be any need to do that," the murderer said as he stepped into sight from the shadows of the auditorium. I could clearly see the gun in Acre's hand, reflected in the soft light from the stage.

"I can't *believe* the police never found those," Jack said as he smiled sadly at the meds. "How hard did they even search this place?"

"You tried to frame us, didn't you?" I asked, staring at the gun in his hand as he walked up the steps to join us. How were Maddy and I going to get out of this one?

"Of course I did. Why else would I use your pizza to poison Luigi? I figured I had several ways to escape detection, but you were absolutely high on my list of people to blame if any of my other plans fell through."

It was obvious that Acre wanted to boast, and I knew that the longer he talked, the better chance we had of someone coming into the auditorium and finding us.

I glanced down and saw the knife Maddy had been fiddling with on the corner of the table; I just hoped that Acre hadn't spotted it yet.

"Go on," I said, trying my best to distract him. "Brag a little. Who are we going to tell? You've got a captive audience."

Acre nodded and smiled. "I do, don't I? Why not? I figured that if I killed Luigi in Timber Ridge at this competition, there would be plenty of suspects around to dilute the attention of the police, and that was assuming that the local yokel cop was even smart enough to figure out that Luigi had been poisoned instead of choked to death accidentally."

"The chief's way smarter than that," Maddy said in Kevin's defense. In a way, it was a shame that he wasn't around to hear it.

"So it turned out. If the police wouldn't believe that it was an accidental choking, then I wanted them looking at you. I used your pizza to deliver the poison, and then I hid the prescription in your fridge. What else did I have to do, send the cops an admission of guilt from the two of you?"

"These are just placebos, aren't they?" I asked as I held the bottle up. "You switched them with the real meds when Luigi made you fetch them from his room."

"I see you were smart enough not to leave any of your prints on it. Well, that doesn't matter. You're going to both die trying to escape, and I'll sadly inform everyone that you'd threatened me before."

"How is anyone who knows us ever going to believe that?" Maddy asked. As Acre's glance moved to her, I searched for anything I could use as a weapon that was within my reach. The knife was too far away to grab without giving myself away. I had an idea, and I realized the second I thought of it that it would be foolishly risky, but at least it was something that might work. I screwed off the childproof top and pretended to smell the pills inside. "How did you think you could fool him with these fakes?"

"That was the easiest part. The pills didn't always work right away, or every time he took them," Jack said smugly.

As I started to put the pill bottle down on the table, Maddy asked him, "But why did you want to kill him in the first place?"

"I didn't know that the fool had changed our agreement behind my back," Acre said with disgust.

"*You* were the one we heard arguing with Luigi in the hallway the night before the contest, weren't you?"

"I figured you must have heard something, but I guessed that you wouldn't even think to suspect me after I feigned sleep when you pounded on my door."

"What were you fighting about? Control?" I asked.

"The man was insane. He warned me that he was going to change everything at Luigi's, but he wouldn't tell me anything specific about what he was going to do. I pushed him for more information, and I even tried to use something I had on him as leverage, but he shocked me and wouldn't back down. I couldn't believe it when he actually *threatened* me. If I'd known the truth at that point, I probably would have killed him on the spot. Can you believe he's letting that moron brother of his run things? The guy gets a million bucks *and* control of the business. It was all meant to be mine, and now that idiot is going to ruin *my* company."

"Frank is smarter than you give him credit for," I said. "He might just fool you."

"Oh, please, don't bother trying to defend the man with your dying breath."

"You still haven't explained how you think you're going to get away with this," I said. I inched forward, as though anticipating his answer, but actually, I was just trying to get closer to the knife on the table.

"Actually, it's pretty neat. I have more than one gun with me, and one of you is about to be unmasked as Luigi's true killer while the other gets shot trying to avenge her sister's death. The only question is which one of you wants to go first."

"Neither one of them," a voice from the back said. I looked to see Hank White standing there in the shadows, but to my dismay, he didn't have a gun with him. All he had was the heavy-duty flashlight we'd borrowed earlier.

"What are you going to do, blind me with that?" Jack asked, laughing as he gestured toward the light with his handgun.

Hank flipped on the light at that moment and sent a powerful and concentrated beam into Jack Acre's eyes. Acre tried to shield his gaze from it with one hand as he fired a shot in Hank's general direction.

I knew that it had hit its mark when I saw the impact of the bullet, and watched Hank's shoulder jerk as he fell.

Without hesitation I grabbed the knife on the table and lunged at the former vice president of marketing and sales for Luigi's. I'd been aiming for his chest, but it struck his arm instead. I realized that it might still work though, as the gun clattered to the stage.

At that moment, Maddy jammed her personal taser into Acre's chest and he went down in a heap. I'd made fun of her for carrying it before, but I was glad she had it with her now.

"Grab the gun while this thing is recharging," Maddy said fiercely.

I did as she asked and grabbed the handgun, holding the barrel less than a foot from his chest.

When Acre recovered enough from the shock, he said, "You don't have the stones to use that."

I cocked the trigger as I moved my aim from his heart to right between his eyes. "Would you care to bet on it?"

"Drop the gun," I heard Kevin Hurley say as the lights came up.

"He just tried to kill us!" I shouted.

"I've got him covered, Eleanor. Drop it!"

I did as he said, making sure that Acre couldn't get it again without going through me.

"Hank White's been hurt," Maddy added.

"I'm fine. It's just a scratch," Hank said as he tried, and failed, to stand up.

"Call for an ambulance, Chief, and then you can take this murderer into custody," I said.

"I knew it all along," Kevin said with a slight grin as he hurried onstage to join us.

"So did we," Maddy replied, lying equally as well as our police chief just had.

Chapter 19

"What made you check the auditorium? Did someone hear the shot?" I asked as one of Kevin's men took Jack Acre away and the EMTs put Hank on a gurney and took him to the hospital.

"I could tell you that it was all just a part of my master plan," Kevin said, "but then we'd both know that I was lying. I was in the lobby when I heard the muffled shot, and I came running. Nobody nearby realized what it was, but I've heard enough shots to tell when it's a car backfiring and when it's the real deal. How did he think he was going to get away with it?"

"He was going to say that I killed Luigi, and when I found out that he knew about it, I tried to kill him. He set us up to look like killers, and he might have gotten away with it."

"What about Maddy?" he asked.

"I was going to die defending my sister, even if she was a homicidal killer," she said dramatically.

"Anybody who knows you would never believe that pack of lies," Kevin said.

"Hopefully, but there would be some room for doubt given the way he tried to set us up. What are the odds that twelve people would recognize that he was lying?" I asked.

"You keep talking about being set up," Kevin said. "How did he try do that?"

"First off he used our pizza to kill Luigi, and then he hid the man's meds in our fridge, which were actually placebos. The more I think about it, I'm beginning to realize that he might not be so crazy after all. He actually might have gotten away with murder."

"Well, I never would have believed it," Kevin said.

"You might not have had any choice," Maddy replied.

"Believe me when I tell you both that I would have found a way to prove you were innocent and avenged your murders," he answered.

"Let's just all be happy that it didn't come to that," I said. My name, as well as my sister's and my pizzeria, have all been dragged through enough mud over the years.

"So what happens now?" Maddy asked.

"Acre's going to jail, Hank's on his way to the hospital, and I'm guessing you two are on your way home."

Maddy and I looked at him in tandem and smiled. "Why on earth do you think we'd give up one last night of luxury here, especially since no one's trying to frame us for murder anymore?"

"Are you telling me that you lunatics are actually going to stay in the place where you were almost murdered?"

I shook my head. "Why not? It's all already paid for, remember?"

"You're both a little odd. You know that, don't you?" Kevin asked.

"We wouldn't have it any other way," Maddy replied.

"As much as I'd love to stay here and chat with you, I have a prisoner back in my jail that I need to interrogate."

"If you decide to go old school on him with pipes and brass knuckles, give me a call," Maddy said.

Kevin just shook his head and chuckled softly as he left.

Gina had been waiting off to one side in the back of the auditorium, and as soon as the chief of police left, she came rushing to us. "I can't believe how close you two came to getting killed tonight."

"Oh, we've been closer before," I said.

"Much," Maddy agreed.

"Don't you two take anything seriously?" Gina asked with a nervous laugh.

"Oh, we were plenty serious when that gun was pointing at us. We're just glad that Hank was there to distract Jack long enough for us to act," I said. "They told us that he was going to be okay before they took him to the hospital."

"He should get hazard pay for what he did tonight," Maddy said.

"Oh, he will," Gina said. "I can't thank you two enough for all that you've done for me over the past few days."

"We were happy to help," Maddy said.

Gina was about to say something else when the back doors opened again, and David and Bob came rushing through.

"We can't leave you two alone for a minute, can we?" David asked with a grin as he wrapped me in his arms.

"What can I say? Even when we aren't looking for trouble, it still manages to find the two of us."

Bob hugged my sister as well, and then took a step back and looked at her. "Are you okay?"

"I'm fine, but I think my taser broke when I jammed it into Jack Acre."

Bob finally let out the breath he'd obviously been holding. "Don't worry about that; we'll get you a new one."

"Can I have a BoltBlaster 2000? They look really sweet," she asked with a huge grin.

"After what just happened, you can have whatever you want. Just name it, and it's yours," Bob said.

"Be careful what you're promising," Maddy said. She looked at all of us and said, "I don't know about the three of you, but almost getting killed tonight has made me a little peckish." She turned to Gina and asked, "What do you think? Could you get your chef to rustle us up something special?"

"You name it, and it's yours," she answered.

"You know, I could get used to this kind of lifestyle," Maddy said.

"If it weren't for the attempted murders and all, I'd have to agree with you," I said as we walked out of the auditorium.

"Gosh, Sis, you want it all, don't you?"

I took David's hand with one of mine, and grabbed Maddy's with the other, squeezing them both. "As a matter of fact, I've already got everything I need. What do you feel like eating, David?"

"A pizza might be nice," he suggested with a wicked grin.

"If you don't mind, I'm not in any hurry to make any more of those," I admitted.

"Hey, I was just kidding."

I thought about it, and then said, "Calzones might be nice, though. I've been meaning to try making them for our menu at the Slice. What do you say? Are you men willing to be my guinea pigs tomorrow?"

Bob and David looked at each other solemnly, and then my boyfriend turned to me and said, "For you, we're willing to risk it."

"I knew there was a reason I liked you both," I said as I put one arm in each of theirs and we made our way to the restaurant. As we walked through the lobby, I realized that they'd probably thought I was kidding, but I was going to make them live up to their promise and taste my first attempt tomorrow.

I glanced over at my sister and smiled, and she returned it in kind.

It meant a great deal to have the men with us, and Gina as well, but I knew that even though I rarely said it, Maddy was my rock, and I was thrilled that she was such an important part of my life.

Who knew? With that thousand bucks, she might just get a raise out of this ordeal.

Then again, I knew that she'd enjoy it a great deal more if we really did decide to blow it and not use it on the restaurant.

Then and there, I promised myself that was exactly what we were going to do, too. After all, we could always find a way to make more money, but we didn't often have an excuse to celebrate our lives.

And after what we'd just gone through, what other excuse did we really need?

MY EASY, QUICK, AND DELICIOUS CALZONE RECIPE

(Square Pegs)

This is quite a simple recipe I use at home myself. It's especially good if you don't have a lot of time and you need to put a meal or snack together in a hurry. These calzones can be prepared as the oven preheats; they are fast to create and are absolutely delicious. You can create your own homemade sauce if you'd like, but the Ragu pizza sauce listed in the ingredients section is an excellent substitute, and has the bonus of being no trouble at all. The only dough I still make by hand with any regularity is the first dough recipe from *A Slice of Murder* (what a shameless way to make you run out and get that book, right?). Lately I've been experimenting with some of the refrigerated pizza dough you can buy at the grocery store, and I've found that Pillsbury's Thin Crust and their Classic Crust are both wonderful for homemade pizzas. I'm not getting anything for saying that, but the crusts are as good as—or in some cases even better than—some of my homemade dough, so they are absolutely worth a try, especially if time is a factor for you. For this book I did a taste test and made calzones for side-by-side comparisons in three different styles of dough, and I was astonished by just how good the premade refrigerated doughs were when judged against my own recipes.

Ingredients

1 package Pillsbury Thin Crust or Classic Crust refrigerated pizza dough (13.8 oz. or 11 oz.)

1 bottle Ragu PizzaQuick Traditional SnackSauce (14 oz.)

4 Tablespoons Parmesan cheese (We like to grate it fresh, but it's your choice)

4–8 pepperoni slices, depending on taste

Any additional toppings, such as mushrooms, peppers, onions, etc., used in moderation (Maximum 1 tablespoon equivalent of each per calzone)

grated Italian cheese mix to taste, prepackaged. We use Sargento Artisan Mozzarella and Provolone Blend

cornmeal (so the dough doesn't stick)

PAM nonstick cooking spray

Directions

Preheat the oven to 400° F, and don't forget to put your pizza stone in so it heats gradually. As the oven warms, carefully unfold the prepackaged refrigerated crust of your choice and spread it open on a greased cookie sheet. The sheets will be approximately 8 inches by 12 inches. Cut the sheets horizontally to get three smaller sheets, each 8 inches by 4 inches. We make this size calzone, but you can also cut each sheet again to produce six 4 inch by 4 inch starters. Make no effort to round them at all. We like the homemade square calzones, which is why we call them square pegs.

For the larger size calzone, place the 4 inch by 8 inch sheet on a plate dusted with cornmeal. Spread 2 tablespoons of grated Parmesan cheese in the center of the rectangle, leaving an inch of free dough all the way around so the edges will seal later. On top of the grated cheese add 2 tablespoons of pizza sauce, followed by the pepperoni slices and any other toppings you like. Then add 2 tablespoons of the Mozzarella and Provolone mix. Fold the dough in half, making a square roughly 4 inches on each side. Take a fork and press the edges of the dough together using the tines. When you are finished, three sides of the calzone will look like picket fences lined up, while one side will be smooth. Once the oven has reached 400° F, place the calzones in the center of your oven on the pizza stone. Bake them 11 to 14 minutes, or until the center crusts are just past tan and more brown than gold. Don't worry if the edges aren't the same color (they won't be), so go by the center of the calzone to tell. Remove the calzones and serve them hot. You can dip these in a little extra sauce on the side if you'd like or add a little olive oil and grated Parmesan, or serve them basically any way you like them. Don't be afraid to play with the recipe until you find exactly what you want!

The only thing Eleanor Swift loves more then A Slice of Delight—her Timber Ridge, North Carolina pizzeria—is her sister Maddy. So when Maddy's cheating ex-husband Grant shows up with some pie-in-the-sky idea to win Maddy back, Eleanor is happy to see her sister swiftly show him the door. But they both know Grant isn't done yet . . .

Especially when he picks a fight with Maddy's fiancé Bob in front of the whole town at the annual Founder's Day Festival. Naturally, when Grant is later found stabbed in the heart with a barbeque skewer, Bob is featured on the police chief's menu as Suspect #1. And when it turns out that Maddy stands to gain a different kind of dough—and lots of it—from Grant exiting this world, she and Eleanor know it's up to them to cook up an investigation to find the real killer.

Was it that female singer at the festival who wanted a word with the recently deceased? Or maybe Grant's haughty sister, who's colder then a day-old pizza? Or Grant's "business partner," who seemingly had the opportunity, means, and motive to mortally skewer Maddy's ex-husband? Only one thing is for sure: Eleanor and Maddy need to turn up the heat and deliver this killer . . . or their next scrumptious pizza may be their last!

Please turn the page for an exciting sneak peek of Chris Cavender's
THE MISSING DOUGH
coming next month from Kensington Publishing!

Chapter 1

"**M**addy, I'm not leaving here until you promise to give me another chance!"

I heard the man shouting all the way from the kitchen of my pizza parlor, A Slice of Delight. It was just ten minutes since we'd opened our doors for the day. I'd been hoping for a quiet shift, but it was clear that I'd have no such luck today. What was going on with my sister now, and who was yelling at her? Whatever was happening, it sounded as though she could use some help. Maddy usually handled the front dining room with no trouble, along with our two part-timers, Greg and Josh, but she was up there alone at the moment, and I needed to see if I could back her up, no matter what the circumstances.

As I hurried up front, I grabbed our security system on the way, an aluminum baseball bat we'd played with as kids. Thankfully, the dining room was empty except for Maddy and a man I thought I'd seen the last of years before.

"Grant, what are you doing here?" I asked as I pointed the business end of the bat toward him like a spear.

"Hello, Eleanor," he said with that greasy way he had about him, lowering his voice and doing his best to smile at me. There was no love lost between the two of us, and I didn't even try to fake a smile in return.

Years ago, Maddy had married Grant Whitmore on the rebound from a bad breakup, though I'd done my best to talk her out of it at the time. The man was almost a cliché: tall, dark, and handsome, a troubled loner that some women found irresistible. I wasn't talking about me, but clearly, some women reveled in his attention. Maddy had fallen for him, and hard, until fourteen months into their marriage she'd caught him cheating with their next-door neighbor. It wasn't all that surprising to me that Maddy had missed his mother more than she had her straying husband. She and her mother-in-law had formed a strong bond that had surpassed the marriage, and the two women had kept in touch long after the dissolution of Maddy's marriage to the woman's son.

"You didn't answer my question, Grant," I said as calmly as I could manage. "Why are you here?"

Maddy looked over at me and frowned. "I can handle this, Sis."

"There's no doubt in my mind that you can, but why should you have all of the fun? If it were possible, I might even like him less than you do." I was normally a pretty levelheaded woman, but this guy was on my Trouble list, a place that no one in their right mind would ever want to be on.

Grant tried to wield his questionable charm on me. "Your sister is right, Eleanor. We don't need your input. We're doing just fine without you."

That was the wrong thing to say to Maddy, and I knew it as I tried to suppress a smile. Grant realized it as well from the instant the statement left his lips, but it was too late for him to take it back.

Maddy answered, "Grant, I don't need your support, your permission, or your acknowledgment of anything I say, think, or do. I threw you out for a reason, and if you think there's a whisper of a chance you are getting back into my life, you are sadly mistaken. I'm happy, I'm engaged, and I'm well rid of you." She looked at me, then glanced at the baseball bat still in my hands. "Could I borrow that?"

"By all means," I said as I handed the bat to her. "But don't hog all of the fun for yourself. I want a shot at him after you're finished."

"What makes you think that there will be anything left after I take my turn?" she asked with her most wicked of grins.

"Ladies, I can see that I've caught you at a bad time," Grant said as he started backing slowly toward the front door. "There's no need to resolve this all at once. There will be plenty of time. I'm not going anywhere. We'll talk again later."

"Or just maybe we're finished here, once and for all," Maddy said. "I meant what I said. There's nothing left to talk about."

Grant made his way to the door and then hesitated before leaving. "Madeline, you can protest all you want to, but I know there's still a spark for me buried somewhere deep in your heart."

"Grant, it's amazing the number of things you think you know about me but don't," Maddy said. She suddenly lunged with the bat, grinned again, and he left quickly.

"What was that all about?" I asked her after we were sure he wasn't coming back.

"What can I say? I guess I'm really just *that* irresistible," she answered with a grin.

"Really? You don't think there's something else going on here?"

"Of course I do," she replied. "Grant is up to something, and I doubt that it's because he is in Timber Ridge to win back my heart. There's only one way to find out, though. I'm calling Sharon."

"Do you really think your former mother-in-law will tell you what her son is up to?" I asked as my sister got out her cell phone.

"Are you kidding? Sharon was hoping to lose him in the divorce instead of me." Maddy listened to her phone for a minute and then hung up. "I got her machine; she's not there. I'll try again later. In the meantime, what say we put this behind us and get ready for our first customer?"

"Aren't you going to call Bob and tell him what just happened?" I asked. Bob Lemon was a local attorney and, more importantly, Maddy's fiancé. "I've got a hunch he might like to know that someone is trying to woo his betrothed."

Maddy glanced at her watch. "Bob knows all about Grant, so there's no way he'll be threatened by anything my ex has to say to me. Besides, he's in court right now. I'll tell him this evening at the festival. I'm glad we're closing the pizzeria at six so we can go this year, too."

"Hey, we only have a Founders Day Festival once a year," I said. "Besides, with all of the street vendors peddling their specialties, it's not like we'd sell much pizza anyway. It was one of Joe's favorite things about this place, you know."

"Oh, you don't have to remind me. I remember that crazy woodsman's costume he wore one year. I thought Grizzly Adams had come to town."

"My dear husband had a unique sense of humor, didn't he?" I asked.

Maddy nodded and then stared at me for a few seconds before she spoke again. "You know, you aren't nearly as sad as you used to be when you talk about him these days, Eleanor. Is it because David Quinton's in your life?"

I thought about it and then admitted, "You're probably right. Joe's been gone awhile now, and I'm doing my best to let go of the pain of losing him and focus more on the wonderful life we had together. I admit that David has helped me do it."

"By being in your life?" Maddy asked.

"Sure, that's true in and of itself, but my boyfriend loves to hear stories about Joe, and some of the stunts he used to pull. I swear, I believe that the two of them would have been great friends if they'd ever had a chance to meet."

"Well, they *do* have something in common," Maddy said. "They both managed to fall for you."

"And you can't argue with good taste, can you?" I asked her with a smile.

At that moment, four older fellows came into the Slice together. To my knowledge, they'd never been in my pizzeria before, and judging by the way they looked around, it was a pretty sure bet. They weren't exactly in their element.

As Maddy seated them, I asked, "What brings you gentlemen here on this fine and beautiful day?"

"They shut down the Liar's Table at Mickey's in Bower," one of them said, clearly more than a little disgruntled by the fact. "We're trying new places this week, until they're finished remodeling."

"Did you just say liar's table?" Maddy asked. "What exactly does that mean?"

One the men grinned at her as he ran a hand through his full head of silver hair. "It's a time-honored name reserved for a group of regulars who tend to exaggerate their stories just a touch to make them a tad more vivid to the listener."

"Exaggerate?" a shiny-domed companion asked. "That's just about the nicest way of being called a liar I've heard yet."

"Give me time, Jed. I'll see what else I can come up with," his friend replied.

"Don't encourage him," a third man said. As Maddy offered them all menus, he held his hand up and said, "Don't worry about those; we know what we want. If this place is anything like the one I used to go to back when I had a full head of hair, give us a large kitchen-sink pizza and four sodas."

"When did you start ordering for us, Henry?" one of the other men asked.

"Forget that," Jed said. "I want to know how you can remember as far back as when you actually had hair."

"Yeah. I resent the implication that I can't make up my own mind," the heretofore silent one chimed in.

Henry looked at them each in turn and then said, "Excuse me. I didn't mean to be presumptuous. So, what kind of pizza would you three like?"

They mulled it over and finally decided that Henry had been right all along. After they placed their order, I went back into the kitchen to prepare it. Maddy and I liked fully loaded pizzas ourselves, using every topping we could get our hands on, so I could make one in my sleep. As it made its way through the conveyor oven we used, I had to wonder about Grant's earlier visit to the Slice. Was he really there to get back in my sister's life, or was there something more ominous behind his sudden appearance? I had to believe the latter, but only time would tell. I just hoped that he'd been bluffing when he said that he wasn't going to give up easily.

Our lives were plenty complicated enough without having one of Maddy's ex-husbands showing up and making trouble for all of us.

"It's really beautiful, isn't it?" I asked David Quinton as I held his hand later that evening when we first arrived at the Festival.

The promenade where my pizzeria was located had been spruced up for the festival, with tiny white Christmas lights spread around the trees spaced throughout the broad brick square. Even the World War II cannon had pretty twinkly little lights on it, but the biggest center of attraction of all was the obelisk. With a shape that was a duplicate of the Washington Monument, it was a scaled-down version, an eighteen-foot-high memorial to the men and women who had founded Timber Ridge. Their names still dominated our town, with Lincolns, Murphys, Penneys, and even Swifts and Spencers spread throughout the region, and there were most likely more folks with ties to the original founders living all around me than otherwise. What I loved most about the focus on the monument to our heritage was that the gray sentinel was bathed in an ever-changing floodlight of colors, and I wondered how they'd managed it.

"Would you like to dance, Eleanor?" David asked me as we neared one of the two stages set up on opposite ends of the square. They were far enough apart to be isolated from each other for the most part, but every now and then music from the bluegrass musicians on the other side drifted toward the stage near us, where a cover band was playing some of my favorite songs from my youth, a soundtrack of my life growing up.

"Why don't we get some barbeque first?" I suggested. It wasn't that I didn't enjoy dancing with my boyfriend, even if there was already a crowded floor of dancers, but it had been quite a while since I'd had lunch.

"I completely get the logic of feeding you first, but the offer's open for the rest of the night," he said with a smile. "But the next time, you have to ask me."

"You've got yourself a deal."

We made our way to one of the three barbeque sellers set up on the perimeter of the promenade, and I nodded to a few of my customers who were working behind the counter.

An older woman with a ready smile laughed the second she saw me approach. "Eleanor Swift! Who would have thought that I'd ever have the chance to serve you instead of the other way around?" Linda Tuesday said from behind the table.

"From those heavenly aromas coming from behind you, I wouldn't suggest trying to stop me. Is your husband cooking tonight?" Linda's husband, Manny, worked the pit at a barbeque place in Lincoln as his regular job, and he was a legend around our part for his skills in slow cooking.

"Try to keep him away from it," she said with a wry grin. "That man was born with barbeque sauce in his veins, and a fondness for cooking perfect pork barbeque that goes behind obsession."

"And it's a good thing for the rest of us," I said. I didn't even have to glance at the menu printed on bright green poster board. "Linda, we'll take two pulled specials, and do me a favor and sneak a bite of bark on my plate." Almost as an afterthought, I turned to David and asked, "Oops. Is that all right with you? I get kind of carried away when I'm around barbeque this good."

"Sure, it's fine with me, but if you're going to order for me, you're going to have to buy, Eleanor," he said with a grin.

"I like this one," Linda said as she looked at David and added another burst of laughter. "This one might just be a keeper. Or is it too soon to tell yet?"

"He's still on probation, but it's looking good so far," I said with a laugh of my own. Linda had that effect on me, and I always loved it when she came into the Slice.

"It's good to know that I haven't flunked out yet," David said good-naturedly as he started to reach for his wallet.

"Hey, what do you think you're doing, mister?" I said. "Put that away. This is my treat, remember?"

"Sorry. I forgot myself for just a second," he said.

Linda dished us up two plates brimming with pulled pork barbeque, baked beans, potato salad, slaw, and a good handful of french fries. Except for the barbeque itself, the portions weren't overwhelming, just a little more than a taste of each, but it was the only way you could get the full experience of the meal. We took our plates, along with the sweet tea that came with them, and found a bench that had just freed up under one of the nearby trees. Sitting spots were at a premium at the moment, even with the extra benches and chairs brought in just for the event, and we were lucky to grab one.

As we balanced our plates on our laps and began to eat, David took a bite of the barbeque, savored it for a few seconds, and then asked me, "What makes this so good? It doesn't even need any sauce."

"That's the work of a master," I said. "You can taste the smoke in every bite, can't you?"

David nodded, sampled a small bite of baked beans, and then asked me, "I heard you ask for bark. Is that the dark piece right there?"

I picked up the bark-edged piece of pulled pork with my fingers and smiled. "It's from the outside layer, and it's where the smoke and flavor are concentrated the most. It's not for everyone, but there's nothing like it as far as I'm concerned. Want a taste?"

"Sure. Why not?"

I offered a bit to David, who took it and took the smallest bite possible. "Wow, that's intense."

I had to laugh. "Hey, I told you that it's not for everybody."

"If it's all the same to you, I think I'll stick with this," he said.

After we finished eating, we found a trash can and tossed away our plates and cups. "How about that dance now?" David asked.

"I thought you were going to leave it up to me to ask the next time."

"I lied," he said with a grin.

"You're not going to stop asking until I agree to a dance, are you?"

"What can I say? I was born to boogie," he said with a smile.

"Then lead on."

We moved toward the crowd of dancers, and I had to admit, it felt good being in his arms once we carved out a place for ourselves. I'd missed that close contact with someone after Joe died, and it had taken me a long time to allow myself to enjoy it again.

I was just getting into the rhythm of the music when I heard a commotion not far away from us. The second I heard Maddy's voice, I broke free of David's grasp and started toward the ruckus.

Clearly, there was trouble, and if my sister was involved, I wasn't going to let myself be very far away.

When we got to Maddy, I saw that the crowd had parted and that Bob and Grant were in some kind of standoff, while Maddy was trying to get in between them.

David stepped forward without being asked and asked Bob intently, "Do you need any help?" as he stared at Grant. I'd neglected to tell my boyfriend about my sister's ex, and I was beginning to regret the lapse.

Bob's face was flushed, but he shook his head at the offer. "Thanks, but he's not worth the effort from one of us, let alone both."

"What happened?" I asked Maddy, who for once looked positively flustered by what was going on.

"Bob and I were dancing when Grant tried to cut in," she explained. "At my urging, Bob refused, but Grant wouldn't take no for an answer. He pushed Bob in the back, and my fiancé pushed him right back."

"I never laid a hand on him. That was someone else shoving him in the back. I was minding my own business when he assaulted me," Grant complained loudly to the audience we were all attracting. "I'm going to have this man arrested for it, and I expect you all to be witnesses."

He couldn't have broken up the crowd any more effectively if he'd used tear gas on them. Soon enough, it was just the five of us standing there, and when I got closer to Grant, I could easily smell the liquor on him. I knew that they sold beer in some of the tents to fairgoers, but it seemed to me that he'd been drinking something quite a bit harder than that.

"You're drunk," I said. "Go back to your hotel room and sleep it off. Nobody's going to say a word in your defense."

"You think you've won," Grant said as he glared at Bob and shook a finger in his face. "But you're wrong. She was mine before, and she'll be mine again."

"Over my dead body," Bob said.

"If you insist, that can certainly be arranged," Grant said, being careful not to slur his words, though he had a bit of difficulty with *certainly*.

"Is that a threat?" Bob asked as he looked up at Grant and took a step closer to the man. Maddy's ex had a good six inches on Bob and at least thirty pounds of muscle. It was clear that he was in much better shape, but that didn't deter Bob in the least.

"It's a promise," Grant said.

David somehow managed to step between them and faced Grant. "Maybe you ought to just move along. It's pretty clear that nobody wants you here."

"And who exactly are you?" Grant asked as he focused on my boyfriend.

"Me? I'm nobody, just someone trying to make the peace. We don't want to ruin this evening for all of these other folks, now do we?"

"I don't give a rat's left whisker for the lot of you," he said, some of his words now beginning to slur in earnest. "Butt out, bub."

Grant suddenly made a lunge in David's direction, and Bob pulled David back half a step. As he did, Grant had no one to support him, and he suddenly fell forward on his face. He was so sloshed that he hadn't had the foresight to break his fall with his hands, and when he stood up again, his nose was bloody from its impact with the bricks of the promenade. "He hit me!" Grant screamed to no one in particular.

"I did no such thing," Bob said calmly, though he didn't look displeased that Grant had managed to bloody his own nose. "You can ask anyone."

"Why should I bother? You already told me that they'll all just lie for you." Grant spotted Police Chief Kevin Hurley just then, who was making the rounds of the fair and had no doubt heard the disturbance. "Officer, arrest that man," Grant said as he pointed to Bob.

"Why on earth would I do that? What's going on?" Kevin asked. "Is there a problem here?"

"That man struck me," Grant said, his voice slightly muffled as he held a handkerchief against his nose, trying to stop the bleeding.

Chief Hurley looked at Bob as he raised one eyebrow. "Counselor, is that true?"

"He was taking a swing at David, so I stepped in," Bob explained.

"To hit him?" the chief asked, a little surprise slipping into his question as he asked it.

"Of course not," I said. "Grant fell down all by himself. We all saw it. He didn't need any help from any of us. He's clearly plastered."

"Eleanor, I don't believe I asked you for your take on this," the chief said.

"No, but I'm sure you just hadn't gotten around to it yet," I said. The chief and I had had more than our share of problems in the past, dating back to our high school years when we'd gone out briefly, but I wanted to make this go away quickly so we could enjoy the rest of the night. "This is Maddy's ex-husband," I explained, "and he's been blustering around town all day that he's here to get her back, something she continues to tell him is impossible."

"Is that true?" the chief asked Maddy.

"I couldn't have said it any better myself," Maddy said. She looked at me and grinned as she added, "And you know that I would have done it if my big sister had been able to let me have a chance on my own."

"Sorry about that," I said with a smile of my own

that showed I wasn't the least bit repentant for my actions.

"You're forgiven," she replied with a nod.

"Okay, I've heard enough." The chief turned to Grant and said, "You've got two choices, the way I see it. You can move along peacefully right now and leave these good folks alone to enjoy the celebration, or you can spend the night sobering up in one of my jail cells."

Grant snapped out, "Why am I not surprised that you'd side with them? Are you in their pockets, too?"

"Excuse me?" the chief asked in the near silence that seemed to surround him for a moment. Though the question had been posed in a restricted voice, all of those around us knew that Grant was on dangerous ground at the moment.

"Never mind," Grant said as he started away. Before he could fade into the crowd, though, he said, "This isn't over," to the group of us.

"For your sake, it had better be," the chief said.

After Grant had disappeared into the crowd, Bob spoke up. "Thank you, but I had things under control here."

Before Chief Hurley could respond, Maddy said, "Of course you did. Now, are we going to finish our dance, or am I going to have to ask the chief of police instead?"

"It would be my pleasure," Bob said as he took Maddy into his arms.

Chief Hurley looked at me, shrugged, and then went back to his rounds of the festival.

David said, "Our dance wasn't finished either, as I recall."

"Then by all means, let's dance," I said.

As we moved in time with the music, David whispered in my ear, "Why do I have the feeling that this isn't over?"

"Probably because you've been around Maddy and me too much lately," I said.

"Too much? Never. I dispute your claim that there could ever be too much contact with you."

"And Maddy, as well?" I asked softly, for his ears only.

"Let's just say that I'm glad I chose the right sister," David answered. When I didn't respond, he leaned back and asked, "Are you telling me that you're going to let me get away with that?"

"What can I say? I'm feeling pretty forgiving all the way around tonight. Now, are we going to talk, or are we going to dance?"

"Yap with you or hold you in my arms? That's not even a fair fight," he said as he pulled me a little closer. After that, I didn't spend too much more time worrying about Grant and why he'd reappeared in our lives.

For now, for that moment in time, I was just content being exactly where I was, keeping the company I was keeping, and being a part of the life of Timber Ridge, North Carolina.